Gray Dawn

ALBERT PAYSON TERHUNE

Gray Dawn

Grosset & Dunlap

PUBLISHERS

NEW YORK

By Arrangement with Harper & Brothers
Printed in the United States of America

MY BOOK
IS DEDICATED TO
THE MISTRESS

Contents

Gray Dawn

CHAPTER ONE

Scared Stiff

It BEGAN on a villainously cold and sleety and tempest-twisted night in mid-December, one of those nights nobody wants. Across the frozen lake, from the white-capped Ramapo Mountains beyond, hooted a ruffianly gale that slapped along ahead of it a deluge of half-frozen rain.

Over the woods and the sweet lawns of The Place yelled the sleet-laden hurricane, buffeting the naked black tree boughs into a hideous goblin dance, hammering against the stanch old rambling gray stucco house with its festoons of seventy-year wistaria vines, wrenching at the shutters and shaking racketily the windowpanes.

The frozen ground was aglare with driven rain and with slush. Borne on the riot of wind and sleet, a spectacular December thunderstorm flashed and rumbled. In the North Jersey hill country minor thunderstorms are by no means rare in late autumn and early winter. But this one was as crashingly noisy and as pyrotechnic as though it marked the finish of a July hot spell.

The Sunnybank humans and the Sunnybank collies were

roused from their gale-lullabyed sleep by the glare and din. The humans were vaguely aware of the phenomenon, and sank back to slumber, wondering drowsily at it. The kennel dogs reacted to it, each after his own nature. A thunderstorm terrifies some dogs to crazy panic; others it excites; a few are indifferent to it.

Wolf, official watchdog of The Place, lay quietly on his sheltered veranda mat, wakeful, alert, but giving no heed to the storm itself. His job was to guard, not to let mere electric tempests distract him. Terror never had found foothold in Wolf's fiery soul.

At first hint of the far-off thunder—long before any human ear could have detected its approach, through the roar of wind and fanfare of sleety rain—Bruce awoke, on his rug in the Master's study. Bruce was a gigantically graceful collie, flawless in body and mind and heart—such a dog for beauty and disposition as is found perhaps once in a generation.

In all normal crises he was calmly fearless. But thunderstorms were a dread to him. Now he got to his feet and pattered softly upstairs to the Mistress's room. Without a sound to waken her, the great dog moved over to the side of her bed. He stood there, mute and miserable, his shaggy body pressed tremblingly close against the edge of the mattress, seeking comfort in his nearness to the sleeping woman.

Thus, ever, in thunderstorms, Bruce would hunt out the Mistress, and would stand as close to her as he could, throughout the time of fear. Though he was the Master's dog and the Master's worshiper, yet in such moments of stress it was the Mistress he came to for comfort. Perhaps,

despite her gentleness, hers was the stronger character, and
the psychic collie realized it.

Lad, too—up to the day of his death, three months earlier
—had always hurried to the Mistress in moments of real or
fancied danger. But in Lad's case he had been the protector,
not the protected. Lad, like Wolf, his son, had not known
the meaning of fear. From puppyhood he had seemed to
feel that the Mistress needed him to stand fiercely in front
of her when hint of peril was at hand. At such times, woe
to any stranger who should chance to come near her!

To-night another Sunnybank collie was sharing Bruce's
terror at the rackety thunderstorm. A hundred yards from
the house was a snugly warm little building containing a
blanket-bedded brood-nest. Here, for the past few nights,
had slept Cleo, a gentle and wise, if temperamental, merle
collie.

Wakened, like Bruce, by the first distant breath of the
thunderstorm, Cleo had jumped up and had begun to trot
nervously to and fro in the narrow confines of the nest. As
the thunder waxed louder and as fitful glares of lightning
illumined the world, Cleo's nervousness swelled to fright.
Around and around the nest she tore, whimpering piteously
in fear.

At last, summoning all her panic strength, she hurled herself at the flimsy window, three feet above the level of the
floor. Clumsily she leaped, goaded on by the fright that
made her mad to escape from these close quarters and to
hide from the lightning in some deeper and darker refuge.

Her gray body smote the window and crashed through
it, carrying along broken glass and slivered casings. A gash

across the nose and a nasty cut on the shoulder testified to her tumultuous plunge through the panes. Floundering she landed on the slush outside, sliding along for a yard or so, then colliding heavily with a heap of cordwood.

She gathered herself together, whining and shuddering. But before she could get into motion for a dash to some safer hiding place she was aware that the thunder and lightning had passed by. The gale was still screeching and the mingled rain and sleet were cascading down through the ice-chill air. But the thunderstorm had rolled on down the valley and had departed.

With the passing of noise and glare, Cleo's panic terror left her. But she was too sick and in too much pain to force herself to the effort of leaping back through the shattered window to the warmth and dryness of her brood-nest. With a sobbing little whimper she cuddled down in a puddle of slush; and lay there.

Gray dawn had scarcely begun to creep sullenly up from the black east when the Master awoke. He woke thus early because something was troubling him. He did not know what it was. He lay there, dully trying to remember. Bit by bit it came to him. He remembered being half awakened by the thunderstorm and of wondering subconsciously whether he ought not to dress and go out to Cleo. He knew her horror of such storms.

He had been dead tired, and the thought had not roused him sufficiently to banish the sleep mists. But now it recurred to him with full force. Getting up, he huddled sketchily into a few clothes, thrust his bare feet into a pair of boots, and left the house at a run, heading for the brood-nest.

Twenty feet from the nest he came to a dumfounded halt.

There on the icy ground, her gray fur drenched, and half frozen, lay Cleo. At sight of the Master she did not spring up as usual and run to greet him. She contented herself with lifting her head and wagging a feeble tail in welcome.

Scattered around her in the slush lay eight inert and rat-like little creatures. They were thoroughbred collie puppies—Cleo's and Bruce's children—soaked and chilled and dead.

They were Cleo's first babies. The young mother had had no idea how to save or nourish this sudden family of hers, nor even the wit to carry them in out of the down-pour of killing sleet. Warmth and dryness are all-needful to newborn puppies. Warmth and dryness had been provided in advance for this litter whose advent had not been expected for another three or four days. But the thunderstorm had wrecked the careful plans of Cleo's human guardians.

The Master saw the smashed window of the brood-nest. He noted the slash across Cleo's nose and the glass scratch on her gray shoulder. He understood—now that it was too late for the understanding to do him any good.

Belatedly he sought to save a situation which his drowsiness had permitted. Ripping off his coat, he gathered up the eight chilly and wet morsels of flesh and fur and wrapped them tenderly in it. Then he turned toward the house, to try to warm one or more of them back to life by means of hot water and the kitchen oven.

He whistled to Cleo to get up and follow the coatful of frozen babies. Wearily she obeyed. As she got to her shaky legs something rolled out of the crease between her flank and her side. The Master chanced to see it, in the faint dawn light, and stooped to pick it up.

It was a male puppy, larger than any of the eight others. He was alive. He was warm. He was vigorous. By some stray instinct of maternity, when he was born, Cleo had nosed him against her furry side as she lay there. He had happened to slip down between her hip and her ribs. There he had lain, sheltered from the sleet, in a pocket of dry fur, whence he had fallen just now when his mother got up.

For an hour, in the kitchen, the Master and the Mistress and the maids and the superintendent of The Place wrought over the puppies. Eight of them could not be wooed back to life, by immersion in hot water, by manipulation, or by wrapping in hot cloths in the warmth of the oven. Five hours of exposure to sluicing rain and to hammering sleet, on the frozen ground, had killed them all.

But the ninth puppy was egregiously alive and energetic. Snuggled to his mother's warm underbody, he wriggled and muttered happily. There could be no doubt of his health and well-being. A third larger than any of the others, he was a queer iron gray of hue, with white chest and legs and tail tip, and with a thin white blaze on his foreface. Patches of golden tan marked his cheek bones.

"That's the way of it," glumly philosophized the Master. "Collie 'futures' are as tricky as 'futures' in Wall Street. Sometimes you can't help raising a banner litter. Then again, you'll take every precaution, and some accident like this will clean out the whole lot. I could have sold those eight pups at one hundred and fifty dollars or more apiece, at six weeks old. Call it one hundred and fifty. That means a thunderstorm and my own thick-headed sleepiness have cost us twelve hundred dollars, at the very least. And——"

"But we've still got this gray puppy," put in the Mistress. "He's a beauty, too. And he's bigger and finer than any of the others were."

"He's a blue merle," objected the Master. "The only merle in the litter, at that. I don't care for merles."

"I've always wanted a blue merle puppy at Sunnybank," said she. "If you don't want him, I'll have him for mine. May I?"

"Take him, if you like," vouchsafed the Master, grouchily. "He's Bruce's son. So he can't turn out altogether worthless. What are you going to call him?"

The Mistress looked ponderingly at the tiny collie. Then her glance strayed out into the dawning day. The downpour had ceased. But the skies were still snarled up with iron-gray clouds shot with silvery tints. A streak and a spatter of shimmering white, in the east, showed where the sun would rise in another half hour. Sere and pale-tan in hue, a branchful of unfallen oak leaves swayed in front of the window.

"Gray, silver, snow white, flecked with ashes-of-gold," she said, half to herself. "The same color scheme as the puppy's. I'll take it as an omen. I'll name him—'Gray Dawn.'"

Thus the puppy began life, under a name as poetic as he himself was materialistic.

He was a blue merle, of unusual purity of shade. Collies

are divided by color into four classes—whites, tricolors (black and white with tan markings), sables (every shade of yellow or brown), and blue merles. The merle's chief hue is a silvery gray—"blue," as the old British fanciers named it. A muddy or brownish gray is off color. The ideal shade is the vivid silver gray with bluish lights in it. Such a merle was Sunnybank Gray Dawn. Often a merle will have one or both of his eyes "marled"—that is, of a whitey-blue color. Dawn's deepset eyes were as darkly brown as those of his glorious sire, Bruce.

In a week Dawn had ceased to resemble a sleek rat. In a fortnight he was a gigantically fuzzy and pudgy baby. The iron gray of his coat had changed to deep silver, strewn with occasional black blotches. As he was unusually large by nature and as he absorbed all the nourishment that nature had supplied for nine youngsters, he was nearly as big at two months as are most puppies at four. Beneath his fat was a mighty structure of bone, the frame of a future giant.

By reason of this he was unbelievably awkward. From much food and from Cleo's individual care and because of the queer spirit that dominated him from birth, he was bumptiously aggressive. Consciously, he was in eternal mischief. Unconsciously, he was in everlasting trouble.

"He's not like any collie pup we ever had on The Place," complained the Master, a few months later. "I think he's a changeling. I think he rained down from some practical-joke planet when the other eight pups died. Some teasing spirit of the dawn sent him here to smash our patience and to smash most of the other things we have."

This diatribe was brought forth by a dual mishap. Gray Dawn, galloping gawkily up on to the porch, had seized the hem of the Mistress's organdie dress and had tugged at it in an effort to draw her into a romp. Under those shaking tugs, the flounce had been torn in a jagged and enormous rent.

The noise of the tearing organdie had so interested Dawn that he relinquished his grip on the skirt. As he was braced backward with all his might at the time, he lost his balance and crashed into a porch jardinière the Master had brought back from Syria many years before.

Under the impact of Dawn's furry body the jardinière flew off the veranda edge and showered into scores of pieces against the hard driveway below. The Mistress's exclamation of dismay at the tearing of her dress and the Master's volcanic outburst of language at his cherished jardinière's destruction rang in the puppy's ears.

From birth Dawn had been abnormally sensitive and prone to take offense or hurt from a single sharp word. Now, ears and tail adroop, he scuttled off the porch and around the corner of the house, for refuge with his gentle mother in her kennel yard.

"When he isn't destroying things, out of fun," raged on the Master, "he's doing Charlie Chaplin stunts of destructiveness, because he's too clumsy and stupid to get out of his own way or out of anything else's way. If he begins like this, he's due to grow up into a wholesale scourge. I'm beginning to hate the sight of him."

"Pick him up, some time, and look straight down into his eyes," counseled the Mistress. "You'll see something there that will show you he isn't all clown. I never saw a steadier, stancher look in any dog's eye, except Laddie's. Dawn is going to turn out all right. Don't worry."

"I wish he had the steadiness in his body, instead of in his eye," growled the Master. "His eye may be all right. But it isn't his eye he does all the damage with."

A wild clamor from somewhere to the rear of the house sent both of them hastening from the porch to find what direful thing had befallen. As they rounded the corner they came upon a scene of carnage.

Gray Dawn had galloped to the kennel yard in search of Cleo and of consolation for his scolding. But Cleo had gone on a lakeside ramble. The puppy set out in search of her. The interest of the quest made him forget his grievance.

Midway across the dooryard he beheld a fluffed-out and noisily self-important Plymouth Rock hen, as tall as himself, convoying her bevy of ten baby chicks from the chicken runs to a forage in the garden.

This hen and her brood were supposed to be quartered safely in a coop with a wire runway, alongside the main poultry house behind the barn. She had pushed aside a rotting slat from her coop, and had emerged into freedom. Calling her babies to her, she sallied forth on a food quest. Clucking fussily and glancing from side to side for possible danger to her puffily soft infants, she hustled across the dooryard, the chicks running for dear life to keep up with her strides.

Gray Dawn saw. He slid to a shuffling stop. Here was by far the most dramatically entertaining spectacle of his three-month career. Not only was it thrilling to look upon, but it offered infinite possibilities in the way of fun. Barking with falsetto excitement, Dawn charged gleefully down upon the hen and her chicks.

Now hens are like dogs and humans; in that no two of them have precisely the same disposition. Where one hen with chicks will fly wildly away from danger, leaving her young to fend for themselves, another will fight for her brood with the courage of a tiger.

This Plymouth Rock chanced to be of a courageously aggressive nature, thanks to a strain of game fowl, and she suffered from a complex that all the world was in league against her beloved chicks. She courted battle. She reveled in it.

Dawn could not have found, in a day's journey, a pluckier or more pugnacious she-fowl. It was like his endless bad luck that he should have singled out this particular gallinaceous Boadicea as the victim of his mirthful assault.

The chicks peeped shrilly and fluttered to their dam for safety as they beheld the clumsy little furry silver-and-snow avalanche bearing down upon them. The hen did not gather them lovingly under her wings and prepare to die defending them. Instead, she carried the fight to her pursuer. She carried it considerably more than halfway.

As Dawn was frisking merrily up to the cluster of chicks and their attractively clucking mother, he was aware of something whizzing toward him with much the speed and aspect of a gray feather duster tied to a catapult. Glad that the hen was meeting his yearning for a romp in such sporting spirit, the puppy swerved from his charge upon the chicks and gamboled to meet her. Then——

One of the men working in a near-by flower border described thus the clash:

"For a couple of seconds you couldn't tell which was

the hen and which was Dawn. They was like one of them fizzing and fuzzing pinwheels we set off on the Fourth. And I can't see yet how only just the two of 'em ever managed to make all them kinds of noises they made. It was like a steam calliope throwing fits in a dog pound."

As the Mistress and the Master came on the scene, they saw Dawn fleeing at incredible speed, his thick feet moving too fast to be seen, his tail tucked far between his legs, his furry throat emitting a blended series of anguished shrieks. Close behind him ran and flew and flapped the irate hen, every now and then catching up close enough to deliver a screech-evoking peck on his flying hips.

Down the hilly lawn raced victor and victim. Dawn ended the chase by plunging frenziedly into the lake, whither the indignant conqueror dared not follow.

The Master's roars of laughter followed the stricken puppy into his watery refuge. Never could Dawn endure to be laughed at. Now, at the sound, he crouched lower into the water, his pecked and disheveled head almost submerged in it.

"Served him right!" exulted the Master. "It's the best lesson he could have had. After this he'll let all chickens severely alone. He'll walk around them as if they were a puddle."

The Master was right. From that day the gray puppy never sought to molest a chicken. But the lesson had more far-reaching and less gratifying results. For example:

A week or so later the Master was making a round of the stables and the vegetable gardens. With him were Bruce and Wolf and Bobby, his constant companions whenever he walked a dozen steps. With him, too, was Gray Dawn, capering gawkily in front of him and behind him and around him.

Dawn varied his rocking-horse progress by dashing alternately at one or another of the older dogs and essaying to lure them into a frolic. Bruce paid no attention to the tumultuous invitation. When Dawn would leap at him or throw himself against the giant collie's side, his stately sire would move away, with a look of disgust on his beautifully classic face.

Wolf was younger and more playful. Often he and the gray youngster romped together across the lawns. But when he was out walking with the Master or the Mistress, Wolf did not care to be fooled with. Accordingly, the fire-colored and fire-tempered collie now met Dawn's first lumbering rush with a snarl and a show of teeth.

"Wolf!" reproved the Master, though with no great earnestness.

Wolf turned away from his youthful tormentor and fell into step at the Master's side. But his momentary flash of resentment checked for the time any further advances on Dawn's part. The puppy was not wholly a fool. Wolf's snarl and snap had not been reassuring.

Then, as they neared the stables, a procession issued from the garage door and moved toward them. The warlike hen had wriggled her way once more out of the ramshackle coop. She was leading her covey of chicks again on a foraging jaunt.

Bruce and Wolf gave not so much as a second glance in her direction. From birth both of them had been brought up to let chickens alone. But Dawn happened just then to be cantering several yards in advance of the others. The hen and her brood emerged from the garage, not fifty feet in front of him.

At sight of the bumptious puppy the hen fluffed out her feathers and prepared for battle. She had no chance to go into action. Dawn was too quick for her. Howling, he turned and fled. Once more to the lake he ran, remembering that the water alone had had power to check the hen's former pursuit. As he ran he emphasized his every jump with a howl of fear.

In disgusted wonder, the Master gazed after him. This time the Master felt no impulse to laugh.

"Scared stiff!" he commented to the superintendent who came out of the barn at sound of the ki-yi-ing. "He wasn't anywhere near her, either. The second he caught sight of her he lit out, howling. He's a coward. Yellow all through!"

"Maybe, sir," doubtfully assented the superintendent, staring after the runaway. "But I don't rightly see how any son of Bruce could be a coward. He's only a puppy yet."

"When Wolf was a three-month pup he sailed into two big Airedales that growled at my wife on the road up yonder," said the Master. "And he'd have fought them till they tore him to pieces if I hadn't interfered. Bobby never whimpered when that delivery car broke his leg in two places, when he was a puppy. But this overgrown bull calf of a Dawn bellows and runs away at sight of a measly hen that pecked him once. Scared stiff!"

The Mistress had come out-of-doors, attracted by Dawn's yells. At sight of her the puppy scrambled out of the lake, his thick coat heavy with muddy water. Up to her he rushed, patting her new sport-suit's skirt ecstatically with his mud-sodden paws, and then happily shaking himself. A shower of mud water spattered the new suit from hem to throat.

Thence he trotted over to the Master, with an air of swaggering bravado, as though to show his own forgetfulness of his late humiliation. The Master called Dawn to him and slipped a leash about his neck. Then, without a word, he led him to the wire yard within which were penned some forty hens and chickens.

At first, Dawn ambled along happily enough. Only recently had he been broken to lead on the leash. He was mildly proud of the accomplishment. But as the hen yard came into sight, he hung back, digging his claws into the earth and struggling to get away.

At once the Master stooped and took off the leash. Dawn scuttled at top speed to seek a place of safety. But at his first jump the Master's command brought him to a halt. He looked doubtfully at the man, then at the yardful of potentially murderous hens. Then he began to back away. A second and a third time the Master's quietly authoritative call stayed the flight.

From the time he could walk, the puppy had been taught obedience, as was every puppy born at The Place. Learning it thus early, there was no need to enforce it by blows or other punishment. The dogs grew up with the idea that obedience was a part of their lives.

But now Gray Dawn was straining against his birthright habit of obedience, as he had strained against the leash.

Over and over, slowly, patiently, at regular intervals, came the annoyingly insistent call: "Dawn! Gray *Dawn!*"

For nearly ten minutes the Master stood there, outwardly firm and patient, inwardly longing to tear the slinking puppy in three pieces and to stamp on the fragments. For this is the magic secret of dog training—lose control over yourself and at once you lose control over your dog. Your strongest and most irresistible weapon is iron patience—or a semblance of it that can deceive him.

Little by little, inch by inch, Dawn came closer to the Master, now and then breaking away at a run, but ever drawn on by that reiterant call of, "Dawn! Gray *Dawn!*"

Meanwhile the Master was inching toward the hen yard. At last Dawn was beside him and within a foot of the yard-ful of puppy-eating hen monsters. The Master patted the silver head mottled with black like a snow leopard's, and he spoke soothingly and in praise of the dog's imaginary courage.

Just then a dragon fly fluttered across the yard toward man and dog. One of the hens saw the fly and gave chase to it. She began to run in Dawn's general direction. With a yelp of terror, the puppy turned and fled for the lake.

The Master gave up the fight and returned surlily to the house.

"It's no use," he reported to his wife. "He's yellow. He's a cur. He was scared stiff. He's hopeless. He has spoiled two of your prettiest daytime dresses in ten days, besides break-ing the jardinière. I could stand that. In fact, I *did* stand it. But we've never had a cowardly collie on The Place, and we're not going to have one."

"What do you mean?"

"The last day you were in town Meagher dropped in for a chat with me, on his way to Paterson. He saw Gray Dawn and he wants to buy him. I told him the pup wasn't for sale. He asked me to give him first chance at him if ever I changed my mind about letting him go. Meagher knows more about collies, from the ground up, than almost any other breeder in America. He went over Dawn as carefully as if he were examining him for life insurance. He says he's got the best bone and framework of any collie he's seen in years. He says he'll outgrow his gawkiness and be a magnificent show specimen. He——"

"But——"

"The pup's ears are a bit heavy," went on the Master, refusing to meet his wife's unhappy eyes, "just as we've noticed they are. But that is the only flaw Meagher sees in him. He says he can correct it. Well, I don't care for all the 'show specimens' on earth, if they're fools and cowards. Dawn is both. I wouldn't care if he turned out to be as great a show collie as his grandsire, Champion Gray Mist. If he is yellow and a clown, we don't want him here. Meagher is going to stop for lunch on his way back from the Rochester show to-morrow. And I'm going to tell him he can have Dawn if he still wants him. He offered me two hundred dollars. I believe I can get him up to two hundred and twenty-five. We'll be well rid of the cur. Dawn is your dog, and of course I'll turn over to you the cash I get for him. But if you'll just think a minute, you'll agree with me we're better off without him."

"Do as you think best," sighed the Mistress. "But somehow I hate to see him go. And I wish it was some one besides Mr. Meagher. He won't be unkind to Dawnie, I suppose, but he treats his dogs as if they were prize pigs. He feeds them and he exercises them and he trains them for the shows. But that is all. He doesn't 'humanize' them. He is like nearly all the professional breeders, that way. Poor little Dawn! I wish I didn't care so much for him. It seems——"

"I know," said the Master. "But he's a coward, and he's born to trouble. And he's a clown and a fool. Apart from that, he's all right, I suppose. I could stand all the other faults if he wasn't an arrant coward. Of course, I won't let Meagher have him if you say not. Dawn's your dog. But I hope you'll see it my way. Why, the pup's got a twist to his brain that makes me sick! For instance, you've seen the way he shakes hands. Every other dog I ever trained shakes hands with his left paw. Every dog does that, I think, unless he has been trained by a left-handed master. They shake with the paw opposite the hand that's held out to them. Well, Dawn shakes with his *right* paw, and I can't make him do it any other way. That's a sample of all the rest of his ways. He's upside down, mentally. And he's a coward."

Dawn gamboled on and blundered on during the next twenty-four hours, joyously ignorant that he was marked for sale and that he was to change from the free and "folksy" life of The Place to a show career with an owner whose sole interest in his splendid dogs was the cash or prestige, or both, which could be wrung from them.

Such dogs live in sanitary huts and runs. They eat sanitary balanced rations. Often they are trained, by a day or more of pitiful starvation, to look gluttonously alert in the show ring. Their lives are about as interesting and jolly as the *Congressional Record* or the telephone directory. As a rule they die before they are nine years old; often much earlier. None of the gay independence of thought and action, the chumminess and the humanizing influences, which are a collie's birthright, are theirs. Their career is the stultified and miserable career of the prize bull or the prize sheep. God help them!

To their owners they are a cash asset. When they cease to be so they are sold sometimes to a trusting novice who pays a high price for them on the strength of their renown, and who is likely to find himself with a prematurely old dog whose intelligence and friendliness have never been developed and whose show value has collapsed.

American collie kennels contain scores of such past-worthy dogs, of both sexes;—palmed off on trustful buyers at fancy prices by shrewd British breeders. Some excellent collies are imported from Great Britain; but also are imported dozens of once-valuable dogs whose cash value has fled and whose purchase price is egregious. There are many Easy Marks in the dogs-game; and several British breeders have profited handsomely thereby.

(Think of some of these things, next time you visit a big dog show.)

A note from Meagher announced he would reach The Place, on his motor trip from the Rochester show, at about twelve o'clock the following day. At ten o'clock Gray Dawn was treated to a tub bath, which he loathed. When he was dry, the Master brushed his shimmering silver-and-white coat till every hair shone forth. Then, to prevent his marring this perfection by a roll in the mud or a gallop through burrs, he was tied in a straw-bedded angle between the stables and the garage.

A few minutes before Meagher was expected the Master went thither to bring Gray Dawn up to the house and to the view of his prospective buyer.

The little collie stood forlornly, hock deep in clean straw. He wore a collar some sizes too big for him—the smallest collie collar then on The Place. His new-brushed coat shone glowingly in the noon sunlight. Bruce and Wolf and Bobby had made as though to follow the Master down to the outbuildings. But they had been ordered back. Dawn might well try to get in a romp with one of them and muss up his well-groomed aspect.

As the Master advanced toward the tied puppy a black shadow swept athwart his path. Glancing up, he saw a tremendous hen hawk soaring above the chicken yard. Often these hawks soared thus, urged by the sight of so much ungettable food. The network of wire, stretched above the yards, made safe the fowls. The hawks seemed to know this. For they never swooped. They were content to prowl the sky above and peer down at the smugly secure prey.

On plodded the Master toward the tied collie. Dawn wriggled and danced and wagged his tail at the approach of his deliverer. The Master felt a qualm of regret at selling anything that so loved him and that welcomed his coming.

Then regret merged once more into disgust. For there was a bumpy sound from one of the ancient coops abutting on the side of the chicken house, and for the third time in ten days the bellicose Plymouth Rock hen broke out of the rotten-slatted hutch in which she was a prisoner. A chirr-r-r of summons brought her ten chicks scampering out after her.

At sight of his feathered tormentor, so near and free to assail him, Dawn slunk back, tail between legs, seeking to hide himself behind an abutting corner of the garage. At the end of his leash he wheeled about and sought to back still further from his olden enemy. The maneuver sent the loose collar over his ears and off his nose. He was free. The first use he made of his liberty was to canter to a goodly distance and then look back timorously at the hen.

The Master was not minded to waste time in another vain effort to accustom the pup to the clucking fowl especially as he hoped to rid himself forever of Dawn within the next hour. But a new sweep of the black shadow across the turf reminded him that the hen or one or more of her chickens might well be in danger from the hawk if they were not returned instantly to the safety of their coop and wire run.

He stepped forward and scooped up in his hands two of the peeping baby chicks. Then he turned to deposit them in their runway before catching the rest of the nestlings. He knelt to push the two into the coop and to put back in place the loose slat.

As he did so something hot and squawking and feathery smote him on the bent head. The hen had flown to the rescue of her two supposedly endangered chicks. Fearlessly, truculently, she assailed the kneeling man, slapping his face with her fast-beating wings and belaboring his cap with her beak.

The Master drew back from the silly onslaught. One of his toes slipped on the wet grass and he sat down hard. Instantly the hen took advantage of his momentary helplessness to fly at him afresh, in a fury of noisy rage.

The Master put out both hands to shove the angry hen aside and if possible to catch her and return her to her coop. His cap had fallen over his eyes. His groping fingers slid off a flashing bit of rough fur, instead of the feathers he sought to grasp. In his ears was a hideous cacophony of squawks and growls.

He pushed his cap up off his eyes, just in time to see Gray Dawn, the hopeless coward, tear past him and fling himself upon the irate Plymouth Rock.

Dawn had seen the redoubtable hen fly at his Master. He had seen the Master slip from a kneeling to a sitting posture, as though stricken down by the foe. This was no time for personal cowardice while the murderous hen was presumably slaying the man who was Dawn's god. The little collie sprang into the fray.

Disregarding the furious pecks of his enemy, he lunged valorously forward and caught her by the feathered breast, pinioning her to the earth, while her wings smote deafeningly and painfully about his ears.

There he pinioned her and there he held her. He had neither the skill nor the desire to kill her. But he was avidly determined to render her helpless to continue her ravages on the Master. The hen squawked and flapped, but she was powerless to escape from the furry gray monster that had caught and held her.

The Master, getting to his feet, choked back the laugh that sprang to his lips at the absurd rescue. After the first moment there was no laughter in his heart. He knew what that gallant attack on a dreaded enemy had cost the craven puppy in nerve and will power.

Dawn had been cringingly afraid of the pugnacious Plymouth Rock; but love for his Master had overcome terror. *"Perfect love casteth out fear."*

To his infantile idea, the Master was undergoing the same agonizing and terrifying treatment from the hen that he himself had had a few days earlier. To save his god from such torment the puppy had risked another dose of hideous pecking and wing beating.

Great was Terror. But infinitely greater was Love. Paladins of old, bravely giving battle to fire-breathing dragons, had been spurred on by no purer courage.

The Master leaned over and caught the screaming hen, thrusting her into her coop and making fast the broken slat behind her. Then he stooped and picked up Gray Dawn.

Rapturously the collie pup licked at the man's face, rejoicing mightily that he had saved his Master from the fearsome peril. Scornfully he squinted down at the helplessly indignant hen he had conquered. Along with his conquest of her he had conquered fear, though he did not realize it. Again he licked lovingly at the Master's face—the face of the man he had rescued from a homicidal hen.

"Gray Dawn," said the Master, roughly stroking the valorous little collie, "there's a man coming here to lunch to-day. He wants to buy you. Well—he can't have you! Get that, Gray Dawn? He can't have you. You belong *here* —here with the rest of the brave Sunnybank dogs."

CHAPTER TWO

The Non-Sacred White Elephant

THE Mistress began it. But Gray Dawn kept it up until everyone on The Place was sick to death of it.

That was Gray Dawn's way. He had an infinite gift for keeping things up, right joyously, after the rest of the world had wearied of them.

Dawn was barely a year old. In size he was gigantic beyond the run of other pure-bred collies, for he stood twenty-seven inches at the shoulder and his gaunt silver-gray body weighed close to eighty pounds. At heart he was still a bumptious puppy.

Now, when a fluffy little roly-poly pup gambols merrily about a room it is an amusing sight, and no great harm is done. When a gawky beast, almost the size of a yearling calf, does the same thing, destruction and curses follow in his wake—even as they followed in Dawn's.

Gray Dawn was the Mistress's dog. She alone had endless gentle patience with his costly blunders. She alone had the foresight to prophesy a future for him; as, ten years earlier, she alone had foreseen the great future of Bruce, his sire.

Because Dawn was the Mistress's dog and because she loved him, the Master allowed the huge ungainly brute to stay on at Sunnybank. For these reasons and because the Master was wont to get flash-brief glimpses of something stanch and clever and loyal and gallant beneath the puppy's appalling worthlessness. But these glimpses were far too few to compensate for the nerve wrack and mischief the big youngster was forever causing.

On a day, the Mistress took him over to the mile-distant village with her in the car. Bruce and Wolf and Bobby, the car's usual canine occupants, were off with the rest of the Sunnybank dogs, tramping the hills with the Master.

The Mistress had taken Dawn with her on several short drives, to "car-break" him. The task had not been easy at first. The pup loved motoring, as do nine collies out of ten. But he was not a restful driving companion. At sight of any passing street dog he would fill the air with thunderous barking that continued deafeningly for the next mile or more. Also, when the Mistress was driving at a speed of something like thirty miles an hour he had a perilous trick of trying to jump out of the car to investigate any or every roadside object which chanced to catch his attention.

A bruised shoulder and a wrenched foot had cured him at last of this unceremonious way of leaving the machine. A series of sharp rebukes had begun to wean him from his clamorous barking. Still, he could scarcely be called an ideal car dog.

This morning, however, he sat so sedately beside the

Mistress throughout the villageward ride that she was genuinely proud of him. She told him so. She was not yet so certain of his reformation as to leave him untied in the car while she made her various morning purchases. Hence she ran a leash through the robe rail and snapped it to Dawn's collar ring, then went into a shop.

The shop was a miniature department store. The Mistress stopped at its kitchenware counter to buy some jelly glasses. The counter's clerk was busy. Two or three minutes passed before he came to wait on her.

Dawn, meantime, curled his enormous bulk on the car seat, preparing to wait in patience. But, as he turned about, the ill-fastened leash slipped from the robe rail. The dog was free. The pleasantest use to which he felt he could put his freedom was to follow his adored mistress into the store. This he did.

Leash trailing after him, he trotted up to her as she stood at the counter. So busy was she in giving her order to the belatedly attentive clerk that she did not see the mottled gray head which sought in vain to rub itself against her hand. Finding that the Mistress was too much engrossed just then to pet or speak to him, Dawn wandered down the store aisle on a tour of exploration. This place was new to him. It promised to be interesting.

At the toy counter he came to an abrupt stop. This counter was small and was a few feet away from the longer ones. Around its base, as well as on its top, were heaped a collection of cheap toys, for a special sale that had been advertised for the day. It was one of these toys that riveted Gray Dawn's delighted attention.

The thing was a puffy white Canton-flannel elephant, about the size of a large cat and stuffed with sawdust. To the casual eye there was nothing very alluring about it.

To the casual eye there is nothing of special allure about the one toy which a small child usually singles out from a pile of far prettier playthings at the foot of a Christmas tree. No one but the child himself knows why he picks out that particular toy for his favorite and ignores the rest.

Nobody but Gray Dawn could know why the young collie singled out that puffy white flannel elephant from among gaudier toys on the floor, or, indeed, why a mere dog should have been at all interested in any kind of toy. The fact remains that many a dog has some such plaything, which is the joy of his life. The fact also remains that Gray Dawn evidently viewed that white elephant as the most ravishingly beautiful and desirable treasure which had thus far come into his youthful life.

Gravely he stared at it. Then he took a step nearer and sniffed it. Apparently it smelled as fascinating as it looked. With no effort at secrecy, he picked it up gently in his mighty jaws and walked back toward the Mistress with it. This new possession of his seemed well worth exhibiting to her.

The toy clerk had been staring trembling over the counter at the formidable gray intruder. Now, as Dawn bore away the elephant, she screamed to the floorwalker.

The Mistress turned from the uninspiring task of buying jelly glasses. A swelling clamor from the rear of the store made her glance around.

Up the aisle toward her was advancing a rowdy procession. In the van of the parade paced Gray Dawn, his leash dangling. In his mouth he carried tenderly something large and soft and white. Every inch of his giant body betrayed inordinate pride in the thing he was bringing to her. He varied his majestic pace with puppy-like "grace steps."

Close behind him, yet ever ready to dodge back behind a counter, stormed the floorwalker, brandishing a yardstick and shouting at every step the shrill command, "Drop that!" Behind the gesticulating man surged the toy clerk and the proprietor and two other store folk, gabblingly exhorting the dog to drop his plunder and imploring the floorwalker to beat him with the futile yardstick.

Loftily ignoring the hue and cry, Gray Dawn marched over to the astonished Mistress. With rapturous pride he deposited the flannel elephant at her feet. Then he looked up into her eyes with a whimsically eager pleading, as though expecting her to share his delight in the toy.

Before she could speak, a multiple babble of protest burst upon her from the excited people who had followed Dawn up the aisle. She cut short the volume of complaint by asking the stolen elephant's price and paying it.

Embarrassed and annoyed, she stooped to pick up the toy and take it out to the car, there to tie Dawn more securely until the rest of her shopping should be done. But Dawn would not have it so. As her fingers closed around the pudgy white flannel, he caught it up again and, wriggling with pride, cake-walked out to the car ahead of her. He was taking no risks of losing his marvelous new plaything.

Thus the white elephant came to The Place, where at

once it proceeded to live up to the traditional reputation of white elephants.

As I have said, the Mistress began the trouble. She began it by being soft-hearted and letting Dawn have the toy he had stolen. His joy in the prize was too great for her first impulse to return the thing to the storekeeper and to pay for any damage the collie's jaws might possibly have wrought upon it. Yes, the Mistress began it. But Gray Dawn kept it up.

From that hour the elephant was the dearest of all Dawn's possessions. He carried it everywhere. He slept with it between his white forepaws at night. He went further. He seemed to take a certain solicitous care in the elephant's appearance. For he would lick it by the hour, even as he was wont to lick his paws when they were dirty.

There was a difference in results. Whereas the pink tongue's ministrations made the paws glisten like snow, yet that same careful licking made the elephant less and less white. That, and the subsequent accidental dropping of the elephant into the dust or the mud, presently imparted to the once-immaculate toy an unwinsome mouse-grayness of hue.

The dog's strong jaws always closed with the most meticulous tenderness on the flannel. Despite this, the many and prolonged soft pressures presently changed the elephantine figure to a semishapeless wad. Dawn loved his plaything none the less for its loss of color and form. The passing of the days did not abate his fondness for it.

True, he would drop it somewhere carelessly and perhaps forget it for hours. But always he would remember it soon or late; and start on a harassingly distressed search which would continue until he had found it again. As time went on, he seemed to realize he might lose it forever if he did not deposit it carefully during such times as he was not playing with it or sleeping with it between his forepaws.

It was his choosing of these safe places that turned the elephant from a joke to a pest, so far as the humans of The Place were concerned. At first, the big dog's fondness for his toy had amused the Mistress and the Master. The latter had scant patience, however, with Dawn's affection for the elephant. He looked upon this as one more sign of the pup's absence of intelligence.

In every kennel yard on The Place there was an old shoe or a slipper that had belonged either to the Mistress or to the Master. From early puppyhood, the Sunnybank dogs were given these shoes as playthings. Not only was the tough leather good for their teeth, but the shoe itself taught them the scent of the humans' steps; and thus was a bit of sound practical training in the following of a trail.

But few of the dogs continued to play with these shoes or with any other such object after they were grown.

Of course Treve, the golden puppy (later to become famous as Champion Sunnybank Sigurd), was an exception. To the last week of his life, Treve used to steal brushes or hats or stable rags or anything else he could carry away. These he would play with merrily. Then, tiring of them, he would leave them in the long grass or lakeside mud, where never again could their owners hope to find them except by accident. But Treve was an exception to every rule. With Dawn it was different.

Wherefore the Master fumed disgustedly at the gawky young giant's fondness for the shapeless toy. But the Mistress, who saw deeper into things, only smiled at the odd devotion. Her own childhood was much less remote than was the Master's. Never had she outgrown its memories, nor a sympathetic understanding of childishness.

A garish and pot-bellied goldfish bowl, containing six gogglingly gaping red fish, was brought to The Place one day by a guest who had stopped for lunch during a motor trip from New York to her Tuxedo country home. The guest was a goldfish enthusiast and paid startling prices for her finny pets. As the globe was carried cautiously from the car and deposited on a stand in the living room, she expounded to her hosts:

"I won't trust these to anyone else to bring back and forth from town for me. I send the other fish in the service car, on a hanging bracket. But these are my prize winners, these six. I have been offered fourteen hundred dollars for them. But I wouldn't sell them for twice that. I bred them myself, and they have taken prizes at every—— Ugh! What has that great ugly brute got in his mouth?" she broke off.

Dawn, as ever when strangers came indoors, had found his beloved elephant and was trotting forward with it for the visitor's inspection. There was something ludicrously pathetic in this constant desire of his that all newcomers should see and admire his toy.

The Mistress started to explain. The guest shrank back with a shudder at sight of the gruesomely mouse-gray and shapeless flannel lump. Dawn peered wistfully up at her, then down at the elephant he had laid at her feet. The announcing of luncheon cut short the scene. With a furtively consolatory pat of Dawn's head, the Mistress led the way to the dining room. Dawn and the elephant—and the six goldfish—had the living room to themselves.

During the meal the guest held forth at much length and eloquence as to the wonders of her prize fish; comparing goldfish breeding with the breeding of collies, to the latter's manifest disadvantage. As soon as luncheon was ended she hurried back to the living room, to prove by illustration with her own specimens the divers points of beauty which she had been describing. In the doorway she stopped, with an inarticulate squawk.

Dawn had trotted forth some minutes ago to hail a delivery wagon that was bringing meat to the kennels. But the elephant remained. Dawn had realized he could not eat such scraps of meat as the market man might toss to him, if he had the elephant in his mouth. So he had deposited it in a place of safety before he went.

There was a pool of spilled water on the floor around the stand. The fourteen-hundred-dollar fish huddled in a panic mass in the globe's pebbly bottom. Three-fourths of the globe's area was filled with an amorphous grayish mass which had sucked up most of the water it had not displaced. Dawn's elephant had gone goldfishing.

While the Master clawed the soggy flannel-and-sawdust mass from the globe, the Mistress sought to soothe the frantically raging guest. The Master flung the soaked elephant disgustedly out on to the lawn. There presently Dawn retrieved it, seeking to lick it dry of its burden of absorbed water.

A week later the Mistress's birthday was celebrated by the arrival of many and pretty presents, among them an enamel-and-silver dish from an ancient relative. In arranging the presents on a table in the library, the Mistress made certain to put this dish in a place of honor, with the donor's card on it. She knew the aged relative was certain to call during the day to note the reception of her gift.

The relative arrived. So did five of her friends, in the same car. The six were ushered into the library to look at the presents. In the center of the table lay a swollen and grayish thing of flannel. From one end of it protruded the elderly caller's card. Dawn had chosen the dish of honor as a repository for his abhorred elephant. It took the distressed Mistress a full hour to explain, and to soften the feelings of the dish's insulted giver.

Even the stoutest Canton flannel will show the signs of repeated teethmarks, be the jaw grip ever so tender. The elephant chose a right unfortunate time and place to suffer its first puncture.

A package of smoking tobacco, such as the Master had been wont to revel in during his sojourn in the Orient, was brought to him by a friend who had just returned from a visit to Syria. The Master had found that the tobacco had an added zest when mixed with a handful of oily black Perique. He had poured it out on to a clean paper on his study floor, and had added the Perique, mingling the two brands with extravagant care.

As the mixture was completed, two things happened. Some one called up on the telephone, and Dawn meandered into the study, shaking his elephant with mock ferocity as he invited the Master to a romp. That was the moment the puncture occurred, as Gray Dawn's big eyetooth pierced the Canton flannel. The dog continued to shake the toy vehemently.

The Master came back, to find his cherished Syrian tobacco mixed still further by something like a half-pound of dirty sawdust which the elephant had exuded during the shaking. More sawdust strewed the rugs and furniture, while Dawn looked on jocosely, with a limp and almost empty bag of flannel hanging from his mouth.

Hugo or the elder Dumas, in his best moments, might have been able to write an adequate description of the ten minutes which followed. It ended by the Mistress fishing out the remnants of the elephant from the ash can into which her husband had hurled it, and stuffing it with cotton wool to comfort her cowed and heart-crushed collie.

But that was the actual end. By way of compromise with the appealing Mistress, the Master at last gave the following weak-kneed verdict:

"This thing has gotten to be a horror. When I land in heaven I shall find my golden harp muted by that unspeakable elephant; or else it will be stuffed into my halo, just as it was stuffed into my silk hat last week and into my bed the week before. You say Dawn loves it and you don't want it destroyed. Very good. Then I'll make you custodian of the Non-sacred White Elephant. It goes into the library closet. There's room for it on the floor there, with my rubbers and hiking boots. There it lives henceforth. When you want to take Dawn out for a romp with it, you'll know where to find it. But as soon as he's through playing with it I'd like you to be sure to put it back there and shut the door. Then——"

THE NON-SACRED WHITE ELEPHANT

"I promise. And——"

"Then perhaps we can keep it from materializing in goldfish bowls and in enamel-and-silver plates," raged on the Master, "or appearing again in the middle of a centerpiece of flowers on the dining-room table when we're giving a dinner. And maybe I won't have to throw away another package of priceless Syrian tobacco because it's full of wet sawdust. Into the library closet it goes, remember. There it stays, except when Dawn is actually playing with it. I feel like a fool to let him keep it at all. I wouldn't, if you and he hadn't both looked so mournful when I threw it away. But the closet is the solution of the crazy dilemma."

The Master was mistaken. The closet was not the solution. The elephant had not been tucked away among the rubbers and odds and ends in a corner of the closet floor for an hour before Gray Dawn missed it and went in search of it. By scent he traced it to the shut door.

He knew it was inside, and he sought to get to it. This he endeavored to do, first by clawing frantically at the closet door until its lower panels' cream-colored paint was a mass of deep and ugly scratches, and then by waking the echoes by a salvo of frantic barking.

For the double crime of mutilating furniture and of barking in the house he was scolded severely and punished, and was forbidden to commit either fault again. Dawn understood the meaning of his scolding and punishment. From babyhood the Law had been taught to him.

Like every other Sunnybank dog with access to the house, he had been taught all things indoors were sacred from tooth or claw—including the Mistress's green-eyed gray Persian cat, Tippy. Whatever havoc he might wreak outdoors, Dawn understood he must walk gently in the house and must not harm anything there. Even when Tippy chose to get temperamental and side-swipe him on the nose as she minced past him across the library rugs, he must hold back from any form of reprisal.

Nothing but anguish over the loss of his dear elephant had made him forget the Law so far as to assail the door of the library closet. Now he had learned that he must not scratch that door or bark raucously outside it, for the sake of getting to his adored toy.

Yet, late that night the Mistress heard a little sound in the library, and she went in to investigate. Gray Dawn was sitting statuelike on his haunches in front of the closet door, forepaws waving imploringly at the closed portal.

All alone there in the dark, he was "begging," as he had been taught to beg for morsels of food. He was begging the door to open and let him get out his bedfellow, the elephant, before he should settle down on his mat for the night's sleep.

Life moved smoothly and sweetly at The Place. Yet a few days later occurred one of the minor unpleasantnesses which mar the serenity of placid country life. During the haying season The Place's very small force of laborers was augmented by the hiring of a foreigner, Atell by name. The man was a fairly competent worker. His duties did not bring him near the house, and the Mistress had not chanced to see him at all.

But one noontime she and Gray Dawn chanced to be passing the stables as Atell sat in the shed, eating his lunch. Dawn was carrying his elephant and was trotting along in advance of the Mistress. On the advent of the big dog and the queer bundle he carried, the man set down a bottle of bootleg whisky he had bought in the village that morning and from which he had been swigging with much frequency during his lunch hour.

Through eyes slightly bloodshot and dazed by his potations Atell blinked at the dog. At sight of the stranger, Dawn, as ever, proceeded to display his wonderful toy. Up to Atell he trotted, and dropped the lump of flannel into the midst of the luncheon spread out on the laborer's knees.

The man eyed with disgust the uncouth object. Then he shook it to the earth, ground it under his heel, and proceeded to kick it across the shed. Enough of his drink-inflamed gust of temper was left to make him lurch to his feet in the same instant and aim a murderous kick at Dawn himself.

Now, at The Place, no dog was kicked. The Master used to say, "A human can show his inferiority to his dog in better ways than by kicking him." Thus this form of punishment was as new to Dawn as it was painful and humiliating. For a moment he looked at Atell in blank astonishment. Then the dual ill-treatment to himself and to his loved toy awoke to life a hot rage such as his gentle nature had never before known.

All his short life Gray Dawn had looked on mankind as his friends. Anger had found no place in his kindly heart. The queer emotion which gripped him now was as strange to him as would have been a set of newly sprouting wings.

But this outsider had defiled and insulted his precious elephant, and then had given himself a painful, if glancing, kick on the shoulder. Hot fury welled into the collie's friendly brain. With a snarl he leaped at the man.

The Mistress had seen, from afar. She came hurrying up

just in time to catch Dawn by the ruff as he sprang. She was as angry as the collie. So angry was she, indeed, that she did not trust herself to speak. Instead, she pulled Dawn back toward her, to lead him out of the shed.

As she did so the drunken man aimed another fervent but wabbly kick at the dog. The Mistress's swift move, in pulling Dawn toward her, made his swung boot miss its mark. It did not find its desired goal in the dog's ribs. Instead, it flew wide, its impetus almost upsetting his groggy balance. A corner of the boot grazed the Mistress's skirt.

At the sight a wild-beast yell of fury burst from Dawn. Ripping free from the Mistress's clutch, he flung himself, roaring, upon Atell.

He had seen the kick. In the past few seconds he had learned from experience the frightful significance of such an action. Apparently this man had just kicked the all-sacred Mistress.

A million generations of collie ancestors called out fiercely to his untrained spirit—collies that had stood ready and eager to sacrifice their lives to protect or to avenge the humans they had chosen for their gods.

This man, to Dawn's way of thinking, had attacked the Mistress. The rest was red blood-thirsty madness.

Back reeled Atell, shrieking with drunken terror, pushing frenziedly at the hot jaws that ravened for his throat. Under the impact of the eighty-pound silver-and-snow avalanche he crashed backward to the ground.

The Mistress dug her little hands into Dawn's ruff, calling sharply to the raging dog. Through the wrath mists Dawn heard and obeyed. Under the mingled tugging and command he drew back, snarling, reluctant, from his prey. Atell gathered himself up, whimpering and gasping, sobered by the shock, and in mortal terror.

"Go to Robert and get your money," ordered the Mistress, in a curiously muffled voice. "And then get off The Place as fast as you can move. In five minutes I shall let this dog loose; and I shall not stop him, next time he flies at you. Go!"

Picking up the squashed and muddied elephant from the corner and still leading the straining Dawn by the ruff, she turned back to the house. There she telephoned the gate lodge, where Robert Friend, the superintendent, was eating his lunch. In a few words she told him that the new laborer was drunk and offensive and that she had discharged him.

Neither then nor for weeks thereafter did she tell her husband what had happened in the shed. The Master wore no ruff wherewith he could be yanked back by her from attempted homicide.

The Fourth of July came around. The superintendent and his family and the maids had gone to the circus at Paterson. The Mistress, with Bruce and Wolf and Bobby, had driven over for the mail before the post office should be closed for the day. The Master and a man guest had been out since early morning, trying to lure bass to their casting bait. In the course of his training as a boat dog, Gray Dawn had been taken along with them. The Place was empty, save for such few dogs as were shut up in their kennel yards and for the live stock in the barn.

A stiff northwest wind swept down from behind Barometer Mountain and broke the smoothness of the lake into a tumult of choppy waves.

"No use fishing any longer in a gale like this," decreed the Master, turning the boat shoreward. "Besides, it's getting too late in the morning for bass to bite. Let's go home. The mail and the newspapers will be there in a few minutes."

Gray Dawn, lying peacefully in the bow of the boat, was mildly sorry the trip was ending. After the first few strenuous experiences, when he had insisted on jumping overboard in pursuit of every floating leaf or feather, he had grown to enjoy boating almost as much as he enjoyed motoring. And to-day he had behaved remarkably well, not more than twice shifting his position in a way to endanger the craft's already cranky balance, and only once patting at the Master's back with rakingly affectionate claws.

The two men debarked in the boathouse and walked up the sloping lawn to the main house itself, Dawn at their heels. As they went indoors, Gray Dawn pushed rudely past them into the hallway and thence to the library, his leisurely trot changing to a gallop.

The men followed, the Master apologizing for the dog's bumptious vehemence.

"He'll never learn sense and he'll never learn not to butt into people and joggle them," he complained. "He's a scourge. If my wife wasn't so fond of him, I'd——"

He broke off with an exclamation of anger. Straight to the library closet Dawn had rushed. Now, barking and growling, he was tearing away at the newly repainted door panels with both sets of foreclaws.

"Look at that!" stormed the Master. "He's at it again!

My wife said he'd never do it any more, after the way he was punished and called down for it. You know what he's after, don't you? It's that measly elephant I told you about. We keep it in there. He wants to get it out and play with it. DAWN!"

At the shouted word the collie turned and came unwillingly back toward the Master. But he was whining with eagerness and he showed no sign of repentance for his breach of the Law. Touching the Master's hand with his nose, the dog wheeled about once more, before further rebuke could be given, and made another snarling dash at the closet door, ripping destructively at its panels and filling the house with his wild din.

The Master took a quick step toward him, then paused.

"Very good, my rackety friend," he said, with ugly calmness. "This time it won't be a scolding. It will be something that'll put a stop to your baby-doll nonsense once and for all. I'm going to take that silly elephant of yours out for you. Then I'm going to tie a three-pound stone to it and sink it in the bottom of the lake, where you can see me do it. Perhaps that will teach you something. Even if it doesn't, it'll rid us of the elephant pest."

Not giving himself time to repent of the plan, and eager to have it over with before the Mistress should return to beg him not to carry out his threat, he strode over to the closet, pushing aside the frantic dog.

He turned the knob and threw wide the door. Before the fast-swung portal was half open Dawn had plunged past him and forced his way inside. Thus the collie always hastened into the closet in quest of his elephant. But this time he did not dive for the floor corner where it was kept. Instead, he leaped straight in air.

A fraction of a second later the door was wide open and the Master and his guest were staring slack-jawed at the sight before them.

Huddled in the farthest corner crouched a man, yelling at the top of his lungs for help while with bleeding hands he sought screechingly to shove back the rabid dog that tore and ravened at his face.

Clanging around on the closet floor with every mad stamp of the man's hobnailed feet were three of the largest and costliest silver cups from the library trophy shelves.

Atell had chosen shrewdly his time for raiding these shelves and the dining room. From the road above he had seen The Place's denizens, one after another, leave the grounds; the Master and his guest first of all, taking the dreaded Gray Dawn with them.

After two hours of waiting, the coast was clear. Fearlessly Atell descended to the unguarded house. But, just as he was stuffing the first batch of trophy cups into the bag he had brought, the unexpected sound of the returning men had sent him scuttling to the nearest hiding place, which chanced to be the closet.

Dawn, at the threshold, had caught the detested scent and had tracked it down. Heedless for once of the Law, he had striven with all his might to get at the man who had stamped on his elephant and then had kicked him and—a trillion times more unforgivable!—had apparently kicked the Mistress, too. These were things to be paid for. Gray

Dawn was there to do the paying, at whatever later punishment to himself.

"Dawn," said the Mistress next day, setting down three large and pudgy objects in front of the collie, "Master and I have just brought some presents back from the village for you. See? We got every one of them there was in stock. We bought out the store."

Gray Dawn looked interestedly up into her face, wagging his plumed tail, as she talked. Then, at her gesture, he turned his gaze on her gifts. They were three immaculately clean and plump and altogether desirable white canton-flannel elephants.

"They're a prize for a gallant and loyal dog named Gray Dawn," went on the Mistress. "They're yours. You can keep them all over the house if you want to. Master says so."

But, to her surprise, Dawn gave but one disdainful sniff at the trio of gifts. Then he strolled away. He did not so much as pause at the open door of the closet where his olden elephant lay in full view.

" 'When I was a man I put away childish things,' " quoted the Master, with some satisfaction as he noted the dog's utter indifference to the flock of white elephants. "Dawn is grown up—at last. He got his growth during his clash with Atell. That taught him something. Toys don't mean any more to him now than a game of marbles would mean to General Pershing. Do they, Gray Dawn?"

CHAPTER THREE

His Mate

IF THE hero of this yarn were a human, instead of a bumptiously gigantic silver-and-snow collie, it would be classified at once as a love story, and a right dramatic love story at that. But as only humans are allowed the right of way in romance, it will have to stand as a mere dog story.

Sunnybank Gray Dawn was barely two years old. That corresponds with the age of twenty-three, among humans. Some of the irritating rowdy clownishness of his earlier youth had worn off, or had been replaced by a calm stanchness and the rudiments of brain and soul.

But enough of it had a way of cropping out, now and then, to remind the Master of the days when he had yearned to get rid of the troublesome young giant, and when the Mistress alone had been the bumptious puppy's champion and protector.

A mile from The Place was the old Van Meyn house. It had been bought and modernized by a Mrs. Reiper, a large woman of newly amassed wealth and much awesome dignity, who brought letters of introduction to the Mistress and the Master.

On a hill, across the narrowest part of the fire-blue lake, her rejuvenated house shone forth; like a nice new glass milk bottle on a fern-framed boulder.

Gray Dawn met Mrs. Reiper before she had been in the neighborhood a fortnight. The Mistress had called on the newcomer, in due and ancient form. Then she invited her to a little dinner at The Place—a dinner of some dozen neighborhood guests.

Mrs. Reiper was the last of the diners to arrive. She appeared at length, in a right glorious creation of white satin and with many jewels. It was a costume that might have been rather more in keeping for a state dinner at Buckingham Palace than at an informal little summertime neighborhood gathering.

But it and its Amazonian wearer were impressive. At least they were mightily impressive when they burst upon the scene. It was entirely the fault of Gray Dawn that they did not remain so throughout the evening.

People had a liking for the big silver-gray collie. He was an ornament to The Place, and he had friend-winning ways that were all his own. So he was allowed in the living room and on the veranda when there were guests. To-day, in preparation for the dinner, the Mistress had brushed Dawn's massive coat until it stood out from his giant frame like hair from the head of a side-show Circassian Beauty. It was burnished and shimmering.

To add a finishing touch to his beauty, the Mistress tied an enormous cerise silk bow to his collar. Dawn was inordinately proud of any kind of personal adornment. The bow was his chief delight on the few times the Mistress let him wear it. Back and forth he strutted now, head erect, walking with awkwardly mincing grace-note steps, challenging the admiration of all and sundry.

In the course of this triumph march through the house his proudly waving tail smote a bowl of roses that stood on a low table in the music room. A busy maid had to spend the next ten minutes on her knees, sopping the widespattered water and picking up strewn rose leaves and shards of broken porcelain.

As ever at such crises, the abnormally sensitive dog was so humble and cringingly miserable that the Mistress had not the heart to scold him for the mishap. But as she did not want the house to be a wreck of upset furniture and slewed rugs, she ordered Dawn into the Master's study, there to remain clean and quiet and out of mischief until it should be time for him to make his appearance before the guests.

She shut the door behind him and left him there. But it did not occur to her to tell him to stay where she had put him. If she had done so, nothing could have made the obedient young collie stir from the spot until her own mandate should set him free.

He did not realize he must remain indefinitely in the uninspiring study, all by himself. A few minutes later he saw William, the superintendent's son, walk past the window on his way indoors with the afternoon mail. He was fond of William and he was tired of being alone. So when the man passed the study window after leaving the mail, Dawn joined him. This he did by the simple process of jumping through the open window and to the ground five feet beneath.

William petted the resplendently brushed young dog and duly admired his big cerise bow. Then he walked on. But Dawn did not go back into the house. It was much pleasanter outside.

A low-flying swallow skimmed over the collie's head. From puppyhood it had been Dawn's joy to chase swallows. As he could never hope to catch one and as the swallows did not seem to object to the vain pursuit, he had not been forbidden to do it. It was his confident belief that he could bring down any swallow which might have sportsmanship to fly low enough and slow enough.

On the chance that this particular bird might be the one he had been hoping to catch, Gray Dawn gave vehement chase.

The swallow skimmed unconcernedly on, flying low above the billowing lawn, and out toward the sunset lake with its circle of soft green hills and the blue-haze mountains beyond.

Out over the water flew the swallow, almost touching the crisp ripples in his search for gnats. And out into the water plunged Gray Dawn, swimming manfully in the bird's wake. In a minute or so the swallow swirled in another direction, rising high into the sunset.

This was rank lack of sportsmanship, according to Dawn's notions. The collie turned and swam reluctantly back to shore; his carefully tied cerise silk bow a soggy and stringy lump that flapped about his throat, staining the snow-and-silver fur to a dirty pink.

Reaching land, Dawn ambled upon the bank and shook a rain storm of water from his drenched coat. Then he trotted toward the house. Several motor cars, at short intervals, had come down the drive. Dawn started houseward to investigate the arrivals.

But as he trotted past the areaway he paused. A barrel of flour had been rolled thither from the storeroom and had been allowed carelessly to thump against the side of the wall. A stave had been joggled some inches out of plumb. Through the aperture had cascaded perhaps thirty pounds of flour.

It was the sight of this white heap that caught Dawn's attention. Perhaps it reminded him that he was dripping wet. Perhaps he was only actuated by the jinx of getting into trouble at all costs—an imp that had pursued him from birth. In any case, the flour gave him one of his horrible inspirations.

Deliberately he walked over to the white heap. Luxuriously and with much thoroughness he rolled over and over in it. The drift of powdery whiteness was flattened out as if by a rolling pin. Most of the flour stuck doughily to the wet dog as he got up.

Then he continued his progress toward the house. He heard voices and laughter in the living room. He was a sociable animal and always enjoyed meeting visitors who called at The Place. (In later years his name was to become a terror to unauthorized strangers who ignored the many "No Trespass" signs. But he was still at an age when almost all the human race were potential friends whom it was a pleasure to meet.)

The door was shut. He had been scolded several times for

scratching for admittance, and had been forbidden to an-
nounce his presence in such a boorish fashion. But he was a
dog that made up his mind with great positiveness and attacked every problem in a score of different ways before
giving it up.

Just now he wanted to get into the living room where all
those talking and laughing people were. The doors were
shut. Very well; there were other ways. He ran down the
veranda steps and around the house to a cellar window that
was kept open in warm weather.

In through this window he wriggled his damp and floury
body, and jumped downward to a heap of coal just below.
The coal avalanched under his weight. He lost his balance
and rolled down the coal heap to the concrete cellar floor.
There, thanks to his momentum, he rolled over once more
before he could check himself. This final roll was taken in
an inch-deep bed of coal dust.

Gray Dawn arose, feeling no worse for his tumble; and
still unswervingly bent on getting upstairs to the living
room. He was a collie of fixed purpose, as I have said.

Meantime, the last of the dozen guests had arrived. The
dreary few minutes before the announcement of dinner was
enlivened by Mrs. Reiper, who beamed patronizingly
about her and said to her hostess:

"Aren't we to see any of your wonderful collies? I have
read so much about them."

"Bruce always comes into the dining room," answered
the Mistress. "He is the only collie allowed there at meals,
since Laddie died. But Gray Dawn is in my husband's study.
I'll let him out, if you like. He is——"

"Oh, do!" gushed Mrs. Reiper. "I'm so fond of collies.

I have a little collie of my own that I brought with me when I moved here. Her pedigree name is Glenarvon Lassie. I call her 'Lass.' I—— But didn't you see her when you called last week?"

"Yes," said the Mistress, "I saw her. She is beautiful."

She did not add that the poor little dog had shrunk away from Mrs. Reiper's attempted caress during that call, in a manner that bespoke consistent harsh treatment on the part of the obese woman who now was talking so loudly of her affection for collies.

"I'll get Gray Dawn," said the Mistress, rising and moving toward the hallway. "Then after dinner, if you like, we can look at the kennels. We——"

Her words were merged into a gasp. Past her and full tilt into the softly lighted living room charged a truly hideous object. Roughly it resembled a collie which had been sketched by an overimaginative and unskillful child, after two lessons in drawing.

The huge and bounding frame was covered by a pulpy mass of something that was alternately black and paste-colored—something that sprinkled grimy drops and clots of dough at every buoyant stride—something all but shapeless; and with a pinkish tinge to its chest, where still dangled the thing that once had been a pretty cerise bow.

There was an involuntary echo of the Mistress's gasp, from the guests. But only Mrs. Reiper put into words the feeling that the others were too civil to voice.

"*Oh!*" she exclaimed, shrinking back into her chair and thrusting her fat and bejeweled arms forward as if to fend off the Horror. "What a frightful brute; What *is* he?"

Gray Dawn answered the question for himself, before

the Mistress could speak and before the Master could make the first move to eject him from the room.

With all a true collie's psychic perception, Dawn realized that his dramatic entrance had aroused an unprecedented throb of interest among the people there. Misreading that multiple stifled gasp, he thrilled to the idea that he was making a hit. And, after his infantile custom, he proceeded to show off.

In front of him was a big woman in shimmery white. She was stretching out her arms to him in apparent invitation. That was enough for the idiotically excited dog.

With a single bound he landed in the middle of the horrified Mrs. Reiper's white-satin lap. There, in almost the same motion, he curled himself around and lay down with a thump. He weighed a fraction more than eighty pounds.

Squashily he lay in the guest's vainly heaving lap, while her gemmed fingers slipped and floundered in masses of coal dust and pasty dough, in her frantic efforts to push him away. It is no simple thing to dislodge eighty-odd pounds of live weight that has planted itself on one's meridian.

To add to the awfulness of a situation that was already overburdened with that dread attribute, the rather unstable old Heppelwhite chair on which Mrs. Reiper was sitting collapsed under its doubled weight. She and Gray Dawn and the remains of the chair went to the rug in one scrambling and unloving tangle.

All this before the Master could jump forward and lift his prostrate guest to her feet and then pick up the abhorrent Gray Dawn by the scruff of his neck and deposit him bodily on the porch outside.

That was the first of it. In the ample bosom of Mrs.

Reiper, thenceforth, blazed a deathless hatred for The Place, its owners, and all pertaining thereto. For the luckless gray collie her hatred swelled into something approaching mania. For which, on the whole, she hardly could be blamed. Perhaps there is nothing so hate-impelling, in all this universe of hateworthy happenings, as the fact that one has been made supremely ridiculous in public.

A week or so later Dawn swam the narrow part of the lake in pursuit of another low-flying swallow, whose own course led so far across the narrows, before it rocketed skyward, that Dawn found it easier to land on the farther bank than to turn and swim home without waiting to get back his breath after the top-speed sprint.

As he climbed the bank a flash of gold and white appeared on the summit a few yards above him. Instantly Dawn stiffened and his hackles bristled, as became a dog meeting another of his species on alien ground. But in the same moment his upper lip uncurled and the newly stiffened tail relaxed into a friendly wag. For this stranger dog was a female.

Friendly he advanced toward her. They touched noses—the silver-gray giant and Mrs. Reiper's dainty little golden Glenarvon Lassie. Just then a rabbit leaped hysterically from a bunch of dead grass near the water edge. By common impulse the two collies dashed off together in chase of it. Running shoulder to shoulder, they clove their crashing way through woods and underbrush.

By the time the rabbit had dived into the ruins of a boundary stone wall, high up the hillside, there were other rabbits to nose for among the wall crannies. Then a dipping swallow afforded a second futile race to the two.

At last, panting and comfortably tired, they ambled toward a house that stood high on the hill, just beyond the woods.

It was Glenarvon Lass that led the way now, toward her own home, while Dawn followed eagerly. The big dog had found a new idol.

And this idolatry, by the way, is far more common among collies than many a human realizes. There is sometimes a genuine devotion between a male and female collie which rivals that of the lifelong wolf mates from which the collie clan sprang. Such a selfless devotion, for instance, as Sunnybank Lad had had for his temperamental mate, Lady, up to the hour of her death. Such a devotion as had now come into the heart of Sunnybank Gray Dawn for this little wisp of gold and white that was leading him toward her owner's abode.

On the veranda of the hilltop house sat Mrs. Reiper. At sight of her, Lassie did not spring forward ecstatically, as did The Place's dogs on coming in sight of the Mistress or the Master. Indeed, Lassie halted momentarily, and lost some of her gay bearing.

Dawn halted, too. He remembered this large and loud-voiced woman. Though even yet he had not been able to understand the commotion whose center he had been on the night of the dinner, yet he did remember those big hands shoving him roughly away and that big voice calling him names. The memory was not pleasant.

The two dogs stood at gaze, fifty feet from the porch

where sat Mrs. Reiper. Glancing up, she saw them. Her rubicund face waxed purple. Snatching up a stick, she advanced angrily on the gray collie, shouting to him to be gone.

At the words and the menacing gesture Lass whimpered, shrinking back in terror. She was no stranger to abuse and to floggings. Dawn instinctively ranged himself in front of her, for protection. In his heart the excited woman roused no fear—nothing but a mildly displeased curiosity. At The Place, women did not make uncouth noises like that. At The Place, neither man nor woman brandished sticks at dogs' heads.

"Get out of here, you nasty brute!" stormed Mrs. Reiper, accompanying the order with a swashing blow of the stick.

Dawn flung himself sidewise, with the incalculable speed of a dodging collie. The stick missed him. It smote the rocky ground with such force as to break it in two and to numb its wielder's arm to the elbow. Lassie, in craven terror, wheeled and bolted for the woods, tail between legs, stomach to earth. Dawn stared after her, then turned and looked gravely at the stamping and gesticulating Mrs. Reiper.

After which, in leisurely fashion, he loafed off into the woods in quest of Lassie. Mrs. Reiper flung three stones after his slowly departing body. But they missed him. He did not compliment her by dodging or by quickening his insultingly slow retreat as the missiles bumped past him.

Thus ended Gray Dawn's first visit to the shiny house on the hill—a visit of which the folk at The Place were not aware until later.

But next morning he swam the narrows again, Leander-like, to roam the woods and chase rabbits with Glenarvon Lassie. Again he followed her home. This time Mrs. Reiper chanced to be indoors and did not see them approach from the woodland.

Lassie trotted around to the kitchen door, with Gray Dawn at her heels. On the kitchen steps sat a cook, peeling potatoes. At sight of Gray Dawn the woman's wide face was widened still further into an appreciative grin.

The maids of the various houses around the lake were all fairly well acquainted with one another. Thus gossip traveled fast. The tale of Dawn's first encounter with Mrs. Reiper had reached kitchens for two miles in every direction. Mrs. Reiper was not loved by her servants. Wherefore the appreciative grin with which her cook now welcomed Gray Dawn, the cause of her employer's humiliation.

"Stay where you are, you big clown," she bade him, getting up and moving into the kitchen. "I've got a bit of a present for you. You've sure earned it."

The cook was built for endurance rather than for speed. Yet in a few seconds she was out on the steps again, a luscious soup bone in each hand.

"Take it," she ordered, thrusting the larger of the bones at the well-pleased Dawn. "And here's one for you, too, Lassie, you poor little baggage. It's more kicks than presents you get in this house. Take it, now."

The two dogs lay down, shoulder to shoulder, to revel in their unexpected feast. Contentedly they ate, now and then rolling an appreciative eye on the cook as she sat at work on the steps above them.

"That's a fine big beef bone you're gnawing, Gray Dawn," expounded the cook. "It's glad I'd have been to buy you a whole beef, for the privilege of seeing you when you got up into her lap that night. I—— Scat, the two of you!" she broke off, at sound of a step on the side porch. "She's coming."

Around the veranda appeared the fiercely advancing figure of Mrs. Reiper. From a window above she had happened to see the feasting collies. Brandishing a dog whip, she bore down upon them.

Dawn was having a beautiful time gnawing the bone. He saw no good reason to cease from his banquet just because this woman hove in sight. So he continued to gnaw. But Lassie, with a whimper of fear, turned tail and fled. She knew by torturing experience the meaning of that whip.

She ran a few yards, then dashed across to the comfortably gnawing Gray Dawn and touched noses with him.

Now nobody dare say whether or not dogs have a language of their own. (Personally, I believe they have, and a very comprehensive one. But I cannot prove it.) Yet no student of canine life can doubt that dogs express certain wishes or ideas to each other in the touching of noses.

At the contact's message Dawn got up and followed Lassie in her flight. He was not scared. But she had called him to what seemed to promise a romping race.

Around the house fled Lassie, with Dawn galloping close beside her. From past performances, Mrs. Reiper read Lassie's move aright. When threatened by a whipping, Lassie always ran around the house in panic terror, eventually coming back almost to where she started.

Thus, instead of chasing her, the angry woman ran **now**

around the opposite corner of the house, whip aloft, to seize and thrash her luckless dog on the return trip.

The ruse was well planned. But it failed. It failed because Dawn put on a burst of extra speed in his supposedly sportive race with Lassie and he forged slightly ahead of her. The gray giant was traveling at express-train speed and with head down as he skirted the house. He was enjoying the romp to the full.

Around the last corner he flung himself, oblivious of everything except the retaining of his lead in the race. Mrs. Reiper ran around the same corner at the same time, from the opposite direction. Dawn caromed sideways, from the shock, his neck jarred and his muscles wrenched by the collision. But Mrs. Reiper sat down very hard indeed. She had been smitten amidships by the charging dog's skull, just when she was off balance.

The cook shrieked aloud in a rapture too sudden to be controlled. Lassie galloped off to the woods, with Dawn frisking along at her shoulder. Gaspingly Mrs. Reiper gathered herself up, purple of face and purblind with fury.

Two minutes later, over at The Place, the Mistress answered a telephone call. At the other end of the wire was Mrs. Reiper. In curiously muffled but heartfelt tones the much-upset woman declaimed:

"That big gray brute of yours has been hanging around my house for the past few days. I tried to drive him away, but I can't. He stole a soup bone out of my ice box just now. When I tried to take it from him he sprang at me and knocked me down. I am severely hurt and I am sending for the doctor. He——"

"But," cried the Mistress, bewildered, "I don't understand! Dawn never stole anything in his life. And as for his attacking any woman——"

"I am not interested in hearing my word doubted," snarled the wrath-muffled voice. "I've called you up to give you fair warning. I have suffered all from that abominable beast that I intend to suffer. I warn you solemnly that I shall kill him the next time he sets foot on my land. Remember that, please. I shall not warn you again."

"But," protested the utterly amazed Mistress, "I didn't even know Gray Dawn had strayed off The Place. I'm ever so sorry if he hurt you, Mrs. Reiper. But I'm sure he——"

A venomous click indicated that her hearer had hung up the receiver. The Mistress went out on to the veranda, carrying along a pair of field glasses which stood always on the library shelf. These glasses she leveled at the hillside across the narrows—the hillside crowned by the shiny house. No sign of Dawn.

Then, as she swept the glasses' focus to one side, she caught a glimpse of a big silver-gray form cantering through the hillside woodland, a smaller and slighter golden collie dancing along beside him. Dawn and Lassie were once more on the track of a rabbit.

The Mistress lifted to her lips a little silver whistle she carried at her belt, and she blew a long and shrill blast on it. Instantly Dawn stopped in his rabbit hunt and stood irresolute. At a second blast he spun about, touched noses with Lassie, and came bounding down the hillside toward the narrows. In another minute his mighty shoulders were breasting the lake water in a swim for home.

"That means another nice little visitation from Old Man

Trouble!" grumbled the Master when he heard the story. "If I can size up human nature at all, that miserable woman will carry out her threat. If Dawn goes back there to play around with her ill-treated little collie, the woman is certain to kill him. And Dawn is one-hundred-per-cent certain to go back there. So what's to be done?"

For answer, the Mistress led Gray Dawn down to the lakeside. Pointing to the water, she said, slowly and emphatically:

"Let it alone, Dawn! Let it *alone!* Do you hear? Don't— go—in—there! *Don't!*"

Dawn understood. He was to keep away from the lake. He looked wretchedly unhappy at the command. He loved to splash about in the cool water after a hot run. Almost alone of The Place's collies, he enjoyed a long swim. (The collie is not by nature a water-dog.) And now he must stay out of the lake. It was just one more of the million senseless prohibitions his owners were forever forcing on him. It did not occur to him to disobey. From birth he had been taught to mind.

"There!" announced the Mistress. "Now we needn't worry any more. I hate to keep him from swimming, on these hot days. But it's better than having him shot by Mrs. Reiper. He can't get across there any more."

The next morning the Mistress was arranging a mass of newly cut roses in the bowls on the veranda when the far-off sound of a bark reached her. There was not another dog on The Place or indeed in the neighborhood that had Dawn's thunderous bark. It was recognizable to anyone who had heard it once. But now it sounded from much farther away than the forty-acre confines of The Place. Also, it sounded from across the lake. It was a joyous welcome-bark, such as Dawn reserved for dear friends he met after an absence.

Sick with apprehension, the Mistress got the field glasses and trained them with none too steady hand on the grounds of Mrs. Reiper's home. She was just in time to see Gray Dawn scamper merrily out from the woodland to the south and caper affectedly toward Lassie as she ran down from the porch to greet him. The bark had heralded his arrival.

Not a hair of the silver coat was damp. Dawn had obeyed the Mistress's orders not to go in the lake. But she had not forbidden him to visit Lassie, and he yearned to visit her. Accordingly, he had skirted the lake shore—a distance of almost three miles—and had arrived dry shod and exultant at the Reiper place.

The watcher with the field glasses waited only long enough to see Mrs. Reiper arise from a porch chair and go hastily indoors—presumably for a gun or pistol wherewith to fulfill her threat. Then, running fast, the frightened Mistress hurried to the boathouse, launched a canoe, and paddled with all her fragile strength across the narrows.

The Master was not at home. None of the men could be summoned from their work in the fields, for several minutes at the very least. There were not several minutes to spare. Even now she might be too late to save her loved dog from slaughter. Frantically the Mistress paddled to the nearest landing place across the narrows. Panting and running, she breasted the steep hill leading to the shiny house.

Dawn and Lassie frisked gayly about on the hillside lawn

at the side of the house for a few moments. Then suddenly they checked their romp. For Mrs. Reiper was coming out of the house. As ever, Lassie shrank back at sight of her owner. But Dawn saw no cause for shrinking. He stood his ground.

This time Mrs. Reiper did not charge furiously at the two collies. Instead, she paused at the top of the steps, eyeing them. Then slowly she came down to the lawn and walked toward them. There was no anger in her face or in her bearing. Indeed, she chirped invitingly to the gray intruder.

In her hand she was carrying something which she held out to Dawn. Scent and sight alike told the dog what she was offering him.

It was a chunk of raw beef, monstrous appetizing to behold and to smell. Apparently this noisily eccentric woman had certain redeeming points. Dawn's plumed tail began to wave appreciatively. Even Lassie halted in her retreat and eyed the tempting morsel with timid eagerness.

But this delicious gift was not for Lassie. Mrs. Reiper made that fact very plain indeed. She waved Lassie back and she held out the meat to Dawn alone.

"Nice doggie!" she cooed, alluringly. "*Good* old Dawn! Catch it!"

As she spoke the last words she tossed the lump of meat to the still hesitant dog. Gray Dawn sprang forward and caught it neatly between his jaws. Then he prepared to sink his teeth appreciatively into it before swallowing the several morsels in a single happy gulp.

Mrs. Reiper smiled approvingly at the catch and nodded her head. Her work was done. This atrocious gray brute never again would upset or otherwise humiliate her; never again trespass on her home. In a "pocket" of the meat lump was the teaspoonful of pounded glass she had been at much pains to prepare in anticipation of to-day's visit.

If—as many good folk solemnly believe—there is a special corner in hell set aside for those who poison dogs, then assuredly Mrs. Reiper had just qualified for a red-hot reserved seat therein.

Before biting into the chunk of meat, Gray Dawn glanced across at Lassie. She had forborne to come farther forward when her owner waved her away. But she had lain down a few yards from Dawn and she was eyeing wistfully the rich morsel of food between his jaws.

Dawn saw and interpreted her appealing look. Without so much as letting his teeth sink into the meat, he carried the chunk across to where Lassie lay, and he dropped it on the ground between her white little paws.

It was generous and it was sacrifice. But it was such sacrifice as many a collie has made for his mate and which myriad collie mothers are forever making for their pups.

Dawn did not even seek to share the gift with Lassie. He gave her the whole tempting mouthful. Then he stepped back, wagging his tail, to enjoy her pleasure in it.

Lass had no compunctions as to accepting the present. Instantly she snatched it up, to bolt it before her owner could change her mind and want it back.

Mrs. Reiper squawked aloud in horror and bore down upon her dog, screeching to her to drop the meat. Lass, fearing lest she was to be robbed of the dainty, ran for the woods, carrying it in her mouth until she should reach a place of safety where she could devour it in peace.

But as she galloped toward the line of shrubbery that separated the lawn from the woodland a hot and panting little figure burst through the hedge and caught her by the ruff.

The Mistress, too breathless from her fast climb to make herself heard by either of the imperiled dogs, had hurried toward the hedge just in time to see Dawn receive the meat from Mrs. Reiper and give it to Lassie. Now, with not a fraction of a second to spare, she was in time to catch the scared Lassie and to wrench the piece of glass-filled beef from her jaws.

Holding the deadly mouthful disgustedly in one hand, the Mistress turned to Dawn, who came dancing happily toward her. Ignoring the gobbling and gabbling Mrs. Reiper, she found enough breath to say, quietly:

"Come, Dawn! Come home."

She started away in the direction she had come. Dawn, with one backward look at the discomfited Lassie, followed obediently at the Mistress's heels. But as they reached the hedge Mrs. Reiper was confronting them. Her wild gurglings had subsided into intelligible words.

"Wait!" she exhorted. "I—I—— That meat was for *your* dog. He gave it to Lass. He——"

"Yes," said the Mistress, without emotion. "I saw. Come, Dawn."

But again Mrs. Reiper barred her way.

"You—you saw me try to poison your dog? And then

you saved *my* dog from being killed?" she blithered. "Why? Tell me that? *Why* did you?"

"I'm afraid I couldn't make you understand why," said the Mistress, gently adding: "We must go, now. Come, Dawn."

For once more Gray Dawn was looking worriedly back at Lassie; and then at the beef his mistress had snatched so roughly from her.

"I—I suppose you're going to take that meat and have it analyzed?" said Mrs. Reiper, sullenly. "Well———"

"No," answered the Mistress, pausing an instant in her departure. "I didn't notice I was still holding it. Here it is. Keep it if you want it."

She handed it to the flustered woman; then, chirping again to Dawn, she continued on her way toward the canoe.

Mrs. Reiper stood staring slack-jawed after her. Twice she made as though to follow. But each time she seemed to think better of it. At last she went heavily back into the house. As she passed by Lassie she stooped on an odd impulse to pat the little collie. As usual, Lassie cringed away from the hand that had meted out so much punishment to her. For the first time Mrs. Reiper seemed to note the shrinking. The woman winced, as if in momentary pain.

When the Master heard the story a few hours later he said nothing at all. The Mistress had been braced for a verbal explosion. But there was none. Presently she saw him driving out of the grounds and toward the village.

He was not gone long. When he came back, a gold-and-white little collie was nestling contentedly on the seat beside him. At sight of Lass, Gray Dawn bounded forward rapturously.

"I've always thought we ought to have a dog on The Place," said the Master, in shamefaced answer to his wife's volley of questions. "So I've just bought one. I paid a stiff price for her. But it was the price I had named myself, so I had no kick coming. Yes—we really ought to have at least one dog on The Place. That's why I got this one. I think they call her a collie. I've heard the breed well spoken of. So——"

"Won't you *please* stop talking nonsense and tell me what's happened?" begged the Mistress, a shade of impatience in her voice. "How did——?"

"I went to call on your dear old friend, Mrs. Reiper," said her husband. "Not as a neighbor, but as an accredited officer of the S.P.C.A. Robert had been telling me a few things that her maids told our own maids—things about the barbarous way she has treated this poor little dog. I told Mrs. Reiper, as courteously as I could, that she could either stand trial for barbarous cruelty to animals or else sell me Glenarvon Lassie for double what the dog was worth. She decided to sell."

"Oh, I'm so glad!" exclaimed the Mistress, stroking the happy Lassie's silken head. "She's a beauty!"

"That's a matter of taste," dissented the Master. "Personally, I think she'd look better with fifty pounds less flesh and with a face and figure less like a bloated British grenadier's. But—— Oh, you mean Lassie! I thought you were talking about Mrs. Reiper."

CHAPTER FOUR

The Adventurer

SUNNYBANK GRAY DAWN was nearly three years old when he went to his first dog show. This is not a tale of that show, nor indeed of any show. So in a mere mouthful of words the results can be told.

The judge was an eccentric man who preferred a collie with strength and size and coat and bone and a clean-cut strong head, to one with greyhound waspiness and narrow chest and a long toothpick nose. Wherefore, Gray Dawn went through his various classes like a silver whirlwind, and at last annexed the coveted purple rosette that gave him "Winners" and the first three points on a championship he was never to acquire.

At the show—it was held in a suburb within an hour's ride of The Place—Paul Lejaren was showing a string of collies and other dogs. Lejaren was a professional handler—a man who makes his living by boarding dogs and by conditioning them for the show ring and by taking them to one show after another for their owners.

The Mistress and the Master had seen Lejaren at shows

They had noted that he treated the dogs under his care with a wise gentleness and vigilance, far different from the cranky negligence of some professional handlers. He looked after their comfort before attending to his own; and he was not drunk or absent when their classes were called.

At the end of Dawn's first show, Lejaren came over to the bench where the Master was making his collies ready for the homeward drive.

"I like that big young merle of yours," said the handler. "I'll watch him with a lot of interest on the spring show circuit."

"You won't see him on the spring circuit," answered the Master. "This is due to be a busy summer for me. I won't have time to take any of our dogs on the circuit. This is my last show, till fall."

"It's a pity," mused Lejaren. "Two or three of the collie judges at the spring shows are men who like Gray Dawn's type. He'd come close to getting his championship before summer, if he doesn't begin to shed till then. Say! What's the matter with letting me handle him for you? Let me take him home with me to-day, and I'll enter him for the four May shows and the early June shows. I guess you know the care I take of my dogs. How about it?"

The Mistress had come up while the two men were speaking. At her husband's query she looked wistfully at the purple silk rosette she was carrying.

"It would be wonderful if he could win a championship!" she sighed. "Just think! 'Champion Sunnybank Gray Dawn!' And he'd only have to be away from home for about six weeks in all. I——"

"Then it's settled?" asked Lejaren.

"He'll be terribly homesick," hesitated the Mistress. "He's never been away from The Place for a single night. Till to-day he has never been away from home for three hours at any one time. I hate to think of his grieving for us, and——"

"Nonsense!" declared the Master, with true masculine intolerance and wisdom. "It'll be a lark for him. He'll be having the time of his life. Why, look how the crowds and the ring thrilled him to-day! He reveled in it."

"He was with us," said the Mistress. "Not away off, with stranger. . . . Well," she finished, reluctantly, "we'll do whatever you think best. And—and, oh, it *would* be splendid to have him a champion! You'll try not to be homesick, won't you, Dawnie?"

And so it was settled. With no other handler would Dawn's owners have trusted their huge collie. But they felt he would be safe in Lejaren's care. Besides, the lure of a championship is insidious and all-powerful, as any dog breeder can testify. Dawn's easy triumphs at this first show of his made the Mistress and the Master avid for more victories of like sort.

The Mistress alone had the heart and the brain to hesitate about sending him on the circuit with Lejaren. She knew the bumptious young dog better than did anyone else. She read his mischievous dark eyes as did none of the others. She knew that under his boisterousness and show of independence lay a childlike capacity for loneliness and for grief. Wherefore, she dreaded the homesickness which might be his, just at first, so far from The Place and from all he loved.

Dawn had had a delightful day. He had not understood

in the least what was happening in that abode of hundreds of dogs and thousands of humans; that enormous tent with its rows of straw-littered benches and its sharp odor of disinfectants and its myriad barks and yelps.

Yet he had enjoyed sitting on his numbered bench and being stared at. He had enjoyed the repeated brushings. He had enjoyed circling the ring in the "parades" of his classes and standing statuelike on the judging block while a man with strong light hands went over his giant body as skillfully as any doctor might feel for a human's broken bones. Most of all he had enjoyed the handclapping and the wholesale petting when the ribbons were awarded, and the Mistress's evident pride in him.

He was still in a jubilant mood when the Master led him, alongside a strange man, to a crate and bade him step into it. With the idea that it was all a part of to-day's nice game, Dawn obeyed willingly. Then the Mistress was patting him and saying good-by to him.

She and the Master moved away. Dawn sought to follow. But the crate door had been shut by the strange man, who stood beside it as the two others departed.

In sudden panic Dawn hurled himself against the stout door of the crate and tore at it with his nails. The crate heaved and rocked under the mighty pressure from within. One of its panels split from top to bottom, but it held firm.

Lejaren spoke soothingly to the dog and tried gently to quiet him. But Dawn was in no mood to be calmed. His adored mistress and master had gone away, leaving him in this strange place, cooped up in a cage. Madly he fought to free himself.

When at last he ceased to battle with the unyielding

boards, and stood shaking and spent, two of Lejaren's men lifted his crate, along with several others, aboard a motor truck.

For hours thereafter the truck chugged on through the late April twilight and dark, Dawn lying helpless and miserable in the bottom of his crate, unable to see out or to recognize any of the myriad odors of the unfamiliar road and woods and countryside.

He was roused from a doze of nerve exhaustion by the halting of the truck. The journey was over.

The truck had stopped in the dooryard of Paul Lejaren's kennel farm, high in the Westchester hills beyond Chappaqua, New York. Crate after crate was lifted to the ground. Dog after dog was let out of the cramped quarters and was led away to kennel house and yard or shut in one of the several roomy outbuildings.

At last Lejaren opened the door of Dawn's crate. The great gray collie whizzed forth in a dash for liberty. Deftly, yet without hurting him, Lejaren caught the bounding giant alongside the ruff and brought him to a struggling standstill.

Petting the unhappy dog and talking quietly to him, Lejaren led him to a shed and put him inside. Presently he came back, unfastened the door, and blocked Dawn's new effort to dart past him to freedom. Lejaren had brought him a dish of tempting supper and a pail of fresh water. He spoke friendlily again to the miserable collie and backed out of the shed, shutting and barring the heavy door behind him.

After repeated attempts proved to him that he could not break out of the new quarters, Dawn drank deeply of the water Lejaren had left for him. But he was far too miserable to eat. By and by he lay down in the straw, head between paws, in silent misery.

Lejaren gave orders to his head kennel man for the collie's welfare. He himself was to start at daybreak for a one-day show, forty miles distant; taking with him three dogs. He would not be back until late at night. He bade his head kennel man to see that Dawn was removed next morning from the shed to a roomy wire yard, and there treated with special care.

Long after midnight Lejaren's handy man came home from an evening in the nearest village. He had overstayed the decreed home-coming hour. Moreover he was drunk. Lejaren was a stickler for sobriety and for regular hours among his employés.

The handy man dared not stumble clumpingly up to his own room, lest he wake his boss and expose his own hazy condition. A light veil of spring rain was beginning to fall. This made it uncomfortable to sleep in the open. He remembered an empty shed in the yard, with fresh straw in it. Here he resolved to slumber, planning to tell Lejaren in the morning that he had lost his door key and had not wanted to wake the household.

He lurched over to the shed and lifted the heavy oak bar that held shut its thick door from the outside. As he did so he was spared the trouble of opening the newly unbarred door. It flew wide. Out flashed something hairy and shapeless and huge.

Between the handy man's wavering legs plunged the lightning-swift creature. The handy man was knocked flat, his head hitting a stone. Half stunned and wholly drunk he lay till sleep overtook him.

By rare luck he was awakened just before daybreak by the raucous crowing of a farmyard rooster, almost in his ear. Drenched and shivering, he crawled into the shed for warmth, pulling shut the door behind him. There he renewed his broken sleep.

An hour after Lejaren's departure for the distant show the head kennel man came to the shed with Dawn's breakfast. There he found the slumberer, but no dog. It was too late to get word to Lejaren. The kennel man did not know to whom Dawn belonged, so he could not notify the missing dog's owner.

He telephoned the police in one or two of the nearer villages and he made a ten-mile détour of search in one of Lejaren's trucks. Drawing blank, he came back to the kennels to await his employer's return.

Meantime Gray Dawn had found the liberty he had yearned for. Having found it, he had no clear idea just what to do with it. To him, liberty meant Home. It meant The Place. It meant his dainty gold-and-white mate, Glenarvon Lassie. But he was fifty miles from The Place and from Lassie. Incidentally, the wide Hudson River rolled between him and his goal.

Of course the lost collie knew nothing of all this. He knew only that he was far from home and that he wanted to get back there with all speed. But he had not the remotest idea how to do it.

For several hours he wandered aimlessly through woods and meadows, across roads and up and down forested hills.

Then day began to pale the stars. Morning was near, the fragrantly cool daybreak of late April. The rain had stopped long ago. The air was vibrant with damp woodland odors and with the song of birds.

On the treeless top of a high hill Gray Dawn came to a standstill. He did not know why. Nor did he know why he stood there with nose upthrust, sniffing feverishly at— *nothing!*

The collie's ancestor was the wolf, the furtive gray brute that could find his way back and forth from one hunting ground to another, across ranges of snow-thick mountains and across pathless deserts. That weird sixth sense—the mystic sense of direction—was implanted by him in his descendants. Even to-day, in the half-human brains of thousands of collies, it lies dormant, ready to serve them in an hour of stark need.

Not at all realizing what he did nor why he did it, Gray Dawn stood there in the spring daybreak, sniffing fast and eagerly, his muzzle pointing skyward. Not a breath of wind was stirring. But it was not for a mere scent that Dawn was sniffing. His home was fifty miles away, many miles too far off for any odor to carry. It was for an occult Something Else he sniffed. Gradually he found it.

He was facing north. Slowly he turned southwestward. There he stood, trembling a little, his muzzle still in air. Then all at once he learned what he had strained to learn. He knew the way home!

Straight across country he sped, traveling at the elusively fast and choppy wolf trot of his ancestors; turning aside for nothing; breasting rail fence or stone wall; plowing through brisket-deep marshes and scaling perpendicular hillsides.

Once, as his line led across a highroad, he paused and shrank back into the wayside bushes. A scent had assailed his questing nostrils—a scent newly familiar to him and keenly distasteful, since it was associated with the man who had taken him away from the Mistress and the Master.

Thus, instinctively, he cowered back into the lush undergrowth at the verge of the road. In another second a truck rounded the turn just above. On its seat were two men. One of them was Paul Lejaren, on his way to the show. Unknowing, he and his crate-laden truck passed within ten feet of the collie that had escaped from his custody.

Not long afterward Dawn paused near a touring car at a curb. His unswerving way led through the main street of a village. In front of a shop stood the car. It was unguarded. As Dawn approached, a furtive-looking man advanced from an alley and snatched a somewhat costly rug from the car's front seat.

The thief caught the rug by one corner, yanking it toward him, preparatory to cramming it under his coat and making a dash for the alleyway whence he had emerged.

Now, from puppyhood Dawn had been taught that The Place's cars and their contents were to be guarded jealously. This was second nature to him, as well as to all The Place's car-riding collies. Just in front of him a man was stealing something from such a car. Acting on instinct, Dawn leaped forward, snarling, and grabbed a loose corner of the rug in his teeth; pulling vigorously on it.

The thief heard the warning snarl. He saw a giant collie,

muddy and formidable, spring at the rug he was stealing. He dropped his own corner of the rug and fled, popping back into the alleyway with the swiftness of a rabbit seeking its burrow.

At the same moment the car's rustic owner issued forth from the shop. To his indignant gaze was displayed his highly prized rug in the teeth of a mischievous dog that apparently had just dragged it from the car seat and was about to make off with it.

The man caught up a rake that stood for sale on the shop's porch. Wielding it and bawling wrathfully, he sprang at the dog. Dawn dropped the rug and shrank backward, with all a collie's lupine agility. The rake's teeth missed him. The rake handle was split in two by its own blow against the sidewalk.

The man sought for a stone to throw. But Dawn had had enough of the raucous scene. He was aiming for home, not for a squabble with this cranky human. Wherefore, dodging the half-pound rock hurled at him, he resumed his wolf trot down the road, ever moving in that direct southwestward line.

But his adventures were not ended. Indeed, they had scarcely begun. From birth, a perverse imp of ill fortune had trailed the big dog. And this imp was right zealously on duty in Dawn's day of lonely effort to get back to the home and the people he loved.

For the most part his way led across country. But here and there it forced him to travel for a time along roads, and once or twice through villages and towns. For example, he came presently to the last street of a busy little town. The center of the town itself he had missed, as it lay outside his direct road.

Yet, even on this street at the moment there was enough traffic to endanger his life. Two trucks were approaching each other from opposite directions. Each had ample room to pass. But behind one of them a fast-driven runabout of high power was spinning. The runabout's driver either did not see or else did not note the truck approaching from the opposite direction. He merely put on speed to pass the truck directly in front of him.

Dawn had dodged this truck by a miracle, and had gained the farther sidewalk in safety. On the curb stood a six-year-old child, a girl. She had been gathering anemones in the field behind her. Now, with her chubby hands full of the blossoms, she was preparing to cross to her own home on the other side of the street.

She stood still until the truck rattled past. Then, with a little dancing step, she began to run across the roadway. Her parents had taught her to look out for motor traffic and always to cross a street rapidly, before other cars should bear down on her. She was obeying her teachings.

But in avoiding the truck she did not see the fast onrushing runabout. Nor had the runabout's driver seen the child, hidden from his view as she had been by the bulk of the truck. Thus she danced out in the runabout's path just as its driver put on extra speed to pass the truck.

If the child did not see the peril, the collie did. With a lunge of his gray body he had cleared the sidewalk and seized her gingham skirt in his jaws. One sharp backward yank and the little girl was rolling over and over on the sidewalk, screeching at the top of her lungs. The runabout had missed her by a hand's breadth. Its scared driver stepped on the gas and vanished down the road.

From the house across the way a man and a woman ran out, at sound of their daughter's panic shrieks. They saw her rolling on the far sidewalk, presumably in agony, while above her towered a great gray dog that seemed to be trying to tear her face open. As a matter of fact, Dawn was seeking awkwardly to lick the frightened little face. The child's cries awoke in him an eager sympathy. He wanted to comfort her.

The woman shrieked aloud and sped across the street to rescue her offspring from the terrible brute that had knocked her down and now seemed bent on devouring her. The father had stepped back into the house. Now he reappeared, gripping a shotgun into which he had slipped two shells.

Gray Dawn eyed the on-coming and irate woman with no favor at all. He remembered his troublous experiences with Mrs. Reiper, the only other noisy woman he had encountered. He had no wish to repeat that experience. Wheeling, he trotted on his way.

As he got clear of the child and her mother the man across the street whipped the gun to his shoulder and took snap aim at the receding dog. But as he himself was in motion when he pulled trigger, the charge of birdshot went wild. One pellet spatted the sidewalk just behind Dawn. The shot ricocheted and stung the collie's leg, like some super-hornet.

Instantly the dog whirled about, flamingly angry at the hurt. He saw the man and the smoking gun. Truculently

Gray Dawn marched across the street to confront his perse-
cutor. The man rested his gun barrel on the fence top, took
deliberate aim and, when Dawn was within three yards of
him, pulled trigger again.

The gun's hammer clicked feebly on a defective cartridge
cap. The man turned and scuttled up the steps, either for
refuge from the on-coming beast or for fresh cartridges.
As the front door slammed behind him Dawn abandoned
his idea of reprisal and set off once more on his wolf trot;
taking up his unswerving southwesterly line of march.

The stung foot hurt him. He was tired and thirsty. But
he kept on. He was going home. Nothing was going to stop
him—on that he was steadfastly resolved.

It was a time when a recurrent mad-dog scare had swept
Westchester County. An edict had gone forth to shoot all
unmuzzled dogs found at large. As no reward was con-
nected with the insensate command and as the bulk of human nature is decidedly decent, no dog hunters were abroad
when Gray Dawn made his southwesterly pilgrimage
through the county.

At length he struck a wide and winding state road. This
he followed a few miles, luck and a dearth of week-day
morning pleasure cars keeping him from death under the
wheels of some passing motor. Then to the right he bore,
down a steep little street, with a mighty tumble of grayish
water at its end. He was in the heart of Tarrytown.

As he trotted toward the water, oblivious of one or two
small street curs that snapped and yapped at his flanks, a
roaring and whizzing wall cut short his progress. Right in
front of him it thundered. It was the Twentieth Century

Express. By rare good fortune, Dawn was still some yards on the hither side of the railroad tracks when it flashed past.

Scarce had he come to a bewildered standstill at sight of this racketing obstacle, before the train was gone, leaving a haze of smoke and cinders to tease his sensitive nostrils.

On he trotted, to where the Tarrytown docks rise high above the water. There again he paused. He did not lose his sense of direction, the weird sense which impelled him ever more and more urgently to travel southwestward. But in his path reared the precipicelike docks. Beyond them stretched the Tappan Zee, the widest part of the Hudson, an expanse whose several miles of width the dog's near-sighted eyes could not penetrate.

It was as though he had come to the edge of an ocean. His way was blocked. Yet, far more powerful now was that sense of Home, together with an instinct that he was much nearer The Place than when his journey had begun. Up and down the edge of the docks he made his confusedly quest-ing way.

Thus it was, presently, that he neared the Nyack-Tarrytown ferryboat, just putting off for its westerly trip, fairly well filled with foot passengers and carrying five motor cars and two trucks.

Being only a dog and with no knowledge as to the nature of ferries, Dawn had not the remotest notion of this scow-like boat's mission, nor that in it he could bridge the other-wise impassable barrier which lay between him and home.

But the boat jutted farther out into the water than did the line of docks he was traversing. Its prow was nearer his destination, if only by a few feet, than was the string piece whereon he was prowling. Hence, on impulse, he padded over to the just-departing boat and cleared with an easy leap the tiny but widening strip of water between the edge of the pier and the edge of its afterdeck.

It was a pretty jump. The one or two loafers and ferry employees on the dock were too slow to prevent it or even to note the dog's purpose, until he had scrambled to safety on the deck.

A few foot passengers and motorists, who had left their cars and were standing on the afterdeck, drew aside in involuntary alarm as the huge and muddy gray collie bounded aboard. But Dawn had no desire to molest them or, indeed, to make their acquaintance. All he wanted was to get to the front of the boat—the part of it that was nearer his home than were the docks. Forward he wiggled his way, among the few cars.

A woman, grasping by the hand her prettily clad little son, stepped out of a limousine, followed by her chunky and overdressed husband. She had acceded to the child's teasing plaint to let him watch the receding town from the rear deck. Tugging away from his mother's slackened clasp, the little boy scampered aft, to the very apron of the boat.

At the same time Gray Dawn came trotting back from the prow. Finding no way of reaching home from the front of the scow, he was coming to the point whence he started, with an idea of going ashore again and pursuing his quest as before.

But a terrifying gap of gray water spread now between the stern and the dock. The boat was wallowing sturdily across toward the Nyack shore. No jump could clear the intervening space. Dawn had sense enough to realize this, and he halted with his forefeet almost over the edge.

Six feet away, the child was venturing in the same direction, deaf to his mother's wailing call and to his father's staccato grunt of command. Both parents ran to drag him back. They were too late.

The tides and currents and crosswhips of the Tappan Zee are tricky. A puffing and overworked old tug was towing downstream a couple of overburdened timber barges. As the tow crossed the bow of the ferryboat the tug's engine developed sudden and acute heart trouble and went temporarily out of business.

The merry current, aided by tide and a gust of new-risen wind, caught the two lumber-laden barges and swung them sidewise. The ferryboat's engines were reversed, but not in time to prevent the foremost barge from slapping the ferry's bow quarter with a jar that sent some of the standing passengers to their hands and knees.

There was no danger. There was no panic. But it was painful and annoying. A woman screamed long and loud and pointed wordlessly to the spot where her child had been standing when the collision happened. The impact had knocked the little boy overboard and into the swirl of the wake. He had vanished.

Gray Dawn had vanished, too. That same shock had robbed him of his own precarious balance on the lip of the stern apron. Over he had splashed into the wake.

Instantly everyone was crowding the stern, peering over. The woman was in noisy hysterics. Her husband and several other men were yanking their coats off, preparatory to a dive. The engines stopped. The ferryboat hung moveless except for the tide.

There was no need for heroics. Before the first man could vault over the rail or off the apron, a paintless motor boat had changed its course from close alongside the ferry's stern and had swung into the still-boiling wake.

Out of the welter its occupants pulled a squalling and panicky child, unhurt except for a soaking. Out of the welter, too, they lifted Gray Dawn by the scruff of the neck. An eddy had sucked dog and child close together, and together they were lifted to the ferryboat's deck.

While the mother seized her son and alternately wept over him and promised him a spanking for the fright he had given her, her husband and other men clustered about the panting collie. Dawn shook himself violently, deluging those around him with a cloud of river spray. But this shower bath could not dampen their admiration.

"It was magnificent!" bellowed the father to all and sundry. "I saw the whole thing. Cleppy lost his footing when that scow hit us. Over he went into the river. Before he could reach the water this hero collie was overboard and after him. But for the dog, Cleppy would have been sucked under and drowned before the motor boat could get to him. It was *glorious*, I tell you!"

Others declared they had seen the same thing, and they were equally loud in their praise of the highly dramatic rescue. They described separate details of the grand episode, as each chanced to recall it. They believed they were speaking the truth.

But the unvarnished truth is that Gray Dawn had not so much as seen the child. He had been knocked overboard. He had been caught in a churning whirlpool from the propeller and had been banged against some squirming object. He did not know this object was a boy who had been similarly knocked into the river. Before he could realize what had happened, he and the child had been picked out of the maelstrom and had been boosted up on to the deck they had so recently and so involuntarily quitted.

Dawn had no notion at all why everyone was surrounding him, patting him and praising him, nor why one enthusiast bought out the boat's candy seller and insisted on thrusting luscious chocolate bars and lollipops at the eagerly receptive collie. Then the mother ceased to weep happily over her dripping boy. Nothing would do but she must fling both arms most discomfitingly around Dawn's shaggy throat and kiss the white spot on top of his head and promise him a solid gold collar.

There must have been a chorus of roaringly delighted laughter among such members of the mythical Imp family as had pursued Dawn from birth. Two hours agone, the collie had rescued a valuable rug from a thief. By way of reward, he had been struck at and stoned. Afterward he had risked his life to thrust a tiny girl aside from the murder wheels of a fast-driven car. For this he had been shot at.

Just now he had done nothing at all except to fall off a ferryboat. Yet all that boat's passengers were smothering him with praise and pettings and with wholesale gifts of deliciously unwholesome candy. They were acclaiming him a hero. Women were weeping over him.

Thoroughly bewildered, yet as ever reveling in the fact that he was in the center of the stage, Gray Dawn suffered waggingly the maudlin caresses of his admirers. In large and appreciative mouthfuls he gulped down the candy that was urged upon him from every side. A soldier receiving a Congressional medal and a captaincy for having fallen out of his bunk could not have been more utterly astounded and pleased.

As the chorus died down a bit the rescued boy's father announced, oratorically:

"I am going to take this splendid animal home with me, to Suffern. He shall live on the fat of the land and he shall be an honored member of my family to the day of his death. I shall write an account of this gallant rescue to all the newspapers. He shall have a jeweled collar, with a plate on it describing his heroic deed. If he has an owner, I am prepared to offer that owner one thousand dollars for him."

He glared around him for applause. He got it. There was a loud murmur of appreciation. Two or three excited people clapped.

Gray Dawn cocked one eye up at the orator from where he himself lay, chewing blissfully on a large slab of cream-filled sweet chocolate. Dawn alone was not impressed by the speech. Being a dog, he had a queer way of deciding what people he liked and what people he did not like. He did not like this loud-voiced chunky man. Not that the man was a villain or that he was reprehensible in any way. But he happened to be the kind of man whom dogs don't care for.

The ferryboat had maneuvered clear of the timber barge and had continued its westward trip. Now the steep hills of Nyack were looming directly over its prow and the raft-like vessel was warping into the dock.

Motorists forsook the group around Dawn and hurried to their inert cars. The chunky man stooped and picked up the eighty-pound gray giant and carried him to the limousine. He stowed the collie inside and then helped his wife and shiveringly wet child in after him.

Dawn had made no objection to being lifted and carried. He was so dazedly surfeited with petting and hugging and feeding that, for the minute, he did not mind anything. It all seemed part of the impossible past ten minutes. Besides, he loved motoring.

He stretched himself contentedly in the car bottom and fell to gnawing afresh at a fist-sized lollipop that had just been doled out to him from the much-diminished stock of boat candy. At The Place, candy was not given to dogs. It is decidedly injurious for them; and they got none of it, though all dogs like sweets. Hence this feast had the thrill of novelty to the excited Dawn.

Off the boat and up the steep hill rolled the limousine, and through a thread of détours and turns that brought it at last on the main highway that runs from Nyack to Suffern.

Dawn finished crunching his lollipop. His much-diverted mind began to swing back to normal.

He had had a most entertaining time. But that was over. The admiring crowd had scattered. The candy was gone.

Dawn had no desire whatever to remain in the company of these three hysterical people who took turns in pawing him and in telling him how wonderful he was.

He wanted to go home. The more so since his odd sixth sense told him he was much closer to The Place than he had been when he was sniffing the river air from the farther Tarrytown docks. As a matter of fact, only the night before he had traversed this very road in Paul Lejaren's bumpy truck. This, of course, he did not know. But he did know he was nearing home.

However, he lacked the logic to tell him he could travel thither faster and more comfortably in the limousine than on foot. He wanted to get clear of these fussy and unlovable people and to strike once more the homeward trail. With Dawn, to want to do a thing was to make an instant and drastic effort to do it.

The car had arrived at the first scatter of houses that heralded the approach to Suffern. Suffern was only eleven miles from The Place.

Gray Dawn got to his feet. He stretched himself and glanced about him. The car's windows were shut. There seemed no practicable way to escape. Yet drawbacks seldom stood in Dawn's way. He gathered himself for a plunge against the nearest plate-glass window.

He was saved a bumped skull and a liberal cutting from broken glass, for the car came to a stop at the entrance of a garish suburban house. The chauffeur got out and swung open the door which Dawn had been about to assail.

The chauffeur made as though to stand respectfully aside while his employers should descend to earth. Instead, he sat down, most earnestly, on the ground. From his lips gushed sounds that were anything but respectful. A huge silver-and-white shape hurdled his semirecumbent body and tore off across the lawn at top speed.

Gray Dawn had left the car in the manner he had planned to. Instead of a hard slab of plate glass, only the more yielding form of the chauffeur had stood between him and freedom. The collie had leaped out as if the chauffeur was not there. Minor obstacles never checked any project of Gray Dawn's.

Disregarding the bellow of the chunky man and the lurid expletives of the upset chauffeur, the gray collie continued his sweeping run until the limousine and its occupants were a mile behind him. Then once more he halted, this time on the southern outskirts of Suffern. Again he sniffed the air, nostrils aloft. Again he got into motion, slipping into his choppy mile-eating wolf trot.

"Yes," the Master was saying as he and the Mistress sat down to luncheon in a corner of the vine-shadowed veranda, "I miss him. I didn't think I would. He's so clumsy and bumptious and trouble-inviting that I lose patience with him oftener than I like to. But there's something about the big dog that makes him mighty missable. The Place doesn't seem quite the same without him. Well, we'll have to make up our minds to it, I suppose. We shan't see him again for at least six weeks. Poor old chap! I hope he isn't as homesick as you thought he was going to be."

"I wish *I* didn't think so," said the Mistress, sadly. "I've been worrying about it ever since we let him go. He's such a baby, in most ways! And I know how he must be grieving and——"

One side of the little luncheon table arose sharply in air, the glasses and plates cascading to the floor. Their crash was drowned in a trumpet bark of rapture.

Gray Dawn, approaching the house from along the lake shore, had beheld his two adored deities and had made a whirlwind rush to greet them. His flying shoulder had smitten a corner of the table as he cleared the porch steps in his ecstatic upward leap.

The prodigal's return was well in keeping with the nature of the prodigal. Dawn could not have devised a more characteristic reappearance.

That night, at late bedtime, the telephone rang furiously. The Master answered it. From the far end of the wire sounded Paul Lejaren's voice, worried and apologetic.

"I've bad news for you," said the handler. "Rotten bad news. Gray Dawn escaped while I was at the show to-day. I have men out everywhere, looking for him. And I'm notifying the police all over Westchester County and offering a reward. I didn't get home till half an hour ago. Then I found he was gone, and I——"

"You're mistaken," said the Master. "He isn't 'gone.' He's sprawling here at my feet, fast asleep. By the way, what do you feed your dogs? He has chocolate smeared all over his jaws, and——"

"He's—he's gotten home to you?" cried Lejaren, in unbelieving amaze. "Gee! I don't understand that, sir. But it's the best news I've had this year. I'll come down there the first thing in the morning and bring him back here. I——"

"No," contradicted the Master, "you won't. At first I was for taking him back to you, myself. But my wife doesn't want me to. So, as usual, we've compromised by doing what she wants. She wants him to stay right here. Next time, his crazy luck might land him in the dog heaven instead of Sunnybank. She says she'd rather have a live chum than a dead champion. Maybe she's right. I find she's apt to be."

CHAPTER FIVE

Outlaw

GRAY DAWN had a talent for friendliness which would have been worth seven hundred votes to any small-town politician. He fairly exhaled an aura of good-fellowship, and he gave the impression to new visitors at The Place that they had won his instant affection.

As a matter of proven record, they had done nothing of the kind.

To some humans is given a hail-fellow manner that has in it no trace of hypocrisy, yet entails none of the exuberant love for all mankind which it seems to imply. It was so with Sunnybank Gray Dawn.

He enjoyed meeting new people. He was intensely interested in everything that happened. That was all. He did not slip away unobtrusively, as did Bobby and as had Lad, when outsiders sought to pet him or to talk to him. He did not suffer such attentions with haughty aloofness, as did Bruce; nor greet them with a snarl and a flash of teeth, like Wolf. Neither did he repel advances with Treve's melodramatically harmless growl.

He found mild pleasure in being admired and praised and in walking with stately benignity alongside of guests who were inspecting the rose garden or the kennels. But he felt not the faintest real fondness for such people. At heart he had all a true collie's exclusiveness of loyalty.

The Mistress and the Master, in the order named, these were the only humans he loved and guarded and whose approval he sought with wistful eagerness. Other members of The Place's official household—the men and the house servants—he regarded with jovial tolerance. The outside world existed for him merely as the actors in an amusing play exist for an audience.

It was the same in his attitude toward the Little People of Sunnybank. He was on comfortable terms with all these animals. To only one of them did he give whole-souled devotion. But toward that one he showed an adoration which made up, fiftyfold, for his lack of love for the others.

This object of Dawn's worship was his gold-white mate, Glenarvon Lassie. She was a dainty and gentle little collie, whose early ill-treatment—in the days before the Master took pity on her and bought her—had left her with an appealing timidity at utter variance with the fearlessness of The Place's other dogs.

From the first, Dawn and Lassie had been loving comrades. It would have been impossible to find two dogs more widely different in character and in tastes—unless it might have been Lad and Lady, in the earlier days of Sunnybank's canine history. Between Lass and Gray Dawn had sprung up one of those queer affinities which are far less rare among high-bred collies than an outsider might imagine.

It was a throw-back to their wolf ancestors' ways—the wolves had mated once and for life and showed an utter fidelity that might shame many a human couple. There are dogs that follow this world-old lupine custom to a marked degree.

Two such dogs were Glenarvon Lassie and Gray Dawn.

It was amusing to note how the giant silver-gray collie's bumptiousness would tone down when he and Lass romped or hunted together. At first he grew thin and she waxed fat. The Mistress found out why. Dawn was leaving his dinner uneaten, daily, in order that his timid little mate might have his and hers. After that their meals were served apart from each other and at different hours. Yet the Mistress sometimes caught Dawn smuggling his best bones and meat chunks to Lass.

Once, as the whole pack of collies were galloping down to the lake, on the way home from a ten-mile hike with the Master, Wolf accidentally joggled against Lass with his shoulder as he ran past her. She was thrown out of her stride and was almost upset. A faint yelp of surprise testified to the shock.

Instantly Gray Dawn flashed across her and flung himself ragingly on Wolf.

Now, since the death of Bruce the Beautiful, there had been no dog on The Place that so much as thought of disputing Wolf's kingship. The fiery little red-gold collie could thrash his weight in tigers. He was a terrible fighter. While he was not quarrelsome, yet he needed only the slightest encouragement to whirl into murderous action.

His reign was absolute. Not even huge Bobby thought

of disputing it. Bobby and Wolf were chums. But Wolf was king; even as Bobby succeeded by acclaim to the kingship, on Wolf's death; and as did Dawn on the death of glorious Bobby, years later.

Yet now, to avenge his hurt mate, Gray Dawn was hurling himself at the galloping Wolf, tearing at his king's fire-red shoulder in blind fury and bearing him down under an avalanche of vibrant gray fur.

Wolf was as nearly taken by surprise as such a dog as Wolf could ever be. Down he went under the eighty-pound impact. But before he touched ground he was tearing his way through Dawn's mass of neck ruff toward the throat.

Luckily, the Master was coming down the hill directly behind the galloping throng of dogs. His shout checked the fight by the time it had fairly begun. He was in between the whizzingly charging and rolling combatants before real damage could be wrought. He had each of the two by the nape of the neck. At the same time, he was ordering back the rest of the collies as they surged excitedly up the hill toward the scene of strife.

A sizzlingly sharp rebuke turned Dawn and Wolf from warriors into a pair of shamefacedly sulking children. They trotted meekly at the Master's side for the rest of the walk, eyeing each other right unlovingly but making no move to reopen the quarrel.

"It's funny," commented the Master, telling his wife of the incipient fight. "Ordinarily, Dawn would no sooner think of tackling Wolf than I'd try to run over a traffic cop. It wasn't a case of jealousy, either. I saw the whole thing. Wolf jostled Lass. He didn't mean to. He didn't even see her. Dawn must have known that. Yet when she whimpered he sailed into Wolf for all he was worth. He'd fight to the death for Lass, the poor quixotic bungler."

After a time Lass ran no more with the pack. When the other collies were loose she was kept in her shaded kennel yard. Even when she was allowed to roam, alone or with Dawn and one or two of the quieter dogs, she was made to exercise in only the mildest way, and she was discouraged from the wild romps and tearing runs that are a collie's delight.

At first there was doubt whether Dawn ought to be allowed to trot around with her on these easy exercise jaunts. The big gray dog was toned down somewhat from the eternally boisterous and blunderingly bumptious puppy of earlier days. Yet even now he was scarcely a reposeful companion, in his merrier moods.

But soon the Mistress and the Master saw their fears were useless. For some obscure reason, during his walks with Lass nowadays Dawn had an oddly solemn gentleness. Sedately he moved along, refraining from any of the bumble-puppy pranks or the rough romping that had been his.

With the other dogs he was as he always had been. But with Lassie he was curiously tender. He used to watch her with a worried glint in his deep-set eyes. At the approach of a stranger or of any fancied peril, he would interpose his giant body between her and the intruder.

Only once before, in his somewhat long experience as a dog breeder, had the Master noted such tender solicitude of a collie for his half-sick mate.

At night, now, Glenarvon Lass was not left in her kennel yard, with its raised house and big oak tree. Instead, she was shut in the largest of the several brood-nests, in a low shed, far from the other kennel buildings.

Dawn formed a habit of stretching himself outside this shed when she was put in there for the night, and of lying there till she was let out in the morning.

One summer night a tumultuous thunderstorm swept across the lake, from the mountains to northward, roaring down upon The Place. The Master went out to the brood-nest to see that Lass was not harmfully frightened by the lightning and by the incessant bellow of thunder. He remembered the storm that had scourged the heavens on the night of Dawn's birth, and the blind terror of Dawn's friendly little gray mother, Cleo, who had been housed in that same brood-nest.

The Master might well have saved himself the trouble of going out there on this later night. Lassie was one of the unusual collies that have no fear of thunder and lightning and whose nerves are rock-steady. He found her snoozing cozily in the bed of the brood-nest, undisturbed by the tempest. As he entered the shed she looked up drowsily; wagged her tail, and went to sleep again.

But just outside the shed's closed door Gray Dawn was standing. Statuelike, grim, he stood there; the sluicing rain pouring from his drenched coat, the thunder jarring the puddly earth beneath him, the ever-dazzling play of lightning making him blink painfully.

With all Dawn's rowdyish gay pluck, he had a doubly inherited terror of thunderstorms. He could sense their approach, hours off. At once he would become restless and feverishly uncomfortable, unable to keep from moving to and fro in nervous disquiet, panting as if from a long gallop.

As such a storm came nearer his uneasiness and fear would increase. At the first loud sound of thunder he would go indoors and seek the protection of the Mistress's presence. If she was not at home, he would lie quietly under the piano —the "cave" that for so many years had been Lad's in olden times. Nor, except at positive command, would he stir forth from that dim refuge.

Yet, to-night, he stood exposed to the full lash of the rain, unprotected from the incessant glare and blare. Nor did he flinch. Rocklike he stood. He was guarding his helpless mate inside there. It was no time for him to think about personal fear or danger.

Silly as was Dawn's idea of the need for guard duty, yet his brave zeal touched the Master, who enjoyed thunderstorms little more than did the big collie. He called Dawn into the shed and let him spend the rest of the night in its shelter, close to the wire door of the brood-nest where slumbered his fluffy gold-white mate.

Early on a morning a week later, the Master came from the house and started toward the stables to let Lassie out for the day. Two of The Place's men were standing uncertainly at some little distance from the shed. At sight of the Master they turned from what they had been watching and hurried toward him.

"Gray Dawn's gone mad!" reported one of them, visibly scared. "He came a-charging at us the minute we tried to go past him there. He was standing in front of the shed;

like he always is, mornings, lately. As soon as we got close to him he made a dive for us. He wasn't in fun, neither. He sounded like a wild an'mal. Soon as we run back a few yards, he didn't chase us any more. But he's a-standing there, and he won't let nobody go past. He's got hydrophoby. He'd ought to be shot before he gives it to somebody."

"He was perfectly well at bedtime last night," answered the Master, impatient at such an imbecile theory. "A dog doesn't develop hydrophobia in that time. Not one dog in two million ever really develops it, anyhow."

As he spoke he hurried past them and toward the shed. As he turned the corner he saw Gray Dawn standing guard as usual at the door. But now there was more than mere patient vigilance in the gray giant's manner. He stood there, braced and ferocious, as if expecting attack and welcoming the prospect of it.

A workman plodded toward the shed from the far side. Dawn growled low and threateningly. The man did not hear, but continued to approach. Dawn flew at him, head down, ruff abristle.

The Master called raspingly to him just as the collie gathered himself for a spring. At the call Dawn halted his charge, almost in mid-air. Wheeling, he came back toward his owner, but he continued to glower threateningly over his furry gray shoulder at the workman.

The Master put his hand on the shed door's latch. Instantly, Gray Dawn intervened his own body between him and the door.

This time the collie did not growl, nor was there threat

in his action. But there was infinite appeal in the worried dark eyes that Dawn lifted to the Master's face. With his braced body the dog sought to shove him away from the threshold.

"Dawn!" said the Master, sharply. "Gray *Dawn!*"

The collie quivered, as at a blow. But he held his ground. He seemed agonizingly aware that he was breaking the Law in thus opposing the man who was his god. Yet there he stood, his huge body a barrier between the Master and the door.

The Master understood, and he felt a foolish throb of admiration for the dog's pitiful bravery in defying thus the powers that swayed his little world. Even as he had withstood the dreaded thunder and lightning, so now Dawn withstood the Master's gesture and voice. Into the man's mind—as when Dawn, in early puppyhood, had battled with the hen—whimsically came the text:

"Perfect love casteth out Fear!"

From beyond the shut door sounded faintly and far a muffled little crooning, in several falsetto keys. It verified what the Master had guessed at first sight of the newly belligerent Gray Dawn.

While the Master gave due credit to the collie for this senseless effort to guard his mate and her babies, yet no breach of obedience can be tolerated in a dog; if a man is to keep his rightful supremacy and if he wants to hold his canine chum's respect.

Wherefore the Master said, still more sharply:

"One side, Dawn! *Back!*"

He gestured as he spoke, his hand indicating where he

wished the dog to go. Dawn stiffened. Pathetically he stared up into the man's face. The face and the voice and the gesture were inexorable. Slowly and inch by inch, under their lifelong domination, Gray Dawn moved slightly aside from the door.

His great body shook as with an ague. His appealing eyes were bloodshot. Stubborn resistance was in his every line and motion. Yet, he obeyed. He obeyed through no fear, but because loving obedience was a life habit with him and his fellow collies—a habit too strong for Dawn to break, even in this moment of stress.

The Master stooped and petted the classic head that trembled under his hand.

"I know," said he, "and you're a good soldier. I'm not going to hurt her. Nobody's going to hurt her and her pups. You can come in there with me if you like."

He opened the door and entered the shed, then crossed to the brood-nest and opened its wire door. Gray Dawn followed close at his heels, pausing once to spin about and snarl furious menace at a workman who chanced to glance into the shed. The laborer backed away again with ludicrous haste. The collie turned and hurried on to the nest at whose entrance the Master was pausing.

The brood-nest was about seven feet long, by a yard wide. At the far end was a raised section three feet square and several inches higher than the rest of the floor. This was railed off from the lower portion by a board perhaps fourteen inches in height. The bottom of the three-foot nest was padded deep with cedar shavings; above which a soft blanket was tacked, like the cover of an easy-chair.

On this padded blanket bed was Glenarvon Lass. She lay wearily on her side. Against her fluffy underbody nestled six tiny newborn pups, the size of well-grown rats and with fur no longer.

Blind, helpless, squirming, they snuggled to their mother, pushing their clawlike forepaws against her, nuzzling for nourishment. Now and then one or another of them would squeal softly, as if in impatience at not finding at once what he sought.

Three of them were of an indeterminate yellowish brown. One was jet black of back and head top. Two more were mouse-grayish, with faint little black spots scattered here and there on them. This pair were merles, like Gray Dawn, their sire. The black pup was what is technically known as a tricolor. The brownish yellow trio were sables —a term applied to collies that are of any hue from the palest of gold to the darkest seal-brown.

Lass looked up as the Master stepped into the nest and bent over her. She gave him friendly if tired welcome, by wagging her gold-white plume of a tail and licking his hand. Whatever foolish fears Gray Dawn may have had, Lass was in no way worried lest the man harm her babies.

Dawn pushed forward alongside the Master, and thrust an interestedly inquiring nose over the edge of the board partition.

It is much more than doubtful if he realized at all that these six squirming and squealing midgets were his own children. The sense of paternity in dogs is an emotion that exists oftener in fiction than in real life.

Yet there could be no doubt he understood that they belonged to his loved mate and that thus they had her own claim on his protection. As the male wild dog and the male wolf forage for their brood and defend it, so was Dawn prepared to take on these vicarious duties for Lass's sake.

But at the outset he received scant encouragement from his hitherto gently loving little mate. As he nosed the pups, Lass snarled up at him in a flurry of maternal rage. To the Master's touch she had been friendlily acquiescent. To the inquiring nosing of her mate she was abristle with suspicion and hostility. Dawn stared wonderingly at her as she snarled. Then, perhaps thinking he had misunderstood her, he sniffed once more at the pups.

Lass forgot her weakness and fatigue. With the speed and accuracy of a striking snake she slashed savagely at his inquiring muzzle. Swiftly as Dawn drew back, he was not quick enough to dodge an ugly graze on the side of his nose.

"Steady, old girl!" soothed the Master, gently pushing her back among her puppies as she gathered her feet under her to fly at Dawn and to drive him from the nest. "Steady! Lie still. Nobody's going to harm them. Quiet!"

Still growling softly and glaring with resentful distrust at her mate, Glenarvon Lass subsided into her nest.

Dawn was eyeing her, thunderstruck. There was something intensely laughable about his blank surprise as he crouched back and blinked in horrified unbelief at the newly warlike Lassie.

Yet, there was a thread of pathos, too, in his hurt dismay. The blood drops trickled unnoticed from the graze on his white-and-fawn muzzle. It was not the sting of her slash that pained Dawn, but her fierce repudiation of his adoring self.

"Come on out, Dawn," ordered the Master, sorry for the

big dog, yet determined not to risk injury to the pups by letting their dam fly into another gust of rage. *"Out!"*

He led the way, closing the two doors behind him. As in a daze, Gray Dawn accompanied him, tail and head adroop. The big dog walked mechanically, refraining from growling at the men who stood looking in or from so much as noticing them.

Had Hero sicked the family Towser on Leander as the swain emerged dripping from his death-daring swim of the Hellespont; had Juliet responded to Romeo's ardent wooing by dumping a pitcher of ice water over the balcony rail upon his upraised face; had Cleopatra chased the round-armed Antony with a rolling-pin—these would have turned fiery romance into slapstick comedy.

Yet, the more the Master thought of the scene in the brood-nest and the more he looked at the crush-spirited and dumfounded gray collie, the less did he see to laugh at. As for the Mistress, when he told her about it, she saw no fun in it at all.

For days Gray Dawn brooded miserably. True, at night, he slunk unobtrusively down to the shed and lay outside its shut door till daybreak. But no longer did he seek to enter. Indeed, when the Mistress or the Master or the superintendent went into the brood-nest, Dawn stalked away, stiff-legged.

He was wretchedly unhappy. His abnormally sensitive feelings were hurt as never before had they been hurt. He was grieving. Always a heavy eater, now he left his food dish almost untouched. He lay around and brooded, miserably.

"Can you blame him?" asked the Mistress during the second week. "A dog can feel such things every bit as keenly
as we can. He can feel them a great deal worse. Because
he can't understand them or make excuses or know they
will be all right later on. All Dawn knows is that his feelings
have been horribly hurt and that Lass doesn't care for him
any more. . . . But I'm certain she does. Would you mind
going down there and letting her out?"

Hitherto, when Lassie had had her brief exercise, two or
three times a day, since the pups were born, Gray Dawn
had chanced to be indoors. Now he was on the lawn, pacing
slowly behind the Mistress and the Master on their afternoon stroll of the grounds. The Master went down to the
stables, at his wife's request, and let Lass out of her shed,
while Dawn remained beside the Mistress.

Out trotted Lassie, glad for a few minutes in the open
after her patient hours cooped up in the hot brood-nest.
The Mistress called. Lass came frisking across the lawn toward her.

At sight of his mate Dawn took an instinctive step forward. Then he halted, and shrank back beside the Mistress,
standing very close to her, with his head turned away from
the gayly advancing Lassie.

But Lass would not have it so. Experience had taught her
that her beloved babies were safe from harm. It had dulled
the primal motherly impulse of the Wild to fend off anything that might come near them.

As she trotted up to the Mistress she saw Gray Dawn.
Instantly her trot merged into a canter. With ears laid back
and mouth agrin, she dashed up to Dawn, pawing at him

with her little white forefeet, touching noses with him and gamboling happily about him.

Dawn stood moveless for a moment, as if dazed. Then with a deafening clangor of barks he leaped around her, patting the ground with his flattened front legs and pretending to snap at her feet, and in all the other familiar ways luring her to a romp. Nor for a second, did he abate that crashing volley of barks.

The dog was insane with joy over this reconciliation with Lassie. He behaved like a crazy puppy. Around and around he tore, in wide circles, stomach to earth, his barks re-echoing across the lake, his face a mask of rapturous idiocy.

"Well," commented the Master, turning to his wife, "it's all right again. You win. As a peacemaker, you're——"

He caught the Mistress, just in time to keep her from falling. Dawn had intermitted his circling gallop long enough to leap up lovingly at her, as he and Lassie scampered past. The impact almost knocked her down.

One of Dawn's foreclaws caught in a soft Venice-lace scarf she was wearing. The scarf was whisked off her shoulder, still impaled by the flying claw. Down the lawn toward the lake whirled Dawn, in his circular rush, the precious strip of lace flapping unheeded from his claw. As he tore past a locust sapling the other end of the scarf caught in a thorn. The jerk freed it from Dawn's foot. It hung, ragged and rent and ruined, from the locust.

"Yes," dryly observed the Master, "he's quite cured, you see. He's well up to his best form again. Even as a puppy he couldn't have done anything more thoroughly Dawnlike. Did he hurt you?"

"No," said the Mistress, somewhat breathlessly, as she

rallied from the collision and looked in sorrow at her wrecked lace scarf dangling in the breeze. "No, he didn't hurt me. And my scarf will be splendid for cleaning silver or tying up cuts. . . . It's worth all that and more, to have him stop being so heartbroken. Besides, you can't blame him for cutting loose just a little, in celebration. He'll quiet down in a few minutes."

For once the Mistress was mistaken. Dawn did not quiet down. True, after a minute more of wild romping he ceased to bark and gallop, and he trotted sedately off with Lassie to the brood-nest to inspect the pups. But inwardly he was still a fool.

For the next few days complaints poured in from all quarters.

Dawn had gamboled playfully across the glass tops of the cold-frames, up alongside the greenhouse, breaking nine panes and cutting his own foot.

Dawn had picked another quarrel with Wolf because Wolf chanced to saunter past the brood-nest shed and to pause inquiringly at its door. (This time, the Mistress and the Master being absent, it took two men and a pail of water and a broom to separate the fighters.)

Dawn had rolled in a lakeside patch of mud and then had rolled on a sheet left to bleach on the drying-ground back of the laundry.

Dawn had done this. Dawn had done that. The collective nerves of The Place were wearing raw, as in the days when Dawn as a half-fledged pup had been a full-fledged pest. His patience and stanchness of later years seemed to have fallen away from him.

Once more the gentle Mistress was his only advocate in

a world of disapproving folk. Once more it was she who declared his idiocy was only a phase and would pass.

It passed, even as she foretold. In a month or so it was gone. But it was succeeded by a newer and more harrowing phase.

By this time the six pups no longer looked like sleek rats. They were as large as rabbits and they looked like an armful of Teddy Bears. They had been graduated from the brood-nest to the puppy yard. There, with Lass, they were egregiously happy, their tottery legs propelling their fuzzily fat little bodies on daring tours of exploration to every corner of the yard's thirty-foot limits.

Dawn would sit by the hour alongside the wire inclosure, peering gravely at them. They were Lass's. Thus they had a claim on his interest and protection. In his queer brain awoke another atavistic trait—the need to forage for his mate's young.

The Mistress learned first of this when the cook came to her, all but weeping, and implored her to look out toward the puppy yard. As the Mistress gazed, the cook expounded.

Dawn had walked straight into her kitchen, so he had, the big ugly brute, and he had gone straight over to the table, as bold as brass, he had, and he'd lifted a fresh-baked loaf of her best bread right offn it, so he had, and carried it out of doors, under her very nose as you might say; and just take a look, will you, at what he's a-doing with it!

The Mistress looked. There was Dawn beside the puppy yard. On the far side of the wire Lass and the six pups were watching him with silent interest. The meshes of the wire were barely large enough for a man's fist to penetrate them. Dawn was gripping the large loaf of bread by one corner and was striving vehemently to push it through the netting.

Failing to shove it through at one place, he trotted on to another, on the theory that perhaps the meshes there might be wider. Still failing, he reared himself on his hindlegs and tried to drop it over the fence. He could not reach to within a foot of the wire's top.

Down he came on his forelegs again, and attacked the loaf as if it were a mortal foe. He ripped it into a score of fragments. These morsels he shoved through into the yard. Then he stood back to observe the delight of the pups he had saved from starvation.

There was no delight to observe, for the pups were not starving. Indeed, they were not even hungry. Almost wholly weaned, they had had two big meals of bread-and-milk-and-egg that day, and they were due to have three more. Thus, they sniffed with scant favor at the chunks of bread jammed through the wire at them, and they did not so much as nibble it.

Dawn looked acutely disappointed. Then he trotted off. Presently he was back again, his white paws dirt-flecked. Between his jaws he lugged a right abhorrent bone he had dug up—a bone that had been buried by him in a non-hungry moment, weeks agone, while it still had much juicy meat on it.

This he nosed against the wire, seeking to edge it through the meshes, and making sloppy work of the effort.

To the Mistress it seemed high time to interfere. The bits of bread would have done the pups no harm. But super-elderly carrion like this might be extremely dangerous diet for such babies. Nor was there any way of knowing what awful thing Dawn might next bring them.

So she ran out to the yard and sternly bade the crestfallen dog to drop the bone and to stop trying to feed his overfed children.

Once more had Gray Dawn broken the Law, and well did he know it. He knew punishment was his due. From puppyhood he and all the other collies of The Place had been taught that the house's food was sacred from them. In normal moments it would no more have occurred to Gray Dawn to steal a loaf of bread from the kitchen table than it would occur to an archbishop to pocket one of his host's coffee spoons.

But the law of heredity had proven infinitely stronger than the law of man. Ancestral instinct had goaded Dawn to forage for his mate's young, and he had foraged in the nearest and most convenient spot.

To the Master did the Mistress take her problem, worried as to whether the dog should be punished for his theft or whether he was not blamable for following the all-powerful instinct of the Wild. The Master solved the puzzle in unworthy fashion. That afternoon Gray Dawn strode half miserably, half aggressively, into the kitchen. On the table lay unguarded a roll of delicious-looking raw meat. Dawn annexed it for the pups.

By the time he had borne it out of doors his mouth was full of liquid fire. In agony he dropped the meat and drew in great gulps of air, to cool his burning tongue and mouth roof and throat. Then he looked again at the luscious food.

Gingerly he picked it up by one corner. Again that anguish of fire tortured his tender mouth and nostrils.

He dropped the murderous stuff and made a bee line for the horse trough, there to engulf half his head. For by this time the burning had extended to his eyes.

"It was the only thing I could do," said the Master as he and the Mistress came out of the pantry, where they had watched the theft. "It was rottenly cruel. But it was less cruel than to punish him perhaps fifty times for stealing. He'll never do it again."

The Master was right. Never again, in all his days, did Gray Dawn commit larceny of food, whether to feed himself or his young. That one blazingly agonizing experience had been enough. A piece of meat, steeped in red pepper and oil of mustard, is a drastic but terribly effective aid to canine honesty.

For a while there was cessation of trouble. The pups grew apace. Gray Dawn spent hours a day playing gently with them or watching them through their fence wire. Otherwise he had lapsed to his more dignified self. No more did he harrow the nerves of mankind.

Then on a day a neighboring farmer, Frayne by name, came to The Place and bought one of the two merle pups, planning to bring it up as a sheep tender and a herder for his cattle. He chose this merle as the strongest and liveliest of the six youngsters, as well as the largest of the litter. So impressed was he with the puppy that he grunted hardly at all when he heard the high price demanded for it.

"The right sort of collie, trained right, is worth the pay of two hired men on a farm like mine," he said, "and this little gray cuss looks good to me. I'll take him."

He paid out the money and stooped to pick up his purchase. He had come on foot and the baby dog was still very light to carry. But as he lifted the pup and turned to leave the yard, Gray Dawn barred his way. Teeth aglint from under his up-curled lip, and hackles bristling, Dawn moved slowly and ominously toward Frayne. The farmer stopped in his tracks. The Master intervened. His own temper was not at its best. For always he hated to sell one of the Sunnybank collie pups. Hence, manlike, he took out his annoyance on Dawn.

"Back!" he ordered. "Go inside!"

He spoke in a tone that did not admit of argument. Reluctant, suspicious, Gray Dawn turned and made for the house. The Master followed and shut him in. Afterward, when Frayne had gone, the Master saw Dawn dart out of the house when a door chanced to be left open, and make for the kennel yard. There he sniffed the ground then set off up the drive at a hand gallop, muzzle close to earth.

"Following Frayne and the pup!" growled the Master. "I've had about enough of this nonsense with Dawn and the puppies. *Come back here!*"

At the call Dawn halted and turned. At its more angry repetition he came glumly back. The Master took him across to his seldom-used kennel house and chained him. There, an hour later, he had his supper.

The Mistress and the Master were going out to dinner that evening in Montclair. They did not expect to reach home again until well after midnight. In the hurry of preparation they drove off, leaving Dawn still tied to his kennel.

The big dog spent a miserable evening. He knew well what had happened. The stranger had taken away one of Lassie's babies. For some amazing reason the Mistress and the Master had not fought to keep him from taking it. The puppy had been carried off and Dawn was not able to go after it, being tied ignominiously by a strong chain.

For hours he lay with his nose between his forepaws, brooding in sullen resentment at what had happened. Thus did the maids, coming home from an evening at the movies, find him. Thinking he had been left chained by mistake and knowing he was always left on guard on the veranda at night, one of them stooped and unsnapped the chain from his collar.

Like a streak of light the collie bounded to the puppy yard. At its gate he sniffed the earth and instantly caught the scent he was looking for. Again—this time with no one to stop him—he went up the drive at a hand gallop, nose to ground, and out into the motor-infested highroad.

Frayne had walked well to one side of the road, to avoid cars. This fact and the lateness of the hour kept Dawn from accident. In ten minutes his hand gallop had brought him to the byway leading to the Frayne farmyard.

The yard and its fringe of buildings were dark. Frayne's old collie had been run over and killed by a speed-drunk motorist a week earlier. Thus no alarm was given as Dawn trotted into the yard. The surroundings were unlighted, but they were not silent. From somewhere in the huddle of outhouses came intermittently a falsetto barking and whimpering.

Lassie's gray baby was terribly lonely and disconsolate

on this his first night away from his furry little mother and his cuddling brothers and sisters. He was making known his plight by howling and barking most lamentably. He had kept up this plaint, at short intervals, all evening. This in defiance of his new owner's occasional angry shouts from an upper window of the house.

Suddenly the pup's wails changed to a whine of delight. He heard and scented a friend. Dawn had located the tool house in which the puppy had been shut for the night and was loping toward it. Twice he circled the small building. Once he scratched and shoved imperiously at its shut door.

There was no mode of ingress except through the open window, nearly four feet above ground. The jump was absurdly easy for Gray Dawn. With no exertion at all he bounded up and through it. Down he came, as light as a cat, on the floor inside where the puppy awaited wrigglingly his coming. The pup was directly under the window. Thus Dawn in dropping to the floor upset him. Though the youngster was more scared than hurt by the overthrow, the night resounded with his terrified screeches.

Twice in the past hour Frayne had gotten out of bed, resolved to go down and whip the puppy that was robbing him and his household of their rest. The second time he had gotten as far as the front door. Then, as silence fell, he was turning back to bed when this new racket broke out. Snatching a carriage whip from the corner of the hall, he stamped forth in punitive wrath.

Gray Dawn was nosing the pup solicitously, to find the cause of his yells. Under this ministration the howler sank his laments to a snuffly sobbing. Dawn lifted him gently by the nape of his neck, to spring out through the window with him. But instantly he dropped him. Some one was coming at a run toward the tool house. Dawn turned and faced its door.

As he did so the door swung wide. This was an improvement on jumping through a window. Dawn caught up the puppy and ambled out with him into the farmyard. Frayne, flashlight in one hand and horsewhip in the other, recognized the kidnapper at once as the dog that had threatened him in the afternoon. Seeing Dawn making off with the high-priced puppy, Frayne's rage flamed high. With all his might he brought down the scourging whip across the collie's gray back.

Scarce had the blow fallen when Dawn let drop the puppy again and hurled himself roaringly at the man. The pain and the humiliation of the blow turned him to a wild beast. Straight for Frayne's bare throat he launched himself, his jaws ravening for the kill.

Frayne flung up his arms instinctively, and recoiled a step. His heel struck the bottom of the tool-house doorway and he tumbled noisily to the floor, his back smiting it resoundingly. As he fell he shouted.

A woman had thrown open a window in the house. At sound of Dawn's roar and at dim sight of the huge brute springing at Frayne, she caught up the shotgun which always stood loaded in the farmer's bedroom, and she fired both barrels in the general direction of the scrimmage.

Two of the birdshot pellets whizzed past Dawn and found irritating lodgment in Frayne's thigh. But the shot perhaps saved his life, for as Dawn was boring in at the bawling and prostrate man he heard the report of the gun behind him and was aware of a hot sting as three of the pellets raked his fluffy gray side. From all over the house folk were shouting and screaming.

For once in his life, Dawn used supreme common sense. Frayne was down and helpless. There was no more fight in him. Reinforcements were at hand. Something that sounded like thunder had been followed by sharp hurts in the collie's side. It was high time to be getting home. He snatched up the panic-stricken puppy and trotted offendedly off into the darkness.

The Mistress and the Master came down the drive from their evening in Montclair, and stopped the car at the front steps. Something huge and formidable arose stiffly from the blood-flecked porch and advanced with sheepish enthusiasm to greet them. On the floor, where he had been lying between Dawn's forepaws, slept heavily and happily the merle puppy.

"Well," the Master reported next day to his wife as she and Gray Dawn came up the drive to meet him on his return from a call on Frayne, "the net results are that we keep the puppy. I've given back Frayne's money. And I have just paid Frayne an extra fifty dollars for doctor fees for excavating a couple of Number Eight shot from under the skin of his hip and for any other damage and scare he got from Dawn's visit. In return, he won't sue and he won't report Dawn to the police as 'incurably vicious,' as he swore he would when I first went there. I——"

" 'Incurably vicious'?" repeated the Mistress, indignantly, "Why, dear old Dawn is——"

"I'd hate to say what he is," morbidly interposed the Master. "In the past six weeks he's taken turns at larceny and kidnapping and attempted manslaughter and several more things. He's broken about every law there is, except the statutes against arson and violation of riparian rights. I suppose we've got to keep that whole litter of rackety pups, if we want to save him from further outlawry or from another spell of infantile idiocy. He is——"

"He is worth it," finished the Mistress, rumpling the collie's ears as he walked lovingly at her side.

"I know he is," grumbled the Master. "That's why I stand for having him around. When he isn't being an unbearable nuisance he's a grand chum. The only trouble is that nobody knows which he's due to be, next. Nobody. Gray Dawn himself, least of all."

CHAPTER SIX

The Hoodoo Mascot

THE Caritas Motion Picture Corporation (Ltd., Inc., etc.) announced loudly and with entire good faith, through its full-page advertisements, that twenty-five per cent of its next picture's net profits were to be turned over to the Samaritan Fresh Air Fund.

At The Place, one morning at breakfast, the Mistress read aloud the announcement. She read it with real pleasure. This Fresh Air Fund was her best-loved charity. She had investigated it and she had found it did glorious work among the heat-sick children of the tenements by taking great batches of them to cool mountain farms and to seaside homes during the hot spell.

From The Place, every summer, the Mistress sent to the Fund as large a check as she could compass. She sent it always in the name of "The Sunnybank Collies." And now a great film company was to devote a quarter of the net receipts of its next picture to the cause. She read the news aloud to the Master as they sat at breakfast in a shaded corner of the vine-clad veranda, with Gray Dawn and his beautiful big red half-brother, Bobby, lying cozily at their feet.

Since the death of Lad and of Bruce and of Wolf, these two great sons of Bruce were the house dogs, far elevated in importance and in affection above The Place's dozen mere kennel collies of lofty pedigree and of dog-show fame. They two were the inseparable chums, now, of their human deities. Dawn was rising four years old. While he still had, and always would have, a genius for getting into every possible form of trouble, yet he had developed marvelously in brain and dignity and beauty.

"Isn't it splendid?" exclaimed the Mistress, as she finished reading the Caritas announcement to her husband. "I do wish we could help in some way."

Seldom is a wish so quickly granted. The Master had laid aside his half-read mail to listen to his wife's perusal of the Fresh Air Fund offer. The next letter he tore open was from the general offices of the Caritas Company, and was signed by Roy Darroll, a director who had been a schoolmate of his.

You will receive a formal application from our office, probably, by the post that brings you this letter of mine [wrote Darroll], but I want to add my personal appeal to it, for old times' sake and for the sake of a charity I know you people are interested in. Here is the idea:

Our office is writing to ask your lowest terms for the use of your lakeside grounds as a "location" for the making of "exteriors" for our forthcoming picture—the one whose profits are to go in part to the Samaritan Fresh Air Fund. (You'll read about that offer in the papers, by to-morrow.)

The picture is taken from Shugg's novel, *Wolf-Soul*. I am

to direct it. The story deals with a chap who has been banned
by society and who has gone to the mountains to live like a
marauding savage. There he tames and raises a wolf cub. As he
and the wolf are on a hike together, they come by chance upon
an estate that a city man has carved out of the wilderness on
the borders of a lake.

The owner's daughter is sitting alone at the edge of the lake
when she sees the wolf prowling through the shrubbery in
front of her. She is so terrified that she leaps up and loses her
balance and falls into the water. The chap springs in and res-
cues her. That is their first meeting. Her love reforms him and
tames his wildness, just as he has tamed the wolf.

There's a lot more of it, but it's all along that line. Some of
the mountain scenes around the outlaw's cabin we are going to
shoot up in the Ramapo wilderness, back of Bear Swamp and
Rotten Pond. And of course we'll shoot the interiors in the
studio. But most of the action takes place at the lake-edge estate
where the girl lives. (Lois Farady is to play the girl.)

Your grounds are an ideal setting. Will you let us use them
for the bulk of our exteriors? I hear you've refused to let other
companies use The Place for location. But this is for a mighty
fine charity. So I'm hoping you'll consent. I'm also hoping
you'll make the charges as moderate as you can. How about it?

"Well," observed the Master, "you said just now you
wished we could help. Shall I write that they can have the
use of the grounds for nothing?"

"No," corrected the Mistress. "Let's tell them they can
have it for such-and-such a sum, if they will promise to
add the money to the twenty-five per cent that they turn
over to the Fund. That will be still better, won't it?"

"Will it?" asked the Master. "Well, any way you like.
I'll call Darroll up at his office as soon as he's likely to be
there. I'll tell him what you say and get him to send us an
agreement."

Thus it was that four closed cars, jammed with men and women, descended on The Place a few weeks later. Their occupants were various actors and actresses in "Wolf-Soul." Their faces were made up in a sickly cream yellow. The director, Darroll, was in a fifth car, with his assistant, two camera men, one or two roustabouts, and a huge and truculently hideous Malemute dog.

Roy Darroll was resplendent in riding trousers (though he was horseless) and shiny high boots, and a white sports shirt open at the throat. He marshaled his tiny army like a general, then came over to speak to the owners of The Place.

The Mistress crossed to where the Malemute was tied in one of the cars; and called away Bob and Dawn, who were barking raffishly at him through the sheet of door glass. The Malemute snarled back at them with indescribable hate, glaring chiefly at Gray Dawn. The Mistress made as though to put her hand through the narrow opening at the top of the window to pat him. But Darroll broke off in his talk with the Master to call warningly:

"Don't go too close to Polaris! He's as savage and treacherous as a tiger. Nobody but his owner can handle him. We have to leave him chained in a car, except when he is actually at work. We couldn't get a real wolf for the part, so we got hold of Polaris, by rare good luck. He's well trained and he's been used as a wolf in other pictures. See how he's had his fur trimmed and faked and painted? On the screen he's the very image of a wolf. He doesn't have to fake his wolf nature. That's real. Almost too real. I advise you to have those collies of yours tied up somewhere. I know how much you people think of them and I'd hate to have Polaris kill them both. He is a murderer. I'll tell his owner to see he stays in the car when we're not using him."

The Mistress looked about her unhappily. It had seemed a praiseworthy thing to let her home be used for the charity. But now——

There was the evilly snarling Malemute in the car. Raffish men were hustling about, unpacking sheetlike reflectors and other paraphernalia. The assistant director and a roustabout were measuring off spaces on the lakeside turf, with a tape. A group of cheap actors and actresses, with yellowed faces and in garish screen costumes, were smoking and chatting together and eyeing superciliously the pleasant sunlit grounds and the riot of flowers and the rambling old gray stucco house with its background of giant oak trees.

An hour earlier The Place had seemed so serene and lovely; well meriting its nickname, "The House Of Peace"! Now it was uproarious and crowded and turbulent—its sweet silences smirched and shattered by this invasion of noisily abnormal outlanders. The Mistress told herself again it was all for charity and she blamed herself for selfishness in resenting the sordid invasion of her placid home.

Bobby hated strangers, even as Lad had been wont to hate them. After one disgusted look at the flashy visitors he stalked off to his lair in the Master's study. Gray Dawn had no such concept of exclusiveness. At breath of turmoil or of excitement of any kind something responsive always awoke in him.

Now, head erect and silver-gray coat shining, he trotted hospitably over to the chrome-faced group.

"Oh, what a beauty!" cried a girl who had been handfrescoing her dainty face in a little mirror. "Come over to me, you gorgeous collie!"

From seeing her so often on the screen, the Mistress recognized Dawn's new admirer as Lois Farady, leading woman of the new picture. The Master frowned as he saw how delightedly Gray Dawn danced up to the actress at her first summons. He did not like the dogs to make friends so readily with strangers.

But Lois Farady loved collies as much as did Dawn's owners themselves. Moreover, she "had a way" with dogs that usually made the crossest of them respond to her advances. Taking Dawn's head between her palms and then rumpling his furry ears, she asked, with infantile naïveté:

"Is he old?"

"No," said the Master, shortly. "He's prematurely gray. In fact, he was born gray."

"I—I meant, because he is so enormous," explained Lois, not wholly relishing the mild giggle that rippled through the group around her at the Master's cranky reply. "So enormous—and so——"

"Quite!" assented the Master, even more ungraciously. "He was born *that* way, too. So was I. Come along, Dawn."

He walked off, sulkily aware of the same feeling of annoyance that had touched the Mistress at this helter-skelter invasion of The Place and its threat to the prospects of his day's work. He was sorry he had been so boorish to the girl. He wanted to go back and say so. But, manlike, he strode on, the more sulky for his regret.

Gray Dawn followed him, but with great reluctance. Much Dawn liked this new friend of his, this girl with the kindly familiarity and the friendly touch. The Master had called him and he obeyed, which was Dawn's way. But as he went he kept glancing back at Lois Farady. He had found a new friend, a new person on whom to lavish his exuberant affection.

Dawn had many and surprising methods of bringing himself to the notice of those he liked. Lois discovered this, with much suddenness, an hour later.

The scene was set for her first appearance at the lake edge. The time was supposed to be late sunset of a summer evening. In elaborate attire she had wandered away from her father's dinner party for a brief spell of solitude on her favorite rustic bench beside the lake. There, in a later scene, she was to see the wolf creeping up on her and was (in the person of a "double") to fall into the water for the hero to rescue.

Toward the lake she strolled now, two cameras playing upon her. She moved gracefully, her flowerlike face wistful, her softly shimmering white-satin evening dress draped in classic outline about so much of her as it covered at all. The dress, by the way, was one of her own, the creation of a Paris super-artist in women's clothes.

Onward she strolled into the nonexistent sunset. The cameras buzzed diligently. Roy Darroll cooed an almost respectful volley of directions from the side lines.

Then, from nowhere in particular, appeared Gray Dawn.

Trotting across the sloping lawn, he saw his pretty new friend on her way to the lakeside. He frisked down to join her. There was a most delightful stunt he had learned in connection with the lake—a stunt of which he was mildly proud and which seemed to him an inspired way of showing off.

Often, when the Mistress was walking near the brink, as Lois now was walking, Dawn was wont to find a stick and bring it to her to throw into the water for him. Then, with a dash and much loud barking, he would plunge in and retrieve it, swimming back with it to shore and laying it triumphantly at her feet for another throw.

Eagerly now he cantered about in a half circle; seeking a stick to bring to the admired Lois, that he might let her see how accomplished a swimmer and retriever he was. The only thing resembling a stick that he could happen upon in that hurried quest was a large and ungainly thorn bush that one of The Place's laborers had uprooted a day or so earlier and had neglected to burn.

Gray Dawn snatched up this thousand-thorned bush, near its roots, so the thorns should not prick his tender mouth. Then he galloped dramatically down upon Lois Farady.

The shouts of Darroll and of the chief camera man did not deter the dog. He was in the habit of taking orders from only the Mistress or the Master. Just now neither of these was at hand. He pranced jubilantly into the picture and up to the wistfully strolling Lois.

Having been told to keep straight on at the same pace, with her gaze on the sunset, she did not look to see what was happening. Yet she was not kept long in doubt. Up to her galloped Gray Dawn, swirling the thorn bush invit-

ingly to and fro. Fifty of its needle-prongs hooked themselves viciously in the soft satin skirt as he swished the bush
against her to call attention to his presence.

Then, still gripping the stem, he capered wildly around
the girl in a narrow circle. The thorns, imbedded in the
satin, did not come out. They held their tenure in the shimmery material.

Lois shrieked as she felt her costliest dress dragged vehemently around her in a corkscrew pattern and heard the
grim and multiple rending of its material. At last Gray
Dawn had succeeded in attracting her notice.

A malicious idiot could not have devised nor worked
out a more comprehensive scheme for destroying utterly
a several-hundred-dollar evening dress. The thorns had
pierced it from hip to hem. Then they had been yanked
all the way about it in rapid centrifugal motion by a fast-
whirling collie weighing more than eighty pounds. The
destruction was complete.

But Dawn was not satisfied. The thorn bush had become
inextricably tangled up in the satin and the satin had become wound so close about its wearer that it could be
dragged no farther. Wherefore the dog let go of it. Gayly
barking, he ran down to the lake, plunging in and then
scampering back to the scene of his crime. His wet feet
stormed through a patch of lakeside mud as he ran.

He found Lois Farady, helped by Darroll and two others, trying hysterically to unwind herself from the tight-
reefed folds of her tattered skirt.

A turmoiled excitement was in the air, such an aura as
Dawn always was swift to note. It went to his head. Ap-

parently his merry prank had caused much interest. Like a human child who has chanced to get a laugh for some unconscious witticism, he sought to retain the center of the stage.

He frisked up to the actress, patting merrily at her skirt with his mud-sodden forepaws. Darroll shoved him crossly aside. Dawn was the most abnormally sensitive of dogs. But just now he was drunk with playfulness. The shove seemed to him a rough invitation for a romp. Blithely he accepted it.

Pausing only to shake his mighty coat free of a deluge of mud and lake water, which inundated the spotless Darroll from head to foot, Dawn leaped up, slapping the director's snow-fresh shirt front with his muddy paws. Then, as he dropped back on all fours, he let his mud-smeared front feet trail pleasantly groundward, athwart the cream-colored riding breeches.

Darroll drew back one spattered boot for a furious kick. It was as well for him that the kick was not delivered. Even in his present roystering mood, Dawn would not have regarded it as a joke. There would have been reprisals, lightning-swift and terrific—reprisals from which Darroll might have been lucky to emerge with a throat no worse mauled than were his erst-immaculate clothes.

It was Lois Farady whose sharp gesture and sharper word checked Darroll's wrathful impulse.

"Don't!" she exhorted, stepping between him and the offender. "If I can stand it, you can. Never kick a collie— or any other dog, for that matter. Gray Dawn didn't mean any harm. Did you, you miserable clown?"

Despite the tearful annoyance in her voice, Dawn read

unabated friendliness and a rare understanding of himself. For some reason the anticipated romp seemed to be at an end, almost before it had begun. But he thrust his cold muzzle into the girl's palm and wagged his plumed tail as she stroked his head.

"It gums things up a little," said Darroll, reporting the tragedy to the Master. "You see, that was the only evening dress she brought out on location with her. So the scene has to wait till to-morrow—or till the first day when the sun casts the right kind of shadows for it. Probably it'll have to wait much longer than that, or else we'll have to make a retake on all the dinner-party scenes we've shot in the studio. That dress was registered in all of them. We can't have the heroine leave the dinner table in one gown and appear a second later on the lawn in another one. We'll have to wait till a dress can be made that looks exactly like the spoiled one."

"I'm sorry," stammered the Master. "Mighty sorry. Dawn's forever doing some fool stunt like that. At least he used to. This past year or so he has toned down a bit. But he's still——"

"That isn't the worst of it," went on Darroll. "It was Lois's own dress. By a clause in her contract we're responsible for any accidental injury to her wardrobe while she's working. That means the Caritas Company has to replace the dress. The price will come out of the budget of the picture. So the cost of 'Wolf-Soul' will be that much larger, and the net profits that much less. Several Fresh Air Fund kids could have had a week or two in the country on the Fund's share of what Dawn has cost us to-day. I mean, what he has cost us in the dress alone; not in the delay, nor the cash we'll have to keep on paying our company for the time wasted. He——"

"Tell her to send me the bill for her spoiled clothes," said the Master, ungraciously. "The cost shan't put a crimp in the Fund's share of the picture. I never thought at my age I'd be paying out several hundred dollars for a dress, for anyone except my own wife. Certainly not for an actress I've hardly spoken to. But it seems one is never too old to pay."

"Thanks, old man. But——"

"As for the loss of time," went on the Master, his temper not at its best, "well, if you people weren't losing it on account of this mix-up, you'd be losing it some other way. I've watched lots of pictures made. I never yet saw one of them where enough valuable time wasn't frittered uselessly away to drive an efficiency expert crazy. Send me the bill for the dress. Put down the rest of the misfortune to profit and loss. I'll see Dawn is kept tied or else in the house while you're here."

For the next week, during the company's working time, Gray Dawn spent his daylight hours either in the house or ignominiously cooped in a kennel yard. In the evenings and the early mornings and on Sunday alone was he free to rove as of yore.

To Darroll's annoyance, the Mistress very gently but very firmly decreed that The Place was not to be used for motion-picture purposes on Sunday. Thus Dawn had an entire outdoor day that week.

On the following Monday morning, the weather being

ideal, Darroll prepared to take the melodramatic series of scenes which began with the hero and his wolf making their appearance through a wall of shrubbery as Lois sat musing beside the lake.

A fortnight earlier, in the Ramapo Mountains, the scenes had been taken which led up to this—the hero's departure from his hilltop shack and his hike through the forest, accompanied by his faithful if sinister wolf. The wolf had disappeared into some undergrowth. Now he was supposed to be coming into sight at the farther side of the same thicket, and to halt in surly surprise at sight of the girl sitting beside the lake. The hero was supposed to be following, some yards behind him, and to come into view just as Lois lost her balance and fell into the deep water.

Much depended on the success of this episode from first to last. Darroll had worked himself into a fine fit of temperament for it.

The Mistress and the Master had come down to the lake to look on. With Lois Farady and with Tevvis, the leading man, they sat on the steps of the summerhouse to watch the Malemute go through the first part of his work. The dog was guided by his Danish owner and trainer, under Darroll's low-voiced directions.

A query from Darroll, a grunted reply from the trainer, and Polaris emerged stealthily from the screen of bushes. So quietly did he step forth that scarce a twig stirred. So lupine was he in look and movement that the spectators could almost have sworn they beheld a gaunt giant timber wolf slink into view from the underbrush.

Polaris was a born actor and he had been well trained. There was something tremendous in his halt of astonishment at the supposed view of Lois (who, by the way, was not actually within his line of vision just then, but was chatting with the Mistress on the summerhouse steps) and in the hideous silent up-curl of his tushed lips.

He was not a pretty sight as he worked thus at his trainer's sharp commands. But he was compelling and grim. No theater audience, after getting that first malign glimpse of him, would wonder at the heroine for leaping in terror from her seat at such a fearsome sight.

"Good!" commented Darroll. "Once more. This time we'll shoot it."

A word to the Malemute from the trainer, an order from Darroll to the two camera men, and the scene was re-enacted. While both cameras buzzed, the wolflike head slipped evilly into view again. The leanly powerful giant body slid snakelike forward from the masking shrubs. Then, as before, at command, Polaris halted crouchingly, his face wrinkled, his fangs bared, as he glared at the imaginary girl.

One camera was busy with a close-up, the other with a long shot. Darroll beamed. Then he groaned in pettish fury.

Across the focus of both cameras—clearly in the long-shot lens and a blur in the close-up—swept a galloping silver-gray shape—a footage-spoiling shape that changed and ruined the whole tenor of the two films.

Gray Dawn had been shut up in the Mistress's room. A maid had gone thither on some errand. Not seeing the sleeping collie on the far side of the dresser, she had gone out again, leaving the door of the room open. Dawn had awakened from his nap and had wandered forth in quest of human society. He found it.

Scent and sound enabled him to track the group sitting

on the summerhouse steps. Eagerly he rushed down the slope of the lawn to join them. Not only did he want to be with the Mistress and the Master, but with Lois. Several times, during his week of semi-imprisonment, she had come into the house to pet him and talk to him. Increasingly he liked her.

Another and less welcome scent was in the still summer air—the scent of Polaris. The Malemute was out of sight at that moment, in the shrubbery. Dawn's nose told him accurately the precise locality of the stranger dog. Much he longed to wheel forthwith into the bushes and dispute Polaris's right to be hiding on The Place. But even more he wanted to join his loved friends on the steps. The finding and ousting of the Malemute could wait until he had greeted the humans.

Dawn flashed past the thicket just as Polaris emerged from it. Thus he spoiled the whole scene. He could not have timed his enthusiastic advent in a more thoroughly Dawn-like way.

To his chagrin, he was not received with an enthusiasm equaling his own. Indeed, he was received with no enthusiasm at all. His almost morbid sensitiveness told him at once that for some obscure reason he was in disgrace again. His head and tail drooped miserably under the Master's vexed reproof.

"I suppose I ought to take him all the way up to the house and chain him," said the Master to the world in general. "But I want to see this. Here, Dawn, come in here."

He opened the door at the top of the summerhouse steps and motioned the collie to enter the little room. Crestfallen and glum, Gray Dawn obeyed, and the door was slammed shut behind him. Once more, for no apparent cause at all, he was a prisoner. These were abominable days—full of strange people and a hateworthy strange dog and incomprehensible prohibitions and much captivity. Dawn was wretched.

"He'll make no more trouble," the Master informed the fuming Darroll. "I'm sorry he spoiled all that footage. More cash to be lopped off the Fund's share of the picture, I suppose."

Darroll did not answer. Already he was busily repeating the shrubbery scene. For the third occasion, Polaris went through his work, this time without mishap; the two cameras registering his every move and look. A fourth repetition, to make certain of success—in true motion-picture tradition—and Darroll was ready for the next step in the story.

Lois Farady left the summerhouse steps and seated herself gracefully on the rustic bench at the margin of the lake. The "double" made ready for her substitute plunge into the waters. The cameras sang busily. Then, as Lois posed there, the machines were shifted. Polaris began his creeping advance from the shrubbery toward the unseeing girl.

Again the Malemute's work drew a nod of approval from Darroll. Creeping low, his fangs glinting, his mask set in a grimace of half fear, half menace, the great brute slunk stealthily forward athwart the patch of lakeside lawn. As a rehearsal or even a retake for so long a scene would be difficult, the cameras were called into action at his first step.

There was something indescribably sinister in the Malemute's wolflike approach. Darroll glanced nervously at Lois; then for reassurance he looked toward the Danish trainer. The latter grinned back his confidence in his own ability to curb at a word the beast he was urging forward. By club and boot toe he had impressed his mastership on the dangerous wolf-dog. He was confident of his power. But the camera man, whose duty it was to take the full-face view of the advance, fidgeted nervously as he ground his machine's shiny crank.

In the meantime Gray Dawn had sulked his fill. To a nature as sunnily optimistic as his, it was desperately hard to remain sullen or sad for any length of time. When he had been shut into the summerhouse he had lain down on the matting floor with a heavy sigh, and had put his head disconsolately between his forepaws. But it was not easy to stay unhappy when he could hear voices and motion all around him, outside his jail.

He got up to investigate. One window of the summerhouse faced westward to the lake, another toward the Ramapo Mountains. The third looked out on the stretch of lawn between the shrubbery and the bench whereon his dear new friend, Lois, was sitting.

Coming at last to this window, in his quest for more intimate knowledge of what was happening, Gray Dawn stood on his hind-legs, and peered out through the unglazed aperture to the lawn six feet beneath him. At sight of Lois his tail began to wave.

Then his tail stiffened to a ramrod and a growl was born far down in his furry throat.

Lois was gazing out across the lake, seemingly oblivious

of everything. Toward her was moving the Malemute. Every motion and every line of Polaris was vibrant with murder. Straight for the unknowing girl he was making his deadly way.

None of the humans scattered here and there seemed to realize Lois's dire peril. But Dawn realized it at a single glance. He had grown mildly fond of her this past week. In any event, it was not in his white soul to permit any woman to be attacked or harmed while he had power to prevent it.

As ever, his mind being made up, Gray Dawn wasted not a fraction of an instant before going into action. The Malemute at this stage of his murderous progress was almost directly under the window. The two cameras were following him, inch by inch. Gray Dawn launched himself into the picture.

With a spring that called into play all his muscular prowess, he shot through the open window that was barely wide enough to give space to him. Out and downward he swooped, like a bolt of silver and snow.

From a height of more than six feet he dropped. Impulsive as had been his leap, it had all of a collie's queerly true sense of direction. He had gauged it to the inch.

If any other creature is as uncannily quick of perception as a collie, it is a Malemute; for in him the wolf strain and the wolf brain still predominate. Polaris was not taken unaware. He flashed backward and sidewise, to dodge the descending avalanche of fur and fury.

Dodge it he could not, even as he could not have dodged a bullet. But he braced himself for the assault. His backward motion caused Dawn's mighty weight to strike him glanc-ingly, instead of with full force.

Before fairly colliding with him Gray Dawn drove his rage-wrinkled jaws downward for his foe's throat. Even as the Malemute braced himself to meet the charge, Polaris slashed fiercely and cunningly for the collie's underbody. Both dogs missed their mark by a hair's-breadth.

In what looked like the same move, the two combatants were locked in death battle. Over and over on the soft green turf they rolled in unloving embrace, roaring and foaming and striking.

Then they were on their feet again, upreared to meet the shock of each other's impact; then tangled in an inextricable mass of writhing bodies and gleaming blood-flecked teeth.

The duel was on. The ever-smoldering hate that had had its birth when they glared at each other through the car window, nine days earlier, had come to a red climax.

Polaris, after the wolf custom, feinted for the head, then lunged low for a bone-breaking grip on one of Dawn's snowy forelegs. Thus does the timber wolf seek to cripple his opponent. Thus do collie puppies (in their play, that is ever the unconscious imitation of a death fight) seek to nip each other's legs.

But if the wolf wit is strong in a Malemute, it is scarcely weaker in a collie. Dawn drew in his forelegs, as might a kangaroo. With his front feet thus tucked under him he drove forward and downward, impelled by his powerful hind quarters, and he struck for the nape of the Malemute's neck. This is another atavistic wolf trait, this effort to sever the spinal cord of an enemy.

Deftly the other shifted sidewise, but not soon enough to

avoid a deep shoulder slash from Dawn's curved white eye-tooth. The Malemute snapped ferociously for the throat, for the tiny vulnerable patch under a collie's chin where the armor of shaggy ruff hair does not grow.

He failed by the merest part of an inch to reach his goal. As a result he found his mouth full of mattresslike fur and a little skin, and nothing else.

Dawn took advantage of the low-headed lunge to strike again for the neck nape. Again he slashed the shoulder. Once more the two reared their enormous bodies, clawing and snapping for each other as they met in air. Both lost their footing and rolled savagely together on the turf.

Followed a moment or two of indiscriminate battling at close quarters. Dawn was the first to gain a firm grip. He drove his teeth into Polaris's broad chest, and he held on. The Malemute swirled madly about under the pressure, ripping one of Dawn's ears with his rending jaws; but he could not shake loose his foe. Deep drove Dawn's white teeth, with instinctive search for the great vein that traverses the chest muscles. Backward, by sheer force, he pushed the maddened Polaris.

Then, in the midst of a supreme heave, his own hind foot slipped on the blood-slippery grass.

Down went the collie in a sprawling heap; his jaws wrenched free of their chest grip by his own impetus. Polaris dived greedily to the slaughter, tearing for the exposed underbody of his overthrown adversary.

But a collie down is never a collie beaten. Over on his back rolled Dawn with the speed of light, driving all four of his legs upward against the pouncing Malemute.

The clawing feet smote Polaris amidships as he dived for

his seemingly beaten opponent. Their shove checked his rush and deflected the aim of his ravening jaws.

Polaris's teeth closed on one of the up-thrust forelegs, but only in the flesh and sinews of it, a too-hasty aim making him miss the bone. At the same time, and without so much as trying to rise or to drag loose his own imprisoned foot, Dawn saw his chance and made instant use of it.

Upward he drove his bleeding head, like a striking snake. His jaws found at last the mark they had sought. He had the Malemute by the jugular, in a grip that could not be shaken off.

Polaris knew his own awful danger, even before the collie's teeth had fairly closed on the momentarily exposed throat. This was the death grip unless the Malemute could break free from it.

With every atom of his giant strength Polaris thrashed about, to shake off that vise hold. But Dawn hung on. Battered and dizzy, yet he hung on. Polaris let go of the collie's foreleg in his own efforts at freedom. His gyrations yanked Dawn to his feet again.

The collie braced himself mightily and threw all his bewildered purpose into driving his teeth deeper through the mass of muscle and fur which protected the other's jugular. The end was inevitable and the end was near.

And now, helpless and hopeless, Polaris showed a new phase of his wolflike nature. Expecting certain death, he broke into a tumult of terrified howls. He was beaten. All the rabid fight was thrashed out of him. He shrieked as if for mercy.

Dawn had made no sound when the Malemute tore into

his unprotected and overthrown underbody. Death had been very close then. Yet Dawn had faced it silently and had fought on. The Malemute was of different mental fiber, as his yells of fright attested.

Then a strange thing happened.

Dawn seemed to realize that his enemy was become merely his victim. For he loosened the death-grinding hold that was working its steady way down to the jugular and he stepped back a pace.

There, swaying a little, he stood gravely looking at the beaten Polaris.

He had not long to look at him in that position. Still bellowing and ki-yi-ing in mortal terror, the Malemute turned tail and ran for the woods at top speed, tail between legs, body humped double. He was seeking only to get as far away as possible from the dog he had sought to kill.

Then and only then did the two cameras cease to grind. Camera men always keep on at their work until the director's call of "Cut!" stops them or until a scene ends. Darroll had been far too dumfounded to give the needful order. Wherefore, from two different angles and distances every move of the wild battle had been photographed; from Dawn's sensational downward leap from the window, to the Malemute's ignominious flight.

The Mistress and the Master had beheld the conflict, but they had forborne to call off their dog. They knew that Dawn would hear their voices through the fight mists and the racket and that he would obey the call.

But also they knew his cessation of hostilities, and his turning away from the scrimmage, would have laid him open to an immediate and perhaps fatal flank attack from the Malemute. For similar reason, Polaris's trainer had not dared to call off his dog. Thus they had waited, tensely, watching in vain for a chance to break in between the whirlwind battlers.

As the Mistress was dressing Gray Dawn's ugly wounds, the Master helping her with the task, Roy Darroll came up to the porch where they sat.

"Hansen has caught his Malemute at last," reported the director, gloomily, "and he swears he'll sue us for the brute's full value. Polaris is pretty badly hurt, but he'll get well. Only he will be too scarred and mussed up and lame and frightened to be any more use to us for another couple of months, at the very least. That means the picture comes to a full stop. We've spent more cash on it already than we meant to. And it all goes for nothing. I'm afraid the Fund offer will have to be withdrawn. The Samaritan's percentage of the net would be a good many dollars less than nothing, after all this 'overhead.' "

"But——"

"If ever I want to go bankrupt and smash every plan I've got in the world," continued Darroll, morbidly, "I'm coming out to borrow that collie of yours for a few days. I'd guarantee him to wreck the League of Nations and the Constitution of the United States and the Republican and Democratic parties, inside of a single month. . . . Well, good-by, folks. This is the last of us. We're off to the studio. It's been a real privilege to meet Gray Dawn. It almost makes up to me for missing the San Francisco earthquake and the Galveston flood."

At eight o'clock next morning a stutteringly excited Darroll telephoned the Master.

"Hallelujah!" shrilled the director. "We got it! We GOT it!"

"Got what?" asked the Master. "I don't——"

"Last evening our president and I had those dog-fight reels run off for us," prattled Darroll, gurgling with enthusiasm. "Say! It's the grandest fight of *any* kind that ever I saw on a screen. The chief went daffy over it. That gave us our idea. We yanked Beemis out of bed—he's our best scenario man, you know—and we set him to work. He was at it all night. So were we. He's just finished. We've *got* it, I tell you!"

"Got what?" repeated the puzzled Master. "Delirium tremens? You sound like it. If——"

"We've got the greatest action picture—greatest animal picture—of the century!" babbled the director. "Beemis has it all worked out. It's a wow! It's a *quadruple* wow! The first scenes will stand—the ones of the hero and his wolf, up in the mountains. Then comes the new part. The hero hates Lois's dad for grabbing his fortune. He brings his wolf down to their estate to sic him on Lois, to kill her and get revenge on her father. See? And Lois's faithful collie sees him going for her. The collie jumps in and fights the terrible wolf to a standstill, and he saves the girl. That beats the old worn-out drowning rescue a hundred miles. He——"

"You mean that Gray Dawn is——?"

"Then the first version of the story can be picked up again, where it goes on after the rescue," babbled Darroll, heedless of the interruption. "See? Dawn can be registered with Lois in a retake of some of the earlier scenes. Dog stuff always goes big with picture audiences. Collies have been filmed too seldom, and police dogs too often. Dawn can go on with her and the hero, through the rest of the picture. See? Beemis has written in some corking scenes for Lois and Dawn. We'll be out to-day and start on the new work. That dog fight alone would carry a screening of the Telephone Directory to a million-dollar success. Yep. It's a wow! We'll——"

"Do you——?" began the Master.

But Darroll talked on, unchecked:

"We'll show how Dawn happened to be shut into the summerhouse. He charges down the lawn to save Lois when the wolf is staring at her from the thicket. She doesn't see the wolf. So she shuts Dawn up there, because she wants to be alone with her reveries. Then Dawn jumps through the window and saves her. We've already got the long shot of his galloping down the hill just as Polaris stuck his head out of the bushes. We can use that. And we can use the comic-relief scene where he destroys her dress with that thorn bush. That's a scream. Oh, this is going to be a reg-lar ol' he knock-out of a picture, all right! It'll net the Fund five times as much as ever we dreamed it would. I'll be up there in an hour or two, with the whole crowd—except Polaris. We won't need the Malemute any more. His scenes are all taken. G'by!"

Dazedly the Master came back to the veranda breakfast table where Dawn lay beside the Mistress's chair. He blinked in dull amaze at the gray collie. The fight-battered dog wagged his tail in jolly reply.

"Gray Dawn!" said the Master, feebly, "I—I've spent four long years in guessing whether you are a hoodoo or a mascot. And I'm blest if I can get the right answer, even yet. If I had your crazy luck, I'd either be President of the United States or—or else I'd be in the poorhouse for life. I don't know which. But it would be one of the two."

CHAPTER SEVEN

Peace and the Pup of War

A HALF MILE of fire-blue water and another half mile of fields and woods lie between The Place and the friendly little hill village of Hampton. Though The Place is in the real country, yet a car spans the distance between it and Hampton in five minutes. Thus Gray Dawn's weirdest exploit was made easy for him, though its scene was in the village and not at Sunnybank.

It began when artist friends of the Mistress and the Master rented the Peasely bungalow in Hampton for the summer. They were Jack Thrale, his wife, and their six-year-old daughter, Sibyl. They had come to the hill country partly to paint, but chiefly to build up the fragile body and nerves of their little girl.

Sibyl was recovering slowly—far too slowly—from infantile paralysis. Once more she could walk, but only with a cane. She was a beautiful, pathetic wisp of a child. Under the outdoor life of the country a new color was coming into her transparent cheeks, a new vigor into her dragging step. She was on the way to full recovery.

The bungalow rented by the Thrales was pleasant enough to the eye of an artist—all of it except the large and peculiarly atrocious bronze dog which adorned the front lawn. This ornament was a relic of the mid-Victorian days when metal animals were used for lawn decorations.

At sight of the hideous thing Jack Thrale gulped in horror. Then he demanded that it be carried down to the cellar, there to be stored out of sight during his occupancy of the bungalow. But at once a complication set in. Sibyl was enchanted by the metal atrocity. She loved it as never had she loved any of her seventeen dolls.

Eagerly she begged that it be allowed to remain where it was. Too recently had the little girl passed through the Valley of the Shadow for her parents to deny her anything. Jack Thrale would have allowed a life-size gutta-percha dinosaur to disfigure his lawn if Sibyl could have derived any joy from seeing it there.

The child used to pat the bronze dog and talk to it and tie violent ribbons around its neck and use it as a lawn seat, and in a dozen other ways she gleaned vast entertainment from it. This during such hours as she did not spend at The Place.

When first her parents brought her across to Sunnybank to see the Mistress and the Master, she was daft with rapturous excitement over the collies. They returned her shy advances, treating her with a queer instinctive gentleness and abstaining from their wonted rough play.

They seemed to understand how frail and weak and small she was, and they accommodated their wild spirits to her feebleness. It was Sibyl's first personal contact with dogs. It opened to her a brand-new world of happiness.

More than to all the rest of the Sunnybank collies, her heart went out to Gray Dawn. The giant dog constituted himself her escort and her willing slave. Everywhere he paced close to the lame child's side, gleefully retrieving sticks at her behest, "speaking" for bits of food, suffering her to plait the longer masses of his silvern fur into teasingly uncomfortable little tight braids and to cap them with bows of ribbon.

Her hauling and her lordly dictation were a delight to Dawn. It was pretty to note how gently the bumptious big collie bore himself toward her and how zealously he guarded her on their halting walks about the grounds. Her helplessness appealed mightily to the chivalrous strength of him. Also she was his first human playmate near his own age and mentality.

Next to Gray Dawn, the child was entranced by Glenarvon Lassie's six puppies. The fluffy youngsters were a revelation to her. For hours she would sit on the rock in the center of the puppy yard and stare blissfully at them, cuddling one after another in her lap. Gradually she settled on a favorite among the six—a rolypoly merle pup, Scotty by name, a puppy which more than all the rest resembled his sire, Gray Dawn.

Covertly, the Mistress had been noting the little girl's marveling interest in the baby collies and her breathless affection for them. When Sibyl announced at last that she loved Scotty better than all the rest put together, the Mistress held council with her husband and with the Thrales.

As a result, one afternoon when Sibyl and her parents were about to drive back to the bungalow after luncheon at The Place, the Mistress lifted the pudgy gray puppy and placed him in Sibyl's lap as she sat in the car.

"Scotty belongs to you now, dear," explained the Mistress as the child stared, wild-eyed, at the puppy. "Gray Dawn has given him to you with his love. He's Dawn's little son, you know. You'll like to have him for your very own, won't you?"

Sibyl could not speak. Into her pale face seeped a flood of vivid red. Her big eyes grew starlike. Her breath came in shaky gasps. Then, catching the wriggling puppy to her breast, she buried her face in his fluffy fur and sobbed hysterically.

Though Gray Dawn, two months earlier, had resented fiercely an effort of a would-be purchaser to carry home this same puppy, yet now he stood beside the car, wagging his plumed tail and grinning from ear to ear.

Thus Dawn's son Scotty became a worshipped member of the Thrale's bungalow household. The bronze dog on the lawn was well-nigh neglected by Sibyl in her devotion to her living puppy. All day and every day Scotty was her inseparable chum and plaything. Only her parents' firm veto kept her from carrying him to bed with her. Reluctantly she consented to let him sleep on a soft mat on the front porch during the hours of darkness, but only on condition he be allowed to come stumbling upstairs to her room the moment she woke in the morning.

Henceforth, on her almost daily visits to The Place, nothing would do but Scotty must go along with her. Which leads by perhaps prosy degrees to the first act of this story.

One afternoon Thrale had driven over to see the Mistress

and the Master about a proposed celebration in the village— an out-door fête to be held as climax to a drive for the American Legion's Orphan Fund. While the artist sat on the veranda talking over the plans which he and the rest of the committee were working on, Sibyl called to Gray Dawn and bade him come for a walk with Scotty and herself.

The three made their way through the soft afternoon sunlight and shade to the rose garden, a rose-bordered vista of emerald turf stretching from lawn to lake. The child walked faster and better than of old. But she limped slightly and had to lean upon her cane.

Gray Dawn, as ever, timed his pace to hers, moving majestically along at her side. Her free arm was thrown over his shimmering silver shoulders. Scotty saw no need in loitering at so slow a gait. He scampered ahead and behind and around, ever discovering some dramatic toad or beetle to bark harrowingly at, or some seemingly uninteresting hole or bush shadow which might harbor a lurking bear or Indian.

Reaching a spot in the rose garden where two interlacing flowery bushes formed a natural arbor, Sibyl came to a standstill.

"Gray Dawn," she said in her quaintly grown-up diction, "this is the 'chanted cave, in the story Daddy read to me. D'you remember it, Dawnie? I told you 'bout it as much as twice. I'm the Princess and you're the lion, Dawnie. I'll sit here and you must lie down and look noble. Then when the Prince comes riding along—Scotty will be the Prince— he'll be ever so 'stonished. Lie down, Dawnie. I *think* I hear the Prince, right now."

A pretty picture they made—the tiny child and the huge collie, there under the swaying red roses, but a picture which Scotty failed to appreciate. The puppy had discovered a small and harmless garter snake. The snake fled from Scotty's harrowing onset. The baby collie followed in noisy pursuit toward the lake.

Now, though the snake was wholly harmless, the chase was watched by a human whom no stretch of charity could have termed harmless. Indeed, in a small way, his spare frame was packed with as much potential harm as a score of snakes.

He was Phineas Rance, an unloved and unlovable official of the borough of Hampton. He was the village's paid dog catcher and pound keeper. His was a lucrative trade just then, by reason of certain borough ordinances.

The law allowed him one dollar for every stray dog he caught and impounded. These luckless dogs were kept in his back-yard pound for thirty-six hours. Then, if no one claimed them and paid the fine for having allowed them to roam unmuzzled, they were put to death. The pound keeper received another dollar apiece for shooting them.

In this way every unclaimed impounded dog meant two dollars in cash to Phineas Rance. There were unkind and unproven rumors that Rance used to hide dogs in his cellar when their worried owners visited the pound in search of them.

The man had no jurisdiction over the dogs of The Place, for they were outside the borough limits. Yet, to-day he paused as he paddled his battered canoe past the foot of the lawn, and he looked with keen interest at the unsuspecting little gray puppy which was chasing the garter snake toward him.

Rance's canoe trip was not one of mere pleasure. Experience had taught him that stray borough dogs often ran down to the water in hot weather, to drink or to swim. A man equipped with a net and paddling close inshore might often earn several dollars in a single afternoon by catching such wanderers.

To-day he had drawn blank in his tour of the lake edge. But the sight of the merle puppy revived his hopes. It was Rance's self-constituted business to know everything knowable about the borough dogs. Thus, a week agone, he had learned that this puppy belonged to the artist fellow who lived in the Peasely bungalow on Paterson lane—the bungalow with the grand bronze dog on its front lawn.

Well, then, the pup had no business on this other side of the lake. Scotty was not at home. He was straying. What easier—since nobody was in sight—than to net the youngster and, if necessary, to report that Scotty had been wandering at large, unmuzzled, on the borough side of the lake?

The pup was helping Rance's plan by trotting straight toward him. A sweep of the paddle grounded the canoe's prow on the gravel of the beach below the rose garden. Rance gathered up his net and chirped wheedlingly.

At the same time, the garter snake resorted to unsportsmanlike tactics by diving into a hole under a larch tree. That ended the exciting chase. Scotty looked disappointedly around him. There, only a few yards away, was a man chirping to him. The puppy was still at an age and at a stage of experience when he regarded the whole human world as his dear friends. Wagging his tail, he frisked down to the water edge and toward the waiting Phineas Rance.

"Dawnie," said Sibyl, getting up from her impromptu throne under the rose bushes, "I'm afraid the Prince isn't going to come here, after all. I'll call him and——"

But it was Scotty, and not she, that called. The puppy's overtures of friendliness were met by a horny hand that clutched him painfully amidships and yanked him aboard the canoe, seeking to cram his pudgy body into a burlap sack. The indignant Scotty let out a yelp of hurt and surprise.

Turning at the sound, Sibyl was in time to see her treasured chum stuffed into a bag by a lanky man who had stepped ashore from a canoe. She cried out in fear. Instinctively she turned to big Dawn for aid in recovering her stolen playmate. Dawn was no longer at her side.

The soft grounding of the canoe on the gravel had not reached Sibyl's ears. But it was sharply audible to the trained watchdog who long ago had learned to associate such noises with trespassing. Hackles abristle, Gray Dawn ran toward the lake. His first stride brought him in sight of Rance and the captured Scotty, and brought to his ears the frightened cry of his little gray son.

Head down, mighty body close to earth, Gray Dawn charged. Without a sound and at whirlwind speed he flashed to the rescue. Trespass was bad enough. But the seizing and hurting of the puppy served to change his professional ire to red fury. As Phineas Rance stepped aboard his canoe the fierce drive of padded feet on grass behind him made him turn.

Rance flung the bag out into the lake and thrust his canoe after it, making a flying leap aboard. Fast as he was, he was not quite fast enough. Perhaps nothing but a striking serpent is as swift as an angry collie. Lucky it was for the dog catcher that he had thrown into the lake the bag containing the yelping Scotty. He had done so with a vague idea of picking it up again when he should be safely afloat. But he had no chance to do so.

Dawn's leap fell short of the man's shoulders. His snapping jaws missed the fast receding neck. But his head smote Rance in the middle of the back, throwing the man off balance and upsetting him and the canoe. It would have been a simple thing, there in the shallows, for Dawn to finish his bloody work of vengeance on the floundering and water-blinded pound keeper. No human was near to call him off.

But even as he drove for the struggling man, came afresh, if muffled, the puppy's frantic yelp. Scotty was writhing wildly in the encumbering folds of the sack. In another few seconds, impeded and smothered as he was, he must sink. Dawn wheeled from the scarce-begun attack and plunged into the water toward the bit of animated sacking which was beginning to settle beneath the surface.

He seized it gently and bore it shoreward. On the bank he deposited the dripping and soggy and squirming bag, just as Sibyl came limping up to receive her rescued pet.

As he laid down the bag, Dawn wheeled to complete his work of punishment. He had done his duty in saving his pup. It remained to settle with the thief. But Rance had not dreamed away the handful of seconds which had been needed for Scotty's deliverance. Scarcely had he struggled to his feet in the waist-deep water when he was swarming atop his overset canoe and grabbing the paddle which floated near by.

With awkwardly vehement strokes he was paddling the upset craft as far and as fast from the bank as he could. By the time Dawn had leisure to attend to him Rance was thirty feet from shore. Slowly and crankily though an upset canoe moves, yet if it is propelled hard enough and skillfully enough, it makes progress of a sort. And Phineas Rance was putting all his wiry strength into an effort to get out of reach of the gray devil that ravened at him from among the shallows.

Dawn, for all his bumptiousness, had the brain of his deep-brained race. He knew that a swimming dog is one of the most helpless creatures alive when pitted against an opponent in a boat above him. Ignorant that the slightest impact would serve to dislodge this man from his wavery perch atop the upset canoe and send him wallowing impotently in the lake, he saw that Rance was out of the water and was paddling away, with an ever-increasing distance between himself and his pursuer.

Wherefore the dog contented himself by growling in futile rage at his escaped prey, and in sniffing instinctively the still air, to familiarize himself with the man's scent.

Rance saw Dawn halt. He knew his own peril was ended. A surge of crazy anger shook him. He had been capsized and doused and made to flee in panic flight, all by a miserable dog—he who made his living by the misfortunes of dogs. He had been balked in an effort to add two easy dollars to his income. Worse, the cheap new suit he was wearing had begun already to shrink irregularly on his sparse figure as the water dried on it. His silver watch, too, was none the better for its bath. Ragingly, Phineas shook his paddle at the distant and snarling Dawn.

"You mangy cur!" he mouthed, sputtering with wrath and from the water that trickled down from his hair into his nose and mouth. "I'll get you for this, if it takes me a year! I'll *get* you and——"

Here his denunciatory promises were engulfed in the lake. When one is sitting astride a slippery overturned canoe it is not wise to wave one's arms in threatening gestures. It does funny things to one's ticklish balance. In the midst of Rance's gesticulating harangue the canoe righted itself, gunwale-deep in water.

The dog catcher sank far under the surface, coming up half strangled and almost too confused to grip the gunwale with one hand and to grope for the floating paddle with the other. As he had gone overside his booted heel had stove a hole in the ancient canvas side of his cherished canoe.

Ten minutes of combined paddling and pushing were required to beach the canoe on the borough side of the narrows. Then, in crawling drippingly ashore, Phineas lost his footing on the slimy rocks and sat down hard upon the precise center of a waterside yellow-jacket nest.

Rance went to bed that night nursing an incipient attack of rheumatism and a variedly painful assortment of stings and an undying hatred of Gray Dawn.

The three talkers on the Sunnybank porch were interrupted by the sound of loud weeping. They sprang up, to find the three wanderers bearing down on them. Sibyl led the way, sobbing aloud and clasping to her thin chest a wet and frightened puppy. Gray Dawn followed, close at her heels, alternately glancing back over his shoulder toward the lake and seeking to lick the tear-stained little face of the child.

Tremblingly Sibyl blurted out her story, the tears flowing anew when she told of Scotty's immersion in the lake. Incoherent as she was, her hearers understood what had passed.

"I know the man," said the Master gruffly, as his wife gathered Sibyl into her arms and soothed her to calmness again. "At least, I know him by sight and by reputation— or rather, by lack of reputation. His name is Rance. Phineas Rance. He's the borough dog catcher. But why he should have been trying to catch poor little Scotty, here on my land, I can't figure out. He's the best-hated man in Hampton. There are a lot of ugly stories about him. Not only about the way he runs the pound, but the brutal way he treated his sick wife and their half-witted boy, until the boy and the woman had the good fortune to escape from him by dying. He'd never have had his present job—in fact, he'd have been kicked out of the village long ago—if he wasn't the mayor's cousin. As it is, all the decent element is yearning for a fair chance to get rid of him—some chance that's too strong for even the mayor to stand up against. Not that the chance will ever come. Better——"

"But——"

"Better keep a sharp eye on Scotty, and don't let him stray out of your yard without a leash. He won't be the first or the twentieth harmless dog that Rance has spirited away."

"Will he hurt Scotty?" spoke up Sibyl from the Mistress's lap.

"No, dear," soothed the Mistress. "Nobody's going to hurt Scotty. Don't worry."

As the child's face was still clouded with apprehension, the Mistress went on, to divert her thoughts from the shock she had gone through:

"I'm going to tell you a secret. There is going to be a wonderful entertainment over on the Square, right close to your house, next week."

"Is there?" asked Sibyl, in no way interested.

"Yes," answered the Mistress, "and you are going to be in it, too. That's what we were talking about just now. First there is going to be a block dance, by moonlight, on the road in front of the Square. A dance out in the street, with people paying admission, for the Orphan Fund. Then, at eleven o'clock, the people will all gather on the grass near the monument. A curtain will be stretched in front of the monument. Presently that curtain will go up and show some beautiful patriotic tableaux, one after the other——"

"*Beautiful* tableaux?" muttered the artist, under his breath. "Oh, beauty, what crimes are committed in thy name! The fattest girl in town typifying Liberty, and the harelipped souse from the garage as Mars, and——!"

"And"—pursued the Mistress, unheeding, as she continued her effort to make Sibyl forget her shock—"and the first and loveliest tableau of them all will be a figure representing Peace. It will be a child—a very, *very* pretty little girl, painted and dressed like a statue. She will have a palm branch in her arms and——"

"If it hadn't been for Dawnie," interposed Sibyl, with a reminiscent shudder, "that wicked man would have——"

"And who do you suppose the little girl is—the little girl who is to be the statue of Peace?" asked the Mistress, hurrying her climax to avert fright memories. "It is Miss Sibyl Thrale! Won't that be ever so nice? With all the people looking on, and the searchlights and——"

"Me?" gasped Sibyl, thrilled into momentary forgetfulness of her terror.

"The kind of tableaux they had at the church last winter," supplemented Thrale. "Don't you remember, daughter? They——"

"Yes," said Sibyl, "I remember. But—but, oh, I wish it wasn't going to be at eleven o'clock at night. That's so late —pretty near as late as it ever gets to be. And I have to be in bed by eight. Mother won't ever let me sit up till——"

"Yes, she will," the Mistress reassured her. "That's all arranged. You're going to have a nice long nap all in the afternoon, and stay in bed for supper and till nine o'clock that night. Then you'll be wide awake and fresh for——"

"Can I have Scotty in the tableau with me?" demanded Sibyl, eyeing her puppy with maternal pride. "He'd make a lovely tableau, Scotty would. He would——"

"He would!" sardonically agreed Jack Thrale. "I can't imagine anything more sweetly allegorical than a fat and fleasome collie pup in a tableau depicting National Peace."

"He might typify one of the Dogs of War," suggested the Master, in like vein. "At least a puppy of war."

"That's it!" approved Thrale. "Call the tableau, 'Peace —and the Pup of War.' Sublime! Then if we can get friend Phineas Rance to pose as 'The Spirit of Brotherly Love'——"

"If Scotty can't be in it," pleaded Sibyl, gathering from this incomprehensible byplay that her request was vetoed, "then I want Dawnie. Can't he, please——?"

"Even better!" laughed the Master. "In all his approximately blameless life Gray Dawn has never been called on to play any sort of rôle in any sort of venture, that he didn't cause more wholesale disaster than two earthquakes and a tidal wave. Remember that motion picture I told you about, Thrale? He——"

"He saved the picture," spoke up the Mistress. "And somehow his blunders almost always work out happily. Just the same, I don't think he would add to the success of the Hampton patriotic tableaux, dear as he is. He——"

"Wait!" exclaimed Thrale. "I have an idea. Sibyl is right. The Peace tableau can be made to look really like something. Will Gray Dawn lie still when he's told to, and stay still? But then I don't suppose he will. He——"

"Of course he will," replied the Mistress. "That's one of the very first things we taught him in the days when he had a genius for being in fifty places at once—and all of them were places he had no right to be. He will lie still by the hour, if he is told to. But what——?"

"Here's the idea," expounded Thrale. "This first tableau is going to amount to something, then, even if the others are a joke. It won't be Sibyl alone. Sibyl will be standing there, with the palm sheaf held forth, as we planned. But at her feet Gray Dawn will be crouching. He will look of heroic size alongside such a little mite as she is. She will have

one bare foot on his back as she stands there. And between
Dawn's outstretched paws we'll have a sheaf of broken
bayonets or a broken rifle. The tableau will be called: 'Peace
and the Dog of War.' It'll be a knock-out, I tell you; with
that great majestic collie lying there, all——"

"It'll be a knock-out, all right," morbidly assented the
Master. "But Dawn will do the knocking out. You can always count on him for that. He has a divine gift for misfortune. We'll lend him to you for the tableau, if you insist.
But I advise against it."

"He will do splendidly," prophesied the Mistress, adding:
"But there's one difficulty: You told us all the characters in
the tableaux are to be coated with bronze paint, to make
them look like metal statues. You can't do that with Dawn.
He can't——"

"Better use that superb metal dog in your front yard,"
proposed the Master. "He may be horrific to look upon, but
you can count on him not to break up the show. Whereas,
Gray Dawn——"

"We can get around the matter of making Dawn look
like a bronze statue," promised Thrale. "We'll dampen his
coat and then sprinkle the bronze powder on it. We can
rub a bit of cold cream on his face, where the hair is shorter,
to make the powder stick there. That's the way we're to do
with the faces and arms and feet of the people who'll pose
as statues, you know."

"It won't harm him?" asked the Mistress.

"Of course not. It'll wash off and brush out in no time.
We'll keep it away from his eyes and nostrils. I know it
isn't harmful to animals and I know it can make them look

like bronze statues. I know, because I tried it when I lived up in the Berkshires. I fixed up a lamb that way, for a 'statue tableau' of Mary and Her Little Lamb. It washed off easily. The lamb lived to butt me into a trout brook two years later. . . . Yes, daughter, I think we can fix it so you can have Gray Dawn in the tableau with you."

"That's nice," observed Sibyl, placidly, "and—I want Scotty, too."

"When Scotty grows up," suggested the Mistress, "there'll be chances to have him in lots of tableaux with you. But this is the only time poor Gray Dawn will have the fun of it."

"The fun will be all his," prophesied the Master, gloomily.

Early on the evening of the Legion drive's entertainment Gray Dawn and his two owners motored over to the Thrales'. On their way they passed the roped space in front of the tiny Square in whose cement roadway the subscription block dance was already in gay progress.

To give the dancers more room, the curtain had not yet been strung on its wires in front of the squat little war monument.

But on the dais which formed the monument's low pediment stood a small rectangular platform, made of braced *papier-maché* to imitate snowy marble, and with its corners adorned by white *papier-maché* statuettes—a soldier, a sailor, a marine, a Red Cross nurse. The front surface of the platform was inscribed in gilt letters with the names of the many Hampton lads who had fought in the war. On this marblelike rectangle the persons in the various tableaux were to stand when the curtain should be in place and when the space between platform and monument should have been sheeted off for a dressing room.

The Mistress and the Master reached the Thrale bungalow just as Sibyl came downstairs from her long nap. Her first question was for Scotty. But the pup had been relegated for the night to his mat on the front porch and there were other things just then for the child to do, instead of playing with him.

Her robe of bronze-spangled green cheesecloth was spread out, ready for her to don it over her bathing suit, before the additional metallic-hued powder should be applied to it. Remained also the task to cold cream her face and neck and arms and feet and then to powder them with the shiny green-brown stuff.

However, Sibyl's make-up was a simple thing compared to Dawn's. Dampening the dog's massive coat, Thrale set to work with the jars of blended green-and-gold-and-brown powders. But he was not satisfied with the result.

"By this light I can't tell whether I'm getting it the right shade," he complained, "or too green or too brassy. It's one thing to make it look right by these shaded lamps, and quite another to be sure the color will pass muster under the glare of those arc lights."

He mused an instant, then inquired hopefully of the Master:

"Feeling strong, to-night?"

"Yes," said the Master, gloomily. "Especially in my presentiments. Why?"

"That bronze dog out on the lawn," explained Thrale; "he's nothing but a thin shell. Not solid. The two of us could easily carry him in here. You see, with all his artistic failings, he's at least the true color of weathered bronze—chiefly because he *is* weathered bronze. If we bring him in here and then let me work over Dawn till he and the bronze dog are the same color by this light, then Dawn's sure to be bronze color by any light at all."

Two minutes later the bronze lawn ornament was reposing on the lighted back porch where Thrale was working. Once more the artist was busy over Dawn's coat. The collie did not object to the process, except that the cold cream on his face had a pungent and, to him, offensive odor. Yet he lay or stood or sat peacefully enough while Thrale toiled deftly upon his silvery coat.

At last the task was done. There at the worker's feet lay majestically a collie of shimmering bronze, a gloriously statuesque figure, making the genuine metal dog look crudely molded and hideous by contrast—which he was, with or without contrast.

Then Thrale bent to the labor of turning Sibyl into a fairylike statue of Peace. So busy were he and the others in this more delicate achievement that they paid no heed to the collie, until Dawn sought to comfort the child (whose nose itched from the powder and who therefore made a distressful face) by licking her cheek. A smear along her bronzed visage from brow to chin rewarded the caress. Thrale said something virulent under his breath. The Master called Dawn out of the house and pointed to a spot on the clean front lawn.

"Lie down there!" he commanded. "And STAY there!"

Assured that the great collie would obey and thus would keep out of further mischief, the Master went back to the house. Dawn lay meekly where he was bidden to lie. On the veranda, in the flood of moonlight, slept Scotty on his mat, slumbering as heavily as only a puppy can. There was no hope of companionship from him. Dawn sulked. The powder made his tender skin itch. The odor of the cold cream sickened him.

Then down the lane from the direction farthest from the Square came a diversion.

Phineas Rance had been doing a fairly profitable evening's work. In his past-worthy little old motor truck he had been driving through the streets and lanes of Hampton. Most of the village was at the block dance. That meant most of the village's dogs were at home alone. No fewer than five of them, large and small, had been lying on their owners' front steps or in front yards.

These unfortunates Rance had enmeshed cunningly in his net and had dumped into the cage at the back of his truck. Now he was on his way homeward. He had stopped at the local speakeasy and had celebrated his lucky evening by a single small glass of beer—an unwonted extravagance for him. While the beer had in no way affected his brain, yet its memory was pleasant.

Through Paterson Lane rumbled the truck with its five whimpering victims. As it drew near to the Thrale bunga-low, Rance cast an appraising eye over the premises. There, gleaming on the moonlit lawn, crouched the metal dog he had seen and admired for years. There, too, on the veranda sprawled the sleeping gray puppy. There was no light in the front part of the house. It was a glorious opportunity.

Rance stopped his wheezy little truck, leaped to earth, and ran lightly up the path. With one deft swoop he grabbed the puppy. He started back toward his truck.

Then happened something so absolutely impossible, so madly unbelievable, that the jarring memory of it never thereafter left Rance.

In front of him, shining in the moonglare, was the familiar couchant bronze dog. But all at once the metal image leaped to its feet, teeth agleam, growling murderously, and launched itself at Phineas with a wild-breast roar.

The smell of the cold cream had dulled Gray Dawn's powers of scent. Thus, he did not recognize Rance until the dog catcher had run past him on the way to the porch.

This was not Dawn's home. He was not on guard here. It was no business of his to challenge the intruder. But as Phineas caught up the puppy the moon fell full on the man's face, so clearly that even the near-sighted collie could not fail to see every seamy line of it.

This was the thief who had stolen Scotty once before—who was stealing the puppy again. That sort of thing was not on the free list. For once in his life, the command, "Stay there!" was wiped from Dawn's mind by all-impelling anger.

With a roar he flew at Rance. The pound master dropped the puppy as though Scotty were a hornet nest, and made a wild plunge to the refuge of his truck. As he sprang for its seat, Dawn caught up with him and also sprang for a seat. Back to the ground dropped the avenging collie, gripping the entire rear expanse of Phineas Rance's best trousers.

Clearing his jaws of this impediment, he hurled himself once more at the panic-stricken Rance, his bronze head and body flashing back a swirl of moonlight.

But Rance had slammed shut the truck door and was dancing madly on the gas. The ancient vehicle bounded forward with a groaning jerk and Dawn tumbled to earth from the impact with the closed door.

As the truck whizzed away at a perilous pace, Dawn recalled belatedly the order he had received. Instead of giving hopeless chase, he assured himself Scotty was unhurt, then eased his own excitement by a luxuriant roll in the dew-soaked long grass alongside the bungalow lawn. After which he gathered up his trophy of the scrimmage—the breadth of torn trousers cloth—and returned to his resting place on the lawn, where again he lay down majestically, the cloth between his forepaws.

Meantime, insane with superstitious panic and ever seeming to hear the miraculously alive metal dog clanking along close at his heels to drag him to perdition, Phineas Rance drove on through the night at a breakneck pace that sent his ramshackle truck to swaying from one side of the road to the other. Through the lane he tore, shivering all over and making raucous static sounds between his horror-blanched lips. Unseeing, mad with fright, he urged his truck onward.

Out of the lane rocketed the crazy vehicle with the crazier man at its wheel. Into the little Square it dashed, snapping the rope which fenced off the block dance. Warned by its noise and by its driver's wild blitherings of panic, the dancers scattered to every side. Swaying tipsily, the truck clove its way through the open space. It smashed into and through the pridefully decorated *papier-maché* stage with its statuettes and its gilded inscriptions, demolishing it. The runaway vehicle smote against the granite pediment and crashingly resolved into its own component parts.

The cage's door was burst open. Out into the crowd galloped unhurt the five scared dogs that represented Phineas's night work. Out from the wreckage crawled Rance himself, by some miracle no worse harmed than by a cut or so and a few bruises.

But the collision had scattered what little remained of the wits Gray Dawn had shaken. To a brace of indignant policemen and to the startled crowd Rance babbled:

"That iron dog—outside the—the bungalow back there! He—he chased me down the street. He—bit me! Don't let him get me! He's after me. He——"

"H'm!" announced one of the policemen, tightening his grip on Rance's torn collar, and inhaling the rank scent of beer on Rance's labored breath. "Iron dog chased you, did he? There's enough smell of booze on you for pink alligators to chase you. C'mon over to Judge Maclay's. He'll have you put where you'll be safe from iron dogs."

At the same moment the Master went into the bungalow front yard to call Gray Dawn indoors. He found the collie lying where he had been told to lie, the tangle of trousers cloth and a dearth of bronze on his coat the only signs that he had stirred from the spot.

On the lighted back porch, the Thrales and the Mistress

caught their breath at sight of the disheveled and awful-looking thing which so recently had been made up to impersonate the Dog of War. A hot touch of actual warfare had wrecked the likeness. There was a hurried conclave. Then the Master said:

"He didn't acquire that cloth and all that disreputableness just by lying still. Something has happened. Thrale, if you'll get to work powdering him again, I'll stroll up to the block dance and see if there is any news of somebody losing part of his trousers. Both the cops are on duty there to-night. If there has been a complaint, they'll know about it."

It was a half hour before the Master came back. Then he burst in upon the placidly curious back-porch coterie at a run.

"Thrale!" he commanded. "Catch up one end of that bronze dog image and help me get it out to its place on the lawn, in a rush. It's got to be on view there if anyone comes down this lane. Don't ask questions. There may not be much time to waste. Lift! I'll explain when we get it done. By the way, while we're gone, will the rest of you clean that powder and stuff off of Dawn? His part of the evening's entertainment is over."

Between them the two men lugged the antique bronze shell of a dog to its wonted resting place. Then, as they came indoors again, the Master told his story.

"Our dear old chum, Phineas Rance, is in the cells," he began. "He smashed into the block dance at forty miles an hour with his truck. He is charged with 'reckless driving and breaking the road laws and destroying public property' —the platform is knocked to pieces—and with 'driving a motor vehicle while intoxicated.' They've got him on all four counts. Maclay has just finished the hearing. He's passed sentence and he's ordered Rance to the cells to sleep off his drunk. Between you and me, Rance has no drunk to sleep off. I was there and I watched him closely. He may have had a drink or two—in fact, the cop says he smelled liquor on him—but he's not drunk. He's only just scared out of his senses."

"But what's that got to do with——?"

"He says he was passing here and the bronze dog on the lawn chased him. That was enough to prove to Maclay he was drunk. That is why I wanted the bronze dog put back in place and the bronze washed off of Dawn. I figure Rance went past here and Dawn remembered him from last week and chased him. Anyhow, Maclay has fined Rance one hundred dollars and sentenced him to ninety days in jail for driving while he was drunk and for endangering lives. Mac has promised to suspend the jail sentence on condition Rance leaves town to-morrow and never shows up in Passaic County again. Rance was only too glad to promise. The sentence hangs over him if ever he comes back, and he knows it."

"Did he——"

"Say, people, didn't I tell you Dawn could be relied on to break up any show within fifty miles of him?" went on the Master. "Now how about your 'Peace and Dog of War' tableau? Dawn can't appear in it. If he did, and if he was covered with bronze, it might set some wise person to thinking. How about it?"

It was the Mistress, as always, who solved the problem.

"We'll use that bronze dog on the lawn," she decreed. "It will have a new interest for the audience, now that Phineas Rance has been driven out of town by it. It may not be artistic, but it will be better than artistic—it will be tremendously timely."

Promptly at eleven the muslin curtain was rolled from in front of the sheet-covered table which replaced the destroyed platform. The first tableau was revealed.

There stood Sibyl Thrale, wondrously pretty and graceful, swathed in shimmering bronze robes and with one tiny foot resting on the head of the bronze dog. At sight of the magic dog a multiple guffaw mingled with the applause. So loud was it that the announcer feared lest the audience might not have heard the tableau's title.

Thus, clearing his throat as the laughter ebbed, he intoned:

"Peace and the Dog of War."

"I'm Peace," explained Sibyl, her high voice carrying clearly, "and this brass dog I've got my foot on is the Dog of War. He lives in our yard. And this," she added, in elfin ecstasy of mischief, as she unfolded her voluminous robe and produced to public gaze the wrigglingly slumbrous Scotty. "THIS is his little son, the *Pup* of War."

CHAPTER EIGHT

The Killing

———

WHEN sixty-eight chickens were found slain in one coop and forty-five in another and eighteen in a third, all on a single morning and all within two miles of the village of Hampton, the Borough Council met in special session. So did the Grange. So did irate groups everywhere.

Not a fowl had been eaten. Not one was missing from the coops. All had been killed wantonly, for the crazy love of destruction. It was the work of a dog or of dogs. Not only did the method of the slaughter indicate that, but the splayed footprints of a dog were found in mud patches around two of the coops.

(No, this is not a tale wherein Gray Dawn did something to make the whole neighborhood suspect he was the killer of the hundred and thirty-one chickens and wherein at last he was proven triumphantly innocent. Gray Dawn was not a chicken slayer. Nobody believed he was. This is a different kind of story. Yet the wholesale slaughter was at the basis of this adventure of his.)

Keene Ruggles was the chief sufferer from the unknown dog's depredations. Ruggles was a farmer who lived about a mile from The Place and from the village. He found his hencoop door broken open and the floor strewn with torn fowls and feathers, when he set forth on his chores at daybreak. He roused his son Lafe and his hired man; and the three began a search for the culprit.

Their hunt was in vain. Apart from the splay-footed prints in a puddle beside the coop, there was no sign of the slayer.

According to local law, if live stock is killed by an unknown dog, the county must reimburse the unlucky owners for the full value of the destroyed creatures. But if it can be proved that the slaying has been done by any known dog, then that dog's master becomes legally responsible for the entire damage.

While Keene Ruggles was trudging wrathfully to the village, clamoring for vengeance and for cash redress, his son, young Lafe Ruggles, went back to the mud patch and fell to studying the footprints there. He had no need to make overcareful survey of them. The first glance had been enough. But he sought, unhappily, to verify what already he guessed.

Lafe was courting assiduously one Thelma Bergman, the daughter of a small truck gardener two miles up the valley. Lafe, incidentally, was working that summer at The Place. One Sunday, the Mistress and the Master being at church, Lafe had brought his sweetheart to see the Sunnybank collies. The superintendent and his family were also at church and the other men were at their homes. So the swain and Thelma had uninterrupted chance to look over the kennels.

Gray Dawn was lying on the porch as they began their inspection. Often he had seen Lafe working about the grounds, so he did not resent the intrusion. Indeed, the big gray collie paced majestically about with the two uninvited visitors as Lafe led his sweetheart from one kennel yard to another.

Thelma was enraptured over the dogs. She besought her wooer to buy one of them for her. Lafe scratched his head. He was earning only fair wages. The Place's superintendent had told him weeks ago that one hundred dollars was the minimum price for even the poorest of these collies in puppyhood, and that most of the grown dogs were valued at several times that amount.

Thelma at first was prettily insistent, but presently she waxed aggrieved and waspish at Lafe's refusal to gratify her modest whim. For the next few days she treated Lafe with icy glumness when he called to see her after work hours. Then had come his solution of the problem.

Lafe visited the Paterson dog pound. There, by good luck, among the score of unhappy prisoners he found a really fine-looking collie. Though Lafe did not know it, this collie had been picked up in a Paterson suburb, ten miles from his Hackensack owner's home, after an all-night orgy of chicken killing.

Young Ruggles paid three dollars for the stray collie, and took him home. There he kept him under lock and key in a shed for two days, until he had taught the decidedly intelligent dog to answer to the name of Buster—he had no

means, naturally, of learning the animal's former name—
and then he led him up the valley to the Bergman truck
farm.

He presented Buster to the meltingly enthusiastic
Thelma, telling her it was a $300 prizewinning collie he had
bought for her at The Place. Luckily, her knowledge of
high-priced dogs was as slight as her eagerness for them
was great. Hence, she made no embarrassing request for a
pedigree or for a registration certificate or even for a trans-
fer form. She was whole-souledly delighted with her gift.
She asked no questions. She restored her recently disci-
plined suitor to an effulgence of favor.

Lafe would have taken Buster to her a day earlier, and
thus would have shortened his own period of chastening,
but the collie had cut the heel pad of his splayed left front
foot very badly on a fragment of glass on the floor of the
shed. The youth waited for the hurt to heal enough to prevent Buster from limping. The cut itself could not be expected to close entirely for another week or two.

This morning the mud patch in front of the Ruggles hencoop door revealed tracks of a dog whose left front foot
had a deep cut on its heel pad.

There could be no doubt of it. Buster was the killer. No
Sherlock Holmes was needed to work that out. Lafe had
washed and bound up that cracked pad too often not to
know the aspect of the cut. Buster was the dog that had destroyed Keene Ruggles's sixty-eight chickens.

Presently Keene himself came back from the village with
an account of the sixty-three other casualties and of the
wholesale neighborhood wrath.

Lafe ate little breakfast that morning. Indeed, he ate less and thought harder than for a year before. He understood the situation as only a farmer's son could understand it.

Were the killer to remain unknown, the county must pay for every fowl lost. Let it be known that Thelma Bergman's collie had been the killer, and Thelma's tight-fisted father must do the paying. Bergman must hand out anywhere from $121 to $150 for the damage done by his daughter's dog.

Lafe was none too popular with the old market gardener, even now. Such a calamity would bar him from the Bergman home as the indirect cause of the misfortune. More than probably it would end his wooing of Thelma. For, in such case, the fact would be made known that this was not a dog bought from The Place, as he had bragged, but was a mere pound purchase.

Carefully Lafe tramped back and forth through the mud puddle, obliterating the pad marks. Then, on pretext of a sympathy visit, he went to the other farm where the mud had shown similar prints. There he performed anew his labor of obliteration. Afterward he set forth for The Place to begin his day's work.

The morning was hot; and was spent in the hayfields. It was tiring and nerve-scratching work. Haying is a beautiful spectacle to watch—from a cool veranda. To the haymakers themselves it has few charms and much discomfort. Its chief agony is the stamping about in a red-hot barn loft and receiving the hay pitched up from the wagon. On a torrid day that is a form of genuine torture.

At noon Lafe Ruggles sought the shade of the highest

new-built stack and prepared to eat his lunch. He took three thick slices of buttered bread from his dinner pail, a fist-sized lump of greasy roast pork, a huge cucumber pickle, and a wedge of soggy apple pie. These delectable hot-weather dainties he arranged on a sheet of newspaper beside him while he swigged deeply from the bottle of cold coffee he had brought along.

As a rule, he ate with one hand while he manipulated the coffee bottle with the other. But to-day nervousness made him thirsty and took away his appetite. He had no immediate desire for food. Back flew his mind to Buster's misdeeds and to the strong chance of their being traced to the dog.

A killer would not be content with one orgy. He would sally forth again, possibly this very night. Perhaps some vigilant fowl owner—and all fowl owners would now be vigilant for a while—might even shoot him. Almost certainly the flaw in his footmarks must soon be discovered. Then would come Lafe's own black hour of reckoning with old Bergman and Thelma.

With a philosophic sigh Lafe drove the worry from his mind, resolving not to dwell longer on it. The mental act brought him momentarily back to normal. He realized that he had breakfasted early and lightly and that he had worked hard all morning. He found he was ravenously hungry. Eagerly he turned to the lunch he had spread out on the newspaper a few feet away.

But the lunch had changed sadly since last he had looked upon its viscid abundance. Indeed, most of it had become invisible. The pickle alone remained. The major part of the repast was shut off from Lafe's view inside a coat of shimmering silver-gray fur and a mighty body.

Gray Dawn, alone of The Place's collies, had the democratic custom of visiting the workers at lunch time, and of trotting up to them with the irresistible hail-fellow manner that was his. True, he did not condescend to beg from them. But he had no need to beg. At his suavely friendly approach, usually, the man who chanced to be singled out thus for a visit would toss him a bit of food from a dinner pail.

It was pleasant to wander thus among the eaters, receiving titbits from them and being petted and told what a grand dog he was. Lad or Bruce or Wolf or Treve or Bobby would have scorned to graft thus. But Dawn had his own ways, even as they had theirs.

On his rounds to-day he trotted first to the haystack in whose shade Lafe Ruggles slumped. Dawn came up, waggingly and mincingly, as usual; expecting his advent to be hailed by a word of greeting and by a bit of meat. Instead, Lafe paid no heed to him at all, but sat with head on breast, seeing and hearing nothing.

Dawn was not chagrined by this coldness. He had only a casual acquaintance with Lafe and neither liked nor disliked him. Sensitive as the big dog was, he was not to be saddened or hurt by the neglect of anyone but the Mistress or the Master. Yet a word of welcome from Lafe might well have been accompanied by a gift of food, which the collie would have relished.

At The Place they did not serve greasy pork nor soggy pie crust—two exotic dainties which Dawn had learned to relish from his acquaintance with the workmen. Yet here in

front of him, lying unheeded on the grass—and thus doubt-
less thrown away by their owner—were spread delicious
pork and pie; and bread all slathered thick with rancid butter. It was a feast fit for the gods. And it was all his own.

It would not have occurred to Gray Dawn, even if he
were starving, to rob a dinner pail or other receptacle, nor
to take food from a table or a chair. But food on the ground
had ever been treasure trove. Voraciously, yet with a certain queer daintiness, he attacked the feast.

In two gulps the pork was gone. A crunch and a few
lightning-quick laps of the pink tongue, and every crumb
of the pie had followed the pork. With less haste, but with
mild appreciation, he ate the fat bread slices with their
heavy and comfortingly rank coating of butter. He sniffed
at the bumpy pickle, then turned scornfully from it.

Yes, the pickle alone remained to sate the hunger of the
man who just then turned so ravenously to devour his
neglected noon meal. All the rest of the lunch was in Gray
Dawn. The collie stood there, waving his plumed tail in
friendly gratitude for the treat, before going on to the two
other laborers, who were eating under an apple tree a
hundred yards away.

Usually it is some ensuing petty annoyance, rather than
a tough misfortune itself, which crumples nerves and tem-
pers. So it was with Lafe Ruggles this day. Stolidly he had
borne the disclosures of the morning, which threatened to
take his sweetheart from him. Yet that self-control had been
maintained at a cost—a nerve cost which soon or late must
be paid.

The theft of his food and the sight of the smugly happy

dog that had eaten it—these were too much for the harassed man. With a yell of fury, he snatched up a two-pound stone that lay close to his hand. With all his muscular might he flung it at the unsuspecting dog.

Finding no response to his courteous overtures, Dawn had turned away. Thus he did not see the punitive gesture. Yet a queer subconscious instinct, always at the back of a collie's brain, now made him jerk his head sharply about, as if to face the infuriated Ruggles.

Before his head had moved two inches the stone smote him glancingly on the skull.

Deflected as it was by the shift of Dawn's head, the rock crashed against its mark with stunning force. The collie lurched clumsily forward and sideways, tumbling prone. He was knocked as senseless as ever a jaw punch knocked a beaten pugilist.

Even as the stone left his hand, Lafe realized what an insanely babyish thing he had done. He realized the probable consequences, too. Other men were within sight. His shout had drawn their attention to him. They must have seen what he had done. The unprovoked murderous attack on this valuable dog might well land the aggressor in jail or subject him to heavy damages. At the very least, it meant the loss of his job.

These possibilities flashed through Lafe's excited brain as the stone whizzed through the air. Then, as Dawn wheeled partly toward him, a more personal fear possessed him. Should the rock miss its mark, short shrift might be expected from the giant collie he had assailed.

By the time the stone struck aslant Dawn's head, Lafe

had made a scrambling spring and was wriggling his panic way up the haystack. From the summit he peered down. Dawn was not pursuing him.

Oddly still and huddled, the great dog was lying where he had fallen. The midday sunlight was turning his shaggy gray coat to spun silver and snow, except where a patch of red had begun to widen on the mottled black-and-silver of his scalp.

It had taken Lafe little more than a second to swarm up the stack. During that time everything else seemed to hang motionless, from the glaring sun in the coppery sky and the limply dust-powdered foliage to the stricken collie on the ground and the two half-arisen laborers under the apple tree.

Then, all at once, the world ceased to stand still. The two men under the apple tree jumped up and started for the haystack on a run. The collie quivered spasmodically from head to tail and lifted his abraded head, blinking dazedly about him. From the hill above, another man came charging down upon the scene at a breakneck run.

The Place's superintendent, coming back to work from his lunch at the gate lodge, had seen the assault on Dawn while he was still far up the hillside. He changed his swinging walk to a sprint; shouting anathemas as he came.

Gray Dawn was best loved by him of all The Place's dogs; since the death of Bruce the Beautiful, whose picture the superintendent still carried in his watch. The sight of Dawn's apparent slaying filled him with homicidal ire.

Fortunate it was for Lafe that Dawn came dizzily to his senses as soon as he did. The superintendent stopped alongside the hurt dog and knelt over him, instead of charging the haystack.

Emboldened by this dearth of aggression, Lafe slid down the stack and stood sheepishly, mumbling:

"I—I didn't aim to hurt him none. It was—it was just a kind of—of joke. I——"

"Get out of here! And get out, *quick!*" commanded the superintendent, truculently, as he glanced up from his ministrations on Dawn. "Go! On the jump! I want you off this land in three minutes."

He was still kneeling beside the collie, his expert fingers examining the scalp hurt. The skin had been grazed harshly. A bump was beginning to appear where the stone had struck. The dog was still confused and dizzy. But the skull was unharmed.

Lafe made the time-honored retort of his favored class, on hearing himself discharged.

"Gimme my money, then," he grunted. "I don't go till I get it."

The superintendent looked up at him as at some offensive insect.

"Your money, hey?" he repeated. "You're playing in grand luck to get off The Place all in one piece. If the Boss had happened to see you smash the big dog, you'd be on your way to the accident ward by now. If you want your money, go ask him for it. I'll come along and tell him what you did. Clear out!"

Mumbling, swearing, sulking, Lafe clumped away. As he passed out of earshot the superintendent turned to the two other men.

"I'll send him word Saturday night to come to me for his pay," said he. "Let him sweat till then over the notion that he won't get it. I'm letting him off plenty light, the swine!"

As he spoke he was helping Dawn to get up. The collie needed little assistance. Already the shock was passing. His mighty muscles were beginning to co-ordinate once more. His brain was clearing.

Gray Dawn had not the remotest idea what had befallen him, nor why he felt so queer and why the friendly earth and trees seemed to be swimming and lurching crazily before his dazed eyes.

He did not know it was his mildly likable acquaintance, Lafe Ruggles, who had smitten him. He did not connect his odd mischance in any way with Lafe. At one moment he had been turning gratefully away from eating a delicious luncheon. At the next moment he was lying on the ground, trying drunkenly to get to his feet. He had not been able to collect enough of his rudely scattered wits to heed or hear the short dialogue between his friend the superintendent and Ruggles, nor the latter's grumbling departure.

In another hour, barring a sore bump on the side of his head, Dawn was no worse for his mishap. In another day the bump was gone and the graze was nearly healed.

Lafe Ruggles did not dismiss the squabble so easily from his sullen brain. He had lost a fairly good job. He had been fired by the superintendent with high words and in the presence of two of his friends. His money had been denied him. All because he had resented the devouring of his noonday meal by a measly gray dog.

Hate rankled hot and morbid in Lafe's alleged soul. He

yearned to punish both Dawn and the superintendent for his misfortune. Hottest of all burned his revenge lust against Gray Dawn.

Meantime the whole valley was abuzz over the depredations of the chicken killer. Not content with his exploits of the first night, the splayfooted dog sallied out on the two succeeding evenings. The sum of his killings was swelled to one hundred and ninety fowls in an area of four miles.

Lafe sickened to cold horror at the news. Farmers and laborers were abroad of nights now, with shotguns, not only guarding their own menaced hencoops, but patrolling the whole valley in hope of winning the $100 reward offered by the Grange for the killer's death. Soon or late, inevitably, they must catch Buster, be he ever so crafty. Then he would be recognized as Thelma Bergman's collie and unmitigated disaster would set in for Lafe.

By Friday, after two sleepless nights, Lafe worked out a plan to save himself. He gleaned the idea by seeing Thelma and her father drive past the Ruggles farm on their way to Paterson with a load of garden truck. That meant the Bergman shack would be deserted for some hours. The collie, Buster, would be alone there, in the absence of Thelma and Bergman.

Lafe knew they would not return until nightfall from their trip to market. That would give him all the time he needed, even though he dared not set forth until a little before dusk. He spent the intervening hours in laying out his campaign and making his few preparations.

His only apparatus consisted of a pocketful of fried liver cut in small chunks, and a rusty old pistol and a stout rope.

With this set of stage properties he intended to go to Berg-man's at early twilight. There, by the almost irresistible lure of fried liver, he planned to coax Buster to the woods. In the forest it would be safe to tie the rope about the collie's neck and drag him far enough to make a shot in-audible from the highroad.

Then—a bullet through the dog's worthless head—the pitching of his carcass into a bush-masked gully—and good-by to all peril from the killer and from the possibility of trouble to himself.

Thelma would suppose her pet had run away. It was a neat scheme and a simple one. Indeed, it had not a drawback. It could have been carried out to perfection. Indeed, most simple plans could be carried out, did not their authors make the mistake of trying to improve on them. Lafe's plan im-provement occurred to him in a dazzle of inspiration, just after he set forth on his two-mile hike toward the Berg-mans'.

His way led him past the outlying woodland of The Place. Through that bit of road-bordering woods Gray Dawn was strolling on a contemplative quest for rabbits. Twice during the past week Dawn had put up a rabbit in these woods. Both times, after a most exhilarating chase, Bunny had dived into the interstices of a stone wall, leaving the collie to bark harrowing threats at him from outside the haven of refuge.

This afternoon no rabbit appeared. Dawn was about to turn homeward when from the edge of the highroad he heard a cajoling chirp.

Lafe had stopped short in his tracks at first glimpse of the silvery fur through the screen of undergrowth. Then he had looked up and down the road. His jaw had set tight in the spasm of a marvelous scheme's birth.

He was on his way to the Bergman house. Very good. Gray Dawn should go along; if quantities of liver and much flattering persuasion could make him do so. Once there, he could be tied up while Lafe should carry out the prearranged program for getting rid of Buster. Returning to the Bergmans', it would be the work of two minutes to force the chicken-coop door, kill a pullet or two, then shoot Gray Dawn and lay him in the hencoop, smearing his jaws with blood and feathers.

Lafe could say readily that he himself had gone, alone, to call on Thelma, and that on entering the yard he had heard a commotion in the coop and had gone to investigate; shooting the killer in the midst of an orgy of slaughter.

Thus, not only would he have disposed of the gray giant to which he owed so much ill luck, but he could claim the Grange's hundred-dollar reward and could rejoice in the knowledge that the many slain chickens of the past week would be charged to the Master and not to the county.

It was a brilliant inspiration. The only difficulty was to make Gray Dawn accompany him so far. Also, the trip could not be made by road, past the gates of The Place and in view of any passing motorists who might recognize the dog. The only safe route was a wide détour through the back stretches of the woods, a détour which must entail much rough going. Yet the idea was worth the labor—always supposing it could be accomplished.

Wherefore he opened operations by slipping into the

roadside underbrush and chirping to Dawn. The collie trotted forward amiably enough, on recognizing the man. Lafe's first vague fear, lest Dawn recall the attack of three days earlier, was allayed at sight of the friendly advance.

He called Dawn over to him and patted him, giving him extravagantly warm greeting and following this up by the gift of a little chunk of fried liver.

Dawn adored fried liver, as do most dogs. The scent of such transcendent food in Lafe's pocket had had much to do with the collie's prompt response to the chirping. Ruggles drew out the length of rope, to slip its noose over the collie's shaggy throat. Then he hesitated. Dawn had the strength of a young bull and was far from meek. Lafe was in doubt as to how the dog would accept an effort to drag him along by force. He resolved to use guile as long as possible.

Accordingly, chirping once more to his victim, Lafe strolled off, a bit of liver twiddling between his fingers. Dawn followed. At the end of a hundred yards Lafe gave him the liver, and drew out another piece of it as he walked on.

Dawn was having a monstrous pleasant time. He loved walking through the woods and over the hills with any friend. True, Lafe was not one of his few friends. But he was an accredited acquaintance—accredited by having spent so many days working around The Place.

Dawn would have scorned to follow any stranger. But this was no stranger, the affectionate human whose lunch he had eaten with joy this very week. It was a pleasure to accompany Lafe on his forest ramble. Moreover, the jaunt's happiness was intensified ninetyfold by the frequent titbits of heavenly fried liver. All in all, this was a very worth-while promenade.

On past the boundaries of The Place they moved, more and more rapidly, and in a wide semicircle which brought them presently to higher and rougher ground as the dusk began to settle down above them.

The Master and the Mistress were coming up the drive from the house, for their evening walk. Wolf and Bobby were with them. At the gate they all but collided with some one who was turning into the driveway at a run. Instantly the two dogs sprang at the intruder as he stumbled against the Master. The man wheeled upon the collies, whipping to his shoulder a double-barreled shotgun.

Sharply the Master called back Bobby and Wolf, at the same time stepping between them and the wildly excited newcomer. By the dim light he recognized the gunwielder as Lafe's father, Keene Ruggles.

But the Master was wholly at a loss as to the meaning of Ruggles's visit and of his frantic excitement. In the peaceful North Jersey hinterland, law-abiding folk do not go about at night brandishing shotguns.

"What's the matter?" asked the Master. "And before you answer, put down that gun. You're not going to shoot either of these dogs of mine. They went for you because you were clumsy enough to run into me. They thought you were attacking me. What's wrong? I—"

"Enough's wrong!" blazed Ruggles, albeit lowering the shotgun as he saw that Wolf and Bobby made no further hostile move toward him. "That big gray cur of yours—that Gray Dawn collie—is he home here to-night?"

"Why, no," spoke up the Mistress, "he isn't. It's the first time he's ever been away at dinner time. We were just speak—"

"I knew it!" exclaimed Ruggles. "But I wanted to make dead sure, first. Besides, it was on my way. That's why I stopped to ask you. My boy Lafe isn't home, either. He was away since before supper time. I didn't think anything of it till a few minutes ago, when Tim Irons stopped by at my house. Tim told me he was taking the short cut from Preakness, through the woods back of Pancake Hollow, about dusk. He was crossing the Snake Brook bridge when he saw Lafe go across the wood road just ahead of him. Lafe was walking fast. He was out of sight in the bushes before Tim could holler to him. Then, right behind Lafe, he sees a big gray dog skulk across the road and foller Lafe into the bushes, like he was stalking him. He—"

"But how did Dawn—?"

" 'Twasn't very light. But Tim could see the dog was as big as a calf and he was silver-gray. Your Dawn is the only dog around here like that. But I wanted to make sure. Don't you see what it means, man?" Ruggles went on, his voice scaling in angry fright. "Lafe got mad at the dog and slung a stone at him, the other day, here. They say collies always remember. Well, your Dawn must 'a' got Lafe's trail in the woods to-day, and he took after him, to get even for that rock slinging. If he's piled on to my boy from behind, out yonder somewheres, what chance would Lafe have against that vicious brute? Likely enough the dog has tore him to pieces by now. I'm on my way to find out. That's all. I'm li'ble to be too late as it is."

Gun on shoulder, he was striding away at top speed, when the Master stopped him.

"Dawn is a collie, not a hyena," said he. "He wouldn't track anyone down from behind, like a wild beast. Besides, you might spend the whole night beating up those miles of woods and mountain sides without ever finding your son. I can guide you straight to him, if you like."

"How?" demanded Ruggles, halting irresolutely. "How can you? If you know where he is, why—?"

"I don't know where he is," said the Master. "But you just told me he and Dawn were seen crossing the wood road in Pancake Hollow, near the bridge. Irons was coming from Preakness, so Lafe must have crossed the road just north of the bridge. Very good. We'll go there. We'll take these two dogs with us. When we get to the bridge I'll tell them to find Dawn. They'll pick up his trail in ten seconds, on the road there, and they'll follow it till they get to him. All we need do is to stick to them. They'll come up with Dawn. If your son is anywhere near—"

"Good!" grunted Ruggles. "C'mon."

For reply, the Master took the gun from the farmer's shoulder and handed it to the Mistress.

"We'll travel lighter without that bar of junk," said he, disregarding Ruggles's angry protest. "Besides, you seem to be in a mood for shooting first and asking questions afterwards. Either we leave the gun behind here with my wife or

else you can take your own all-night chances at finding
Lafe."

Surlily, mutteringly, Keene Ruggles set off at a sham-
bling run across country, toward the mile-distant Snake
Brook bridge in the hill cleft known as Pancake Hollow.
The Master was at some pains to keep up with the panic-
scourged oldster. Bobby and Wolf frisked ahead of them,
mightily enjoying the fast hike and the men's eager excitement.

Arrived, panting and sweating, at the bridge, the Master
paused. Then he pointed up the narrow grass-grown byway
and said to the collies:

"Dawn! Where's Gray *Dawn?*"

The dogs understood well the simple query. From puppyhood they had been taught to seek out any of The Place's
humans or animals by name, at command. At once both of
them dropped their noses to earth and began to cast about
for their kennelmate's trail. In a few seconds they had found
it in mid-road, and were following it through the underbrush; crashing forward at top speed.

The Master called them back. Ripping his handkerchief
in half, he made impromptu collars for them, through which
he slipped the pocket leash he carried. He held the leash's
two ends, coupling the dogs into a hunting brace. Ruggles
fumed and swore at the brief delay.

"If we let them go ahead," soothed the Master, "they'll
be out of sight and out of sound of us inside of a minute. On
the leash, they'll have to go at our own pace. Now, then,"
he added, to the dogs, "Dawn! Find *Dawn!*"

For another full mile the search party stumbled on, the Master all but yanked off his feet by the dual tug of his questing dogs. Ruggles pattered noisily alongside, strong flashlight in hand to guide his blundering steps.

Upward the trail led, and in a rough half circle to the right, where Lafe had détoured to reach Bergman's house from the rear and out of sight of chance passers-by. Through bushes, around big trees, along the sides of steep hillocks and rocky outcrops they toiled, out of breath and leg weary.

Then, of a sudden, Wolf and Bobby ceased to sniff the rough ground as they struggled on. Both lifted their heads, but in a steady certainty far different from the confusion of dogs that have lost the trail.

"They're hunting by sight, now," panted the Master. "They see him. He's close by. Dogs see much better in the dark than men."

He drew tight the double leash, ordering the collies to a standstill. At the same time Keene Ruggles turned on his flashlight again, sweeping the hilly ground before him and presently focusing the vivid shaft of radiance on one spot.

Ruggles gasped in blank horror and the light wabbled crazily in his palsied grasp. From Bobby and Wolf burst a harsh growl of rage. They tugged fiercely at the leash.

In front of the searchers, and some twenty yards away, a fissured granite crag arose irregularly to a height of perhaps thirty feet. At the foot of the crag was an open space of grass and dead leaves, marking a natural clearing in the underbrush.

In this space and just below the rocks sprawled the moveless body of a man. The dead-white face was toward the shaft of flashlight. The man was Lafe Ruggles.

Above the still figure of Lafe crouched Gray Dawn—gigantic, horrible in the wavering light, his jaws blood stained and hideously snarling.

For an instant the two searchers stared slack-jawed and aghast at the sinister tableau. The Master's heart went sick within him. He saw, but he could not believe. The scene told its own awful story. There could be no doubt. And yet—

Ruggles slumped weakly against a tree, beginning to blubber like a scared child. The sight was too much for him. It verified his worst terrors as to his boy's fate.

"You—you made me leave my gun!" he sobbed, incoherently; then screaming with senile fury, as he lurched forward: "But I'll strangle him with my two hands. With my ten fingers I'll—"

Bobby and Wolf had not ceased to growl fiercely, nor to tug at the restraining leash. The Master turned to catch Ruggles by the arm as the farmer reeled past him on his furious mission of vengeance. The leash slipped from his hand.

The dogs, freed and uncoupled, hurled themselves forward like twin thunderbolts. But it was not at Dawn nor at the motionless Lafe that they sprang. Past these they sped and into the dense darkness to one side of the flashlight's radius. From the black void issued suddenly a bedlam of unearthly din and warfare.

Still holding Ruggles back, the Master trained his flashlight in the direction of the ear-splitting racket. Dawn had left his place above the fallen Lafe and was plunging right zestfully into the babel of battle.

Two hours later the Master mounted the veranda at The Place. The Mistress came forward nervously to greet him, and then stared wide-eyed at three torn and tousled and thoroughly disreputable collies that limped up the steps behind him.

"Let's get some hot water and witch hazel and rags, and fix up these battered warriors," he suggested in answer to her volley of amazed questions. "I'll tell you about it while we're working over them. None of the three is in bad shape, but they've got a few ugly flesh wounds. We'll get to work on Gray Dawn first. He's the real hero of the day."

As they washed and sponged and anointed and bound up the hurts, he told his tale.

At late dusk, Lafe, with Dawn sometimes trotting after him and sometimes bounding ahead, had neared the crag where the Master and Keene Ruggles had found the youth lying. There was light enough for Lafe to see a she wildcat run up the fissured cliff with a killed rabbit in her mouth, and disappear in a cave cleft midway on its surface. This could mean but one thing. In that cleft was the lair where her babies were waiting for their evening meal.

Wildcats are few and yearly fewer in that region. Yet there still is a ten-dollar bounty paid for them by the county authorities. If Lafe could shoot the mother and then catch and kill her kittens, he would be able to claim a goodly cash reward from the authorities. His real mission could wait while he stopped to annex this windfall of wealth.

Accordingly, pistol in hand, he began to climb the crag face, Dawn standing below and watching him with thrilled interest. The collie had caught the wildcat scent and was fiercely on the alert.

Just as Lafe's head topped the rock cleft, the mother wildcat launched herself forth upon the intruder who was seeking to molest her young. She sprang for his face. There was no time to use the pistol. Lafe shrank back from the raking claws that menaced him. He lost his footing and fell to the ground below, the pistol bouncing far out of reach. In the fall his left leg doubled under him and was broken.

The wildcat's leap carried her to the ground beside him. In maternal fury she sprang at the prostrate man. But even as she came hurtling downward from the cliff Gray Dawn went into action. There was an instant of wild scrimmage. Then the cat emerged from the mix-up with a useless fore-leg and a gashed back. But Dawn's face and shoulder bore deep marks of her slashing claws.

Too crippled to venture back into the fight on equal terms, the cat set up a miaouing howl which brought to her aid her mate, that had been foraging among the nearer hills. The two made rush after rush, not at the formidable dog, but at the man who had invaded their lair. Helpless and in agony, Lafe could not have coped with them for a moment. But athwart his writhing body Gray Dawn stood, facing the cats and holding them at bay.

Perhaps it was the presence of the man—impotent though he was—which kept them from coming to grips with the giant collie. Assuredly it was Dawn's grim defense which kept them from ripping to death the wretched Lafe. In any event, they contented themselves with prowling about the two, seeking vainly for some opening in the collie's savage guard, and in making abortive rushes to try to draw Dawn away from the man he was protecting.

And so the time went on; Lafe in anguish of body and of terror. At last he heard his father and the Master coming up the hill to his aid. In sheer relief, he fainted.

So much the shaken and tortured and nerve-broken youth had babbled as he was carried home. His story even included a weepingly penitent confession of his design on Dawn's life and the truth about the Bergman dog. He was too broken to keep his own secret; too hysterically grateful to the great gray collie that had saved him to withhold any of it.

"The three dogs went at those cats in gorgeous fashion," finished the Master. "I always said Wolf could 'lick his weight in wildcats.' Now I know it. How they might have fared if the she wildcat's foreleg hadn't been put out of commission by Dawn, I don't know. They'd have gotten much worse punishment than they did.

"They'd have gotten worse punishment, too, if old Ruggles hadn't found the pistol on the ground and put a bullet through the she cat's head. That stopped the battle. For her mate was down and out. He wasn't the fighter that she was.

"Lafe Ruggles begged me to give him back his job here, as soon as his leg gets well. He says, when his work is over, every day, he'll 'brush Gray Dawn's grand coat for half an hour, and he'll cut up all his meat for him, and let him have half his own dinner pail for lunch, and won't charge a cent for doing it.' Shall we give him the job? What do *you* say, Dawn?"

CHAPTER NINE

The Tartar-Catcher

———

"When boys get out of college and have no equipment for making a living, they get jobs as bond salesmen," moralized the Master. "They know nothing about investments, but they learn just enough Wall Street patter to sell a few bonds to 'easy' friends of their parents. When the supply of friends gives out, most of the callow bond salesmen go hunting real jobs.

"When an old man fails in business he gets a job as an insurance solicitor. He knows nothing about insurance, but he is supposed to have sympathetic friends who will take policies out of pity. When middle-aged people, nowadays, have no other way of getting on, they move out of town and start a tea room or a gift shop or sell antiques."

The Master's harangue was prompted by a letter to the Mistress from a friend who asked her to patronize a just-started antique shop, a few miles from The Place. The friend wrote most enthusiastically of the man and his wife— a couple named Heethe—who had come out into the country to sell delectable antiques to persons of discrimination.

"We aren't 'persons of discrimination,'" objected the

Master, "if that means we are willing to spend a fortune on a lot of junk whose only value is that it is old. What's the special advantage of having 'old' things, anyhow, if they aren't one's own family heirlooms? Generally, they're hideous. Most of these antiques are worthless, too. That's why they are of a style that isn't made any more. Ancient styles that were worth perpetuating are still copied. . . . But who wants to pay fifty dollars for an ugly Stiegel-glass rum bottle; or a hundred dollars for a poison-blue urn; or five hundred dollars for an elderly samplesize desk that is too rickety to write at? Who wants to pay high for the privilege of being tortured by a cane-bottom chair with a precipice back, or to slide off a horsehair sofa?"

"Just the same," argued the Mistress, "we'll have to go there. And we'll have to buy something. Mrs. Banning is certain to ask me about it next time I see her."

"And you're too kind to tell her we don't want to be suckers or to clutter our house with rickety rubbish?" suggested the Master. "Oh, all right. Every letter of introduction carries some sort of sting under its tail. Let's drive across there to-day, and get the ordeal over with."

Thus it was that the Master and the Mistress stopped their car an hour later in front of a ramshackle stone farmhouse on the Wyckoff road—a house bearing the legend, on a pseudo-artistic wooden signboard:

"*Ye Heethe Antique Shoppe.*"

Mrs. Heethe met them at the Dutch double door of the big front room which had been converted into a repository for ancient furniture and the like.

Despite its newness, the shop had the air of gloom and

dust and dark decay common to places of its sort. All manner of olden furniture was arranged with optimistic tastefulness here and there over the wide floor space. The shelves were abristle with luster ware and with Stiegel glass and "flowing blue" platters and other crockery. The walls were hung solid with faded prints and lithographs and etchings and samplers, except for a half-dozen tapestries that filled one end of the wall space.

The shopkeeper was a slackly pretty woman, small and with a persistently scared and deprecatory mien. From the back room emerged her husband, dapper and with the manners of an early-Victorian dancing master. The couple all but fell upon the Mistress and the Master. Apparently, customers were discouragingly few.

Into the room, in the wake of his owners, stalked Sunnybank Gray Dawn. He had been taken along, as usual, in the car. At a motion from the Mistress the great gray collie crossed to a corner less littered than was most of the shop. There he lay down.

Dawn was wholly at ease in these unfamiliar and strange-smelling surroundings. He had ridden almost everywhere with the Mistress during the past two years since he had been promoted by Bruce's death to share Bobby's rank as car dog. He was accustomed to all kinds of places.

True, this particular room of furniture clutter did not appeal to him. Nor, at first glance, did he care at all for the dapper man who snapped such friendly fingers at him. But it was all a part of the ride. And Dawn behaved with the stately dignity that befitted the occasion.

The Heethes were going through an interlapping duet of

salesmanship for the benefit of their two customers. Everything, from spavined flax wheels to near-Sheraton gate-
legged tables, was exploited to the visitors' view. But as
soon as might be, the dapper Heethe took up a position in
front of the carefully hung tapestries.

"Here are our real prizes," he declared. "Museum pieces,
one and all. This bit is a fifteenth-century gem, for instance.
Of course, you know the fifteenth-century tapestries
showed more sincerity of workmanship, if less elaborate
technique, than the sixteenth. This is a treasure. Please examine it as the south light strikes across it. Not a flaw, not a
moth hole, not a frayed spot. Perfect. Yes, that is our star
bit. We refused twenty-nine hundred dollars for it just before we moved up here. But, of course, all the expenses of
opening this shop, and our wish to establish ourselves in this
neighborhood——

"Then, this undoubted Gobelin, over here," he hurried
on, as his hearers made no move to buy and as he caught the
Master swallowing a cavernous yawn, "this is a treasure for
any country house. Very precious. Above a fireplace it
would——"

In his enthusiasm Heethe stepped to one side, to give a
better view of the tapestry. The step brought his heel down
on the end of Gray Dawn's plumed tail.

To have his tail stepped on in this painful manner, by an
unliked stranger, was more than the collie's company manners could withstand. Dawn uttered no sound. But his
silver-and-snow dappled head moved with the swiftness of
light and his jaws came together with a snap on the offend-
ing foot's ankle.

Luckily for himself, Heethe had hopped aside with instinctive suddenness as he felt the tail under his heel. Thus, Dawn's mighty jaws closed only on the flaring cuff of the trousers leg, biting a crescent raggedly out of it.

"Dawn!" cried the Mistress, as Heethe sidled away, blithering with nervous terror.

The collie ceased at once his punitive efforts and subsided to the floor, whence he looked reproachfully from the Master to the Mistress, and truculently at the hopping shopkeeper.

"I'm so sorry, Mr. Heethe!" exclaimed the Mistress. "I do hope he hasn't hurt you! You must let us pay for the damage he has done. He meant no harm. You stepped on him and——"

"Oh, it's quite all right!" Heethe assured her. "Quite all right! It was my own carelessness. I couldn't think of letting you pay anything. He's a grand collie. Let's forget all about it."

"Good breeding!" mentally decided the Mistress. "We must buy enough to make up to him for it, if he won't take money for the damage."

"Good salesmanship!" mentally decided the Master. "He knows we'll never go out of here, now, without buying more than we want. He'll get ten times the price of his ready-made trousers."

And so it proved. When at last the Mistress and the Master left the shop with their dog they had bought far too many things to carry home in their little car; and Heethe had promised to drive over to The Place with the purchases on the morrow in his station wagon.

"Dawn," observed the Master, as he and his wife got into the machine and the collie leaped in after them, "once more you've managed to get into the middle of the picture, and with the usual results. You can always be counted on to do something costly. If you'd bitten both of his ankles, instead of one, we'd have had to buy the whole junkheap."

As the customers drove away, Heethe turned back into the shop and faced his scared wife. She had braced herself for one of his fits of peevish rage over the injury to his best trousers. Instead he smiled benignly on her.

"Lucky bite!" he commented, adding: "I remember Mrs. Banning told you they think the world of that great ugly gray dog. Do you know, I have an idea we can make enough out of Dawn, perhaps, to pay for a pair of fourteen-karat gold trousers, with radium seams. Now don't bother me. I want to think. It's worth thinking over."

Next morning Heethe drove to The Place, bringing along only part of the things the Mistress had bought. With much volubility he explained that an Adam lowboy had developed a shaky leg which even now was in process of mending and soon would be ready for delivery. Similarly, the cane-work on a peasant chair was frayed at the back and must be repaired. An eighteenth-century bee-clock had proven erratic as to keeping time, and was in dire need of regulating.

"I'll bring each article over here the very minute it is in repair," he promised.

"Don't take all that trouble," exhorted the Mistress. "Wait till everything is ready and then make one load of it all."

But Heethe would not have it so. Fussily, he declared his intent of delivering each unwanted item of the lot as soon as it should be in condition.

As he talked he made wistful advances of friendship to Gray Dawn, stroking the collie's head and feeding him bits of cake from his pocket. Dawn had taken no fancy at all to the little man, nor had he liked Heethe the better for stepping on his tail. Yet, the cake was undeniably toothsome. Dawn loved cake of any kind. For the sake of it, now, he permitted the stranger to pet and praise him.

Heethe was an authorized visitor, as was proven by the civil treatment he was receiving from the Mistress and the Master. Hence, there was no question of resenting his well-meant advances. Besides—the cake was delicious.

Next day Heethe brought over the lowboy. Again he made excuse to stay for a chat. Again he made much of Gray Dawn, feeding him even more cake than before. Dawn began to forget his distaste for the man and to think of him only as a gift-bearing admirer.

It was so on the third day when Heethe appeared at The Place with the repaired peasant chair. This time Dawn, of his own accord, trotted up to him and nosed discourteously at his pocket for cake. The cake was there.

On the fourth day Heethe did not make his usual call. But the following day was Sunday. The Mistress and the Master and the maids were at church that morning. So were the superintendent and his family. The other men were at their homes, as usual, for the day of rest.

Heethe drove down to The Place in his truck a little after eleven o'clock, bringing the newly regulated bee-clock.

Gray Dawn was on guard, on the veranda. Bobby was in-doors. The other dogs were shut into their kennel yards. Recognizing Heethe, Dawn came forward, with an eye on the cake pocket.

Heethe got out of his truck and smote loudly at the door knocker. Finding no response except a salvo of barks from the imprisoned Bobby, he looked warily about him. It was then, for the first time, that he seemed to note Dawn's presence. One of the man's hands was behind him. With the other he proffered a hunk of cake to the dog.

Dawn swallowed it at a gulp and looked interestedly at the pocket for more. A second bit was forthcoming. As Dawn reached for it, Heethe's other hand came stealthily from behind his back.

In another instant a stout canvas bag incased the collie's head and its drawstring was tight around his neck. Before the amazedly indignant Dawn could claw loose the impediment he was picked up bodily and strugglingly, and was thrust into a crate in the truck.

A dog—almost alone of all the animal kingdom—has but one set of weapons—his jaws. Dawn's jaws were hampered and made useless by the tough folds of canvas.

Off drove the truck, its closed canvas sides masking the crate, and the crate's tight-slatted sides hiding the dog. In two minutes Heethe was free of The Place's grounds and was speeding toward his antique shop.

Arrived there, he drove to the rear of the house. Calling his wife to help him, he lifted the swaying crate to the ground, with much effort. Between them the two lugged it to the cellar, and faced its door against the opening of a coal bin which Heethe had converted into a stockade cage.

Whipping the bag from the half-smothered dog's head, he thrust Dawn deftly into this cage, slamming its gate just as the collie wheeled about to escape.

"He can howl his head off!" panted Heethe, mopping his wet forehead and relaxing from the unwonted exercise. "Nobody'll suspect anything. It'll just be Tige, that we put down cellar these hot days to keep him cool. Plenty of people around here saw Tige before I sent him away last night. I'll just have time to wash up before I go for my train."

The Mistress and the Master came home from church. Dawn was not on the steps to welcome them. The Master whistled for him. There was no reply. As the Mistress opened the front door, Bobby came dashing out, full of an oddly fierce excitement. Bobby had been asleep in the study when the family went to church, but he had waked as Heethe hammered on the knocker. His nose and ears told him most of what had happened on the porch. Hence his excitement.

The Master came back from a futile search for the missing gray collie.

"This is the first time Dawn ever deserted his post when we left him on guard while we were away," he said, annoyedly. "I felt we could trust him to hold down the job. But, with Dawn, all you can count on is that he'll do something nobody expects him to. Why, a dozen mangy Sunday trippers might have come up here from the lake and stolen every flower and every motor tire when we were gone! Nobody could have gotten into the house. Bobby would have seen to that. But I relied on Dawn to guard the grounds. I told him to. I don't understand it."

As the Master was getting out of his church clothes and into his beloved everyday disreputable khaki and flannel, the telephone rang. He answered the summons. A voice, muffled as by distance—a voice hoarse and elaborately rough and smeared with a foreign accent—called him by name, then went on, hurriedly:

"I have your big gray collie. I have him here. He——"

"We missed him when we got home," said the Master. "I never knew him to stray before, when he was on guard. Thanks for letting me know. I'll come for him at once. Whom am I talking to, please?"

"My name does not matter," answered the hoarse foreign voice. "You do not know me. You never saw me. I——"

"But where do you live?" asked the Master, vexed by the note of mystery in the other's speech. "Tell me how to get to your house, please, and I'll be over there as soon as I——"

"Talk less and listen more," adjured the voice, gruffly. "I shall not tell you my name nor where I live. I have your gray collie. If you doubt it, the license tag of his collar has '397, P.L.' on it. I have him here, safely. I am willing to give him back to you—if you are willing to pay me for my trouble in bringing him here. I——"

The Master put his palm over the transmitter and said hurriedly to his wife in the next room:

"Will you go to the study phone, please, and find out from Central where this call comes from? Some one has stolen Dawn and wants to hold me up for cash." Then into the transmitter he continued: "I didn't catch the last part of that. Somebody here was talking too loudly. What did you say?"

"I said," resumed the accented voice—"I said, if you want your dog you will pay me fifteen hundred dollars for him."

"You're crazy!" cried the Master. "Why, he isn't worth seven hundred at most. He has passed his prime as a show dog. He——"

"I chance to have good information that he is worth fully fifteen hundred dollars to you and your wife," replied the voice. "If you wish to see him again, you will pay me fifteen hundred dollars, in fifty-dollar bills, in a manner I shall dictate to you in a letter you will receive from me to-morrow morning. If you do that, the dog will be turned loose within two miles or less of your home and be allowed to find his way back to you."

"I——"

"If you do not accept my terms, those terms will become harder. They will become harder than either you or your wife may choose to pay. Especially your wife. I shall say no more now, for I think you stopped listening to me a minute ago in order to use some other telephone to find where I am calling from. I shall call another time. I do not care to be traced. Good-by."

There was a click. The interview was ended. Presently the Mistress hurried upstairs with news that the call had come from a coin box in the Hudson Terminal in lower New York City, and to demand eagerly the full details of the kidnapping.

"I'll see him in blue blazes before I stand for a hold-up

like that!" raged the Master. "The whole thing is too mixed
for me to figure it out. Two hours ago Dawn was on the
veranda here. Now some-one calls up from New York that
he is held there for this preposterous ransom. I suppose
Dawn strayed out on the main road. Some thief was passing
by who recognized him. He coaxed the dog into his car
and sprinted to New York with him. He——"

"You know as well as I do that nothing of the kind could
have happened," argued the Mistress. "In the first place,
Dawn never in his life left a spot where we told him to stay.
In the second, he knows too much to wander out on the
highroad. We've taught him that ever since he was a puppy.
In the third, he'd never get into any stranger's car. As for his
being lifted in by force, it would have been as easy to lift
a fighting wolf. Besides, everyone for miles around here
knows him by sight. No thief would be silly enough to
drive through this region with Dawn. No, that can't be the
solution, at all. It——"

"No," glumly assented the Master, "it can't. But neither
can anything else. None of it makes sense. I'll call up the
police, of course, and I'll notify the State Patrol. But that's
all I can do. It isn't as if he was straying anywhere. He'll be
hidden too safely for anyone to find him."

It was a drearily unhappy afternoon the dog's two owners
spent. Nor was it made cheerier by the arrival, at three
o'clock, of the dapper Mr. Heethe, bringing the bee-clock.
He told them he had driven over with the clock during the
morning, but, finding nobody at home, had taken it away
again.

"Hold on!" spoke up the Master, in momentary interest.

"You remember our merle collie, Sunnybank Gray Dawn, don't you—the one that tore your trousers—the one you gave some cake to, the other day? Well, when you came here this morning, was he on the porch or anywhere in sight?"

"No," said Heethe, regretfully, "he was not. I know because I looked around for him. I—I had a fresh-baked little cake I brought over here for him. Would you mind very much if I give it to him now? I've taken a tremendous liking to that beautiful dog of yours. You won't think me silly if I ask leave to give him this cup cake? It is such a tiny one, it can't harm him."

"He's not around just now," said the Mistress, unwilling to listen to the dapper little bore's wordy sympathy, should she tell him of the collie's mishap. "I'm sorry. Won't you come over again, to see him?"

"Thank you very much, indeed. I shall be——"

"What time were you here this morning?" demanded the Master.

"At—let me see—I should say somewhere around eleven. Why?"

"We wondered if it was soon after we started for church or just before we got back," interposed the Mistress. "Thanks again for all your trouble in coming over so often with the things."

Monday's first mail brought the Master a neatly typed letter with no signature. It read:

To confirm our telephone talk:—You may have your collie by paying $1,500 in fifty-dollar bills to me. You will put the bills in a package and you will drop them at ten o'clock on

Monday evening, just outside the entrance to the grounds of Paradise Inn, at Pompton Lakes. You will drop them in the middle of the road, at that time, without stopping your car; and you will continue to drive on at full speed, not looking back.

I shall be in the underbrush near the road; and I shall pick up the package. The next day your dog will be loosed not far from your house, and will find his way home. This if I find the bills genuine and unmarked.

I beg you will not post detectives in the undergrowth there, nor warn the Paradise Inn management; nor try in any way to have me watched or tracked. If you do you may be able to catch me. But if you do there is a solemn certainty you will never again see the dog. For I have arranged, past all mistake, that he shall be killed in the event that I am traced or arrested. And I swear to you he shall be killed in a way that first will torture him to the utmost.

So play fair with me and I shall play fair with you. I am not cruel, but I am in desperate need of money. I wish no harm to you or to the dog. But if you double-cross me in any way, the dog shall die in torture. You may have it in your power to get me caught and imprisoned. If you prefer to do this, rather than have your dog returned to you safe and well, do so. I am taking that chance.

"Well," commented the Master, "I suppose I ought to be grateful to him for not writing the smudgy and illiterate letter of the conventional anonymous blackmailer. What shall we do about it?"

"We are not going to pay the money," said the Mistress, with quiet firmness. "I'd pay ten times as much, sooner than have anything happen to Dawn. But—oh, I can't explain it! Something keeps telling me *not* to do it! I can't explain it. But——"

"You don't have to explain it," answered the Master. "I've played your hunches before, and I've never lost on them. I'll chance this one."

But both of them were miserable and sick with apprehension for the great dog they loved.

At six o'clock on Tuesday morning the telephone summoned the Master from bed. Again the hoarse voice with its elaborate accent was addressing him.

"You did not do as I told you," it began. "I waited until midnight. You did not bring the money. If you don't bring it, to-night, then to-morrow morning you will receive a package. It will contain your dog's ears. If you do not bring the money to-morrow night, to the place I named in my letter and at the same hour, you will receive, next day, a package containing his forepaws; and so on until not enough of him will be left to mail to you. Good-by."

As before, at her husband's signal, the Mistress had run to the other telephone and had asked Central to locate the call. It was from the Broad Street railroad station in Newark.

"The fellow has been reading dime novels, based on the old Corsican bandit yarns," said the Master, uncomfortably. "The wheeze about sending a captive's ears as a reminder that a ransom will be acceptable—it's as old as the hills. Well? How about it?"

"We won't pay," declared the Mistress, her sweet voice a trifle unsteady. "I don't know why. But we won't. And we're going to get Dawn back."

The converted coal bin in the antique shop's cellar was a right dolorous cell for an outdoor dog like Gray Dawn;

apart from his rage and homesickness. For hours after his incarceration he ravened up and down it in helpless fury, hurling himself against its stout sides, gnawing at its wire-enforced slats, seeking to leap its inward-sloping top boards.

Then, tired and sullenly despairing, Dawn lay down on the straw and brooded. Thus Heethe found him that night, and thus the next morning and throughout the day. Dawn ate practically none of the food thrust through the slats to him, though he drank greedily from the gallon pail of water in one corner. He greeted Heethe's several appearances with a deep-throated growl, but he made no active move to break through barriers whose unbreakableness he had proven.

"He's easier to handle than I thought he'd be," Heethe told his wife. "This is going to be a very simple transaction. Those people aren't going to be able to hold out. I know enough of human nature and of fool nature to know that. I'm surprised they haven't paid the money before now. The threat about his ears will bring it in a rush."

It was Tuesday morning. Heethe had just returned from his telephone trip to Newark. He was tired from his vigil in the underbrush on the preceding night and from his early ride to and from Newark. Yawning, he went upstairs for an hour's nap before any possible customers should happen in.

His wife went into the kitchen to finish her morning work there. In the sink was a plateful of table scraps she had set out for her husband to carry down to Gray Dawn. Heethe had been too drowsy to remember the captive's breakfast. The woman picked up the plate and took it to the cellar.

Dawn heard her step. He did not raise his head as he lay asprawl in the straw, nor did he give sign of noting her approach. Yet, as always when Heethe or his wife drew near the bin, the collie's nerves and muscles tensed with angry expectation.

Mrs. Heethe peered through the slats at the dimly seen dog. On a plate inside the bin was the supper Heethe had brought him on the evening before. Dawn had not touched it. The woman felt a throb of pity for the prisoner, who apparently was bent on starving to death. She chirped to him. Dawn did not stir. In the faint light, he seemed already to be dead, so still and inert was he.

Again she chirped; then sharply she called him by name. There was no responsive motion. Dawn was lying as she had seen him lie when she came down for a last look at him on Monday night. It did not seem possible that a living animal could remain thus, without motion, so long.

As a matter of fact, it was not possible. Nor had it happened. Scarcely ten minutes earlier Dawn had cast himself down there again, after prowling gloomily around his cell. But Mrs. Heethe had a complete ignorance of collies and of their ways.

She rattled the bar of the gate. She had seen her husband do this on Sunday evening, and she had seen Dawn spring at him with a wild-beast roar. But now the provocative action had no effect on the statue-still brute. Fear gripped the woman—fear lest the fifteen hundred dollars should be lost irretrievably, by reason of the prisoner's death.

More loudly she rattled the bar. No responsive move nor sound. Dawn was sulking. He refused to be drawn into another impotent assault on his prison by the tempting rattle. He lay sprawled in the straw, without deigning a glance at his visitor.

Resolved to prove what she felt was true, Mrs. Heethe lifted the bar. The dog was dead or dying. That seemed certain. If he was able to move he must surely have given some sign when he heard the bar clicking.

She opened the gate an inch or two and peered in, hoping to get a clearer view of the collie than could be obtained through the close slats.

As she put her eye to the opening she was thrust violently back against the cellar wall.

The bin door flew wide, with the force of an explosion. A shadowy silver shape swept out, past the staggering woman. The collie circled the cellar at a tearing run. Then he found the stairs leading upward. In two bounds, he had reached the first floor and he was launching himself at the nearest window. But, though the glass panes shivered at the impact, he was knocked back to the floor again.

To add an ancient-looking adornment to the modern casements of the ground floor, as well as to serve as protection against burglars, Heethe had equipped every downstairs window with a fragile-appearing wrought-iron grill, strong enough to withstand much force. Not only could these dainty bars keep out intruders, but now they were baffling an inmate that was most eager to get out.

Dawn gathered himself together and dashed along the passage to the big front room which served as shop and in which were hoarded the most costly of the antiques. The shop's front door was shut. The windows were grilled. At a glance Dawn saw he was in an impasse. Turning, he made to retrace his steps and to seek egress elsewhere.

But Mrs. Heethe had scuttled tremblingly up the cellar stairs in his wake. She was in dire fear of the savage beast. But she was in far greater fear of her dapper husband's bullying wrath, should the collie escape. As Dawn came toward her from the shop, she slammed shut in his face the passage door leading to the rear of the house.

Caught in this new jail, the dog went berserk with fury. Around and around the shop he galloped, seeking a way out. In his first circling run he upset three or four spindly antique tables and chairs and a flax wheel. His mighty shoulder caught a mahogany shaving stand obliquely, sending it sailing into space, whence it smashed through a seventeenth-century mirror propped in a corner of the room.

The crash and jingle may have awakened in Dawn his never soundly sleeping devil of mischief, or it may have stirred him merely to a rage of destruction after his two days of unhappy idleness. For he charged back through the splintering and flying furniture, wreaking wholesale ravage. In front of him on one wall he saw thick hangings which might well mask some outlet from the room. He leaped at them.

Under his clawing forepaws the two most precious of the six tapestries came down from their wall pinnings. They fell atop him. In wrath he wriggled from under their dusty embrace. Seizing them, one after another, he held them to the floor with his front feet while his terrible jaws rent them to rags.

A third tapestry came slithering down on him as he was at work on the two others. He treated it as he had treated them. Then he rolled on the three.

This done, he reared on his hindlegs and sought to mount a broad shelf above which was a stovepipe hole leading out to open air. It held hope of exit. Dawn's effort to draw himself atop this ledge ripped the heavy shelf loose from its brackets. Down it came. Down with it tumbled a mass of Stiegel glass and pottery and Colonial china. Dawn and the shelf fell atop the strewn heap of breakables.

Rising from the wreckage, Dawn sprang for the next shelf, still hoping to reach the stovepipe hole. Under his muscular weight, down came dog and shelf and a really valuable collection of Stafford ware and flowing blue platters and two genuine luster tea sets.

Dust and din filled the room while Dawn continued to charge merrily to and fro among fragile curios. Now and again he paused in futile effort to shake loose something which clung persistently about his neck.

Downstairs pattered Heethe, half dressed, his eyes red from sleep. He found his wife crouching weepingly in the passageway outside the shop door. From behind the door issued a continuous noise whose nature could not be mistaken—a noise that would have struck horror to the heart of even a novice collector of antiques.

Without stopping to ask questions and aware only that his meager capital, in the way of stock in trade, was undergoing demolition, Heethe opened the door. Out of the dust clouds and through the inconceivable wreck of glass and china and tapestry and furniture, something huge and murderous charged ragingly at him. Dawn had a score to pay his kidnapper-jailer.

Heethe leaped back. There was no time to close the door.

There was time for only one move of self-preservation, and Heethe made that move. Slipping behind his wife in the narrow passageway, he caught her by the shoulders and thrust her in front of him as a shield.

Gray Dawn was almost upon his prey. But the collie checked himself, practically in mid-air, as he found a woman confronting him and not the man who had mistreated him so vilely.

To the floor he came, still growling thunderously, snarling and seeking fiercely to push past Mrs. Heethe to the man who cringed behind her.

So far as the woman was concerned, Dawn could have gone past her with entire ease. She had no desire to oppose his rush. In panic she was shrieking for help and was straining to wrench loose from her husband's grip.

But Heethe, with the cunning of a trapped rat, was maneuvering her slender body, in the narrow space, so as to fend off the furious dog from himself, the while he sought to back to the kitchen door. The house rocked with screams and growls.

Through her wild terror, Mrs. Heethe noted that a square yard of the priceless fifteenth-century tapestry surrounded Gray Dawn's furry throat like a ruff. In his rending of it, or while he was rolling in it, he had somehow gotten a fragment of the material around his neck, by an accidental thrust of his head through one of its countless rips.

The woman had scope to observe no more, for just then Heethe thrust her forward against the dog, as he himself jumped backward across the kitchen threshold and slammed the door shut after him.

The man was safe. So, for that matter, was his wife. For
Dawn saw his prey had escaped. He had no desire whatever to injure this woman or any other woman. Instantly
he moved back from her and stood looking up with worried sympathy into her weeping face.

It was then that a passing neighbor, attracted by the up-
roar, reached the house at a run and swung wide the shop's
front door. The neighbor halted on the threshold, blinking
aghast at the scene of destruction.

Across the wreckage and out through the open doorway
dashed a gigantic silver-and-snow collie, a faded but still
gaudy collar of tapestry flapping wildly from about his
neck.

The Mistress and the Master were drawing up to the post
office for the morning mail when a confused shout of "Mad
dog!" came to their ears. The Master paused as he stepped
out of the car, and looked about him for the cause of the
outcry.

Down the village street and heading toward the mile-
distant Place a huge and muddy collie was running at
express-train speed. From around his neck a varicolored
rag was flapping in the wind. Behind him a troop of scared
boys were bawling, "Mad dog!"

To the dismay of these youngsters, the tapestry-collared
animal veered suddenly in his break-neck flight and rushed
over to where the Master stood.

Screeching with delight, Dawn threw himself bodily
upon the astounded man, licking his face, beating a tattoo
with muddy and glass-cut feet upon his white linen suit.

Then, catching sight of the Mistress, Dawn hurled himself into the car, landing heavily in her white organdie lap and screaming more loudly and more ecstatically than before.

The next three minutes were pandemonium. As Dawn subsided at last in a furrily blissful heap at the Mistress's feet, the Master found chance to take from the dog's neck the outrageous rag of many colors, and to examine it.

"Where on earth did you come from, Dawnie?" demanded the Mistress. "We ——"

" 'Fifteenth-century tapestry,' " said the Master, dreamily, " 'shows a more sincere workmanship than the sixteenth —if less elaborate technique.' I seem to have heard that precious truth somewhere, lately. I heard it the same time I saw a mangy tapestry with pink-nosed war horses and bench-legged hounds worked on it. See, here's the head of one of the horses and a hind leg of one of the hounds. . . . Dear, will you drive home with Dawn, please? I'm going to take a taxi and run over with this bit of tapestry to the Heethe Antique Shoppe. It belongs there. Besides, I'm just beginning to think of a lot of nice neighborly things I want to say to Heethe. . . . I wish he wasn't so little!"

CHAPTER TEN

Flame!

"There is only one flaw in this home picture," commented Maclay as he sat back smoking lazily his after-dinner cigar and letting his eyes stray in idle appraisal about the oak-ceiled living room of The Place.

The early September night was prematurely chill—one of those nights whose bitter frost fingers slay a million wildflowers and cosmos and salvia and asters and heliotrope, and leave the next morning's sun to rise sorrowfully on wilted black flower beds and borders and terraces. Weeks of tenderly warm weather follow before the next frost. But the damage is done. Save for plucky battle lines of chrysanthemums, the sweet gardens lie dead.

On this cold evening there was a jolly wood fire on the big hearth of the living room. Its reflections danced athwart the time-darkened oaken walls or centered winkingly on the metal of weapon or armor or trophy cup, lending a flicker of life to the glassy eyes of stag or mountain-goat heads on the walls.

Masses of autumn flowers were heaped in bowl and jar.

Drowsy comfort and warmth and sheltered peace brooded over the rambling big room.

On the fur hearth rug, his head across one of the Master's feet, snoozed big Sunnybank Bobby, the firelight turning his shimmery auburn coat to scarlet. On the Mistress's lap was curled a mass of incredibly long and soft gray fluff, whence two jade-green eyes blinked contemplatively at the blaze. A closer look resolved this drift of fluff into Tippy, the Mistress's temperamental Persian cat.

Close at the Mistress's feet snuggled Sunnybank Jean, her worshiping little collie chum, Bobby's sister, and sole living daughter of Bruce the Beautiful.

In a dim corner of the room, as far as possible from the fireplace, slept a huge and dim-seen shape, silver and snow of hue. On this slumberer did Maclay's glance fall last of all. He repeated:

"There is only one flaw in this home picture."

The repetition stirred the Master from the hypnotic lure of the flame flickers to a sense of civility.

"Well," he asked, in no great interest, "what's wrong with this picture? Ought there to be a row of stockings hanging from the mantel or a Christmas tree in the corner?"

"Not a tree in the corner," corrected Maclay, "but a collie out of the corner. Why is Gray Dawn lying over there in the coldest part of the room? Why doesn't he get into the picture, like Bobby and Jean? He ought to be posing on the hearth rug with the firelight playing over him.

" 'The housedog with his paws outspread,
    Lays to the fire his shaggy head.'

"I thought all dogs loved to lie in picturesque attitudes in front of the fire on cold nights. They do in stories and poems. But then Gray Dawn never does quite anything the way other dogs do, does he?"

At sound of his name, Dawn lifted his classic head sleepily from the hard floor and thumped his tail once or twice against the boards. The Master laughed.

"No," he said, "Dawn doesn't do much of anything the same way other dogs do. He's always been a law to himself. But that isn't why he gets as far away from the fireplace as possible. He hates fire with a mortal hatred. It's the only thing except thunderstorms that he's afraid of. It dates back to the time he was a crazy four-month-old puppy. He was capering around the lawn one afternoon, like a drunken rocking-horse, when he lost his balance and sat down hard in the very middle of one of the smoldering heaps of dead leaves the men had been burning."

"And the burnt child dreads the fire ever since? I——"

"Not quite. He got over it in a few months—or he seemed to. He got so he would lie happily on the hearth rug. Then one winter evening, when he was sound asleep there, a little lump of blazing pine knot snapped out of the fireplace and landed just behind his ear. He was so sound asleep that it made a good hard burn before he woke up enough to shake it off.

"Just after that an old shed on a farm near here caught fire. Some of us went over to help put it out. He went along, and his inspired blundering led him over a pile of red-hot boards that had just been torn away from the shed. They burnt his feet so he was lame for a week. That was the climax. Ever since then he has given every fire as wide a berth as he can. Why, if my wife and I weren't here, he wouldn't even stay in the same room with a hearth fire. The very reek of smoke and the snapping of sparks make him nervous, wherever he happens to run across them!"

"He used to love the kitchen," spoke up the Mistress, "till one day he saw the cook spill some fat on the range. It flared up, and Dawn bolted. He has never set foot in there again. He used to growl and then snarl threateningly when he saw anyone start to build a fire on the hearth here. We cured him of that. But we can't cure him of staying as far as possible from it. He'll come to the fireplace if we tell him to, but he scuttles away again as fast as we'll let him. He's queer, in that way—and in several hundred other ways. But, next to Bobby, he's the dearest dog we have left, now that Lad and Bruce and Wolf and Treve are gone. He and Bobby are the last of the long line of Sunnybank's great house dogs. When *they're* gone——"

She didn't finish the sentence. Maclay changed the subject by saying:

"I'm going to run up to Rainbow Lake next week, for some of the fall bass fishing. We didn't plan to open the camp at all till my wife gets back from Scotland. But I'm going up there for a few days, just with my Jap to run the house for me. I wonder if both of you won't take pity on my loneliness and come there for the week-end. I'm not asking anyone else and it'll be more or less a case of roughing it. But the fishing is great, just now. And you'll remember there are some rather beautiful hikes around the hills. Won't you come?"

"If the invitation were baited with smallmouth black bass," answered the Mistress, "my husband would say 'yes' to spending a week-end in jail. We———"

"Good!" exclaimed Maclay. "I'll meet you at the five-o'clock train Friday afternoon, then. You won't mind being bounced about a bit, on the way to the house? It's a rotten road, straight up the mountain, you know. It's even worse than when you people were there last year."

When the Mistress and the Master made ready to drive to the station for their seventy-mile train trip to Rainbow Lake on Friday, Gray Dawn was acutely miserable.

Like Bobby—and like Wolf before them—the great collie knew instinctively whenever his two human gods were planning to leave The Place. He moped about, close at their heels, from morning to night, refusing food and giving a heart-stricken impersonation of Misery.

To-day he was so mournful that the Mistress thought to lesson his woe by letting him ride as far as the station with her. As a rule, Dawn reveled in motoring. But now he climbed listlessly into the rear of the car and cuddled down at the Mistress's feet, his head against her knee.

The Master's watch was slow. The train was pulling into the station as the car dashed up to the gate bars. The Master helped his wife out of the machine and bundled her and the suit cases up the steps of the train's rear platform just as the locomotive got into motion again.

"That was touch and go," he commented as he opened the door and then followed his wife into the train. "We'll have to get our tickets on board. See, we've started. We didn't have three seconds to spare. If——"

He stopped speaking and turned impatiently to see who had given one of his suit cases such an uncivil shove as he passed down the aisle of the rear car.

Beside him in the swaying aisle stood Gray Dawn.

The big dog's moroseness had fallen away. Vibrant with glad excitement, he wagged his plumed tail and his whole mighty silver body in delight.

As the Master and his wife had clambered up the platform steps of the starting train, Dawn's longing to remain with them had overcome his teachings as an automobile dog. He had leaped easily out of the car and in one spring had reached the platform's steps. Scrambling up them he had rejoined his human deities halfway along the aisle, making known his presence by bumping merrily against the suit case. His owners stared at him in unbelieving dismay.

"What in blazes is to be done about it?" demanded the Master. "This is the last train to-day that stops at Rainbow Lake. We can't get off at the next station and send him home in a taxi, for we couldn't get to the lake to-night. We'll have to go back with him. The fishing trip is off! As usual, Gray Dawn is playing true to form and making toad pie of our plans. He——"

"He didn't do it out of mischief," said the Mistress. "He did it because he loves us and wants to be with us. And he is *going* to be with us, too. You're not going to lose your fishing. Take him into the baggage car, won't you, and tip the man there to keep an eye on him till we get to Rainbow

Lake? Mr. Maclay likes dogs and he likes Gray Dawn. I'm certain he won't mind our bringing him along. Please don't be angry with the old dog, dear. He didn't mean any harm. He——"

"He never needs to 'mean any harm,'" grumbled the Master. "He can do more harm, without meaning to, than anything short of an earthquake. But you're right. The only thing to do is to take him along, unless we want to go back, too. Mac won't mind. And some miracle may keep Dawn from trouble while he's there. Or it may not. I'll take him to the baggage car. But I'll have to stay there with him. If I don't, he'll break any rope he's tied to and jump out of the moving train to see what's become of us. Come along, Dawn."

The collie's acceptance of his own invitation to join the week-end party at Maclay's wilderness camp was not the day's sole upset of calculations. Arrived at Rainbow Lake railroad station at six o'clock, the voyagers looked in vain for their host among the few rustics who were loafing around the platform.

A wiggling little Japanese manservant stepped forward to greet them. He handed them a note, then picked up their luggage and carried it to a muddy car. Over his shoulder the Jap peered interestedly back through slitted eyes at the giant collie that stood so eagerly expectant beside the guests. Dawn was gorgeously happy. Always new environment thrilled him, as did any form of adventure.

"H'm!" mused the Master, after a glance at the note. "Mac says he was called to town in a rush, at four this afternoon, to a conference. The two biggest men in that merger he told us about have just come on unexpectedly from the West. They sail to-morrow for Europe. This is the only time they can have the meeting. Something big has turned up, Mac says, and they have to see him at once. He'll try to get the noon train back here to-morrow. In the meanwhile he sends all manner of apologies to you, and he says his man will make us comfortable and that we're to consider the house is ours."

They followed the Jap to the disreputable little car and squeezed into its tonneau along with their suit cases, Dawn sitting in joyous self-importance on the front seat alongside the apprehensive Jap who served as chauffeur.

Maclay was a corporation lawyer of much wealth, and with three homes and seven cars. But he was happiest when he could steal off to his elaborately rough cottage camp on the shore of his private lake, high among these mountains—a home reached by a trail which only this small and weather-battered car could climb with any ease or certainty—there to spend a week or two in what he chose to consider a Spartan simplicity, waited on by one super-costly manservant, and fishing or shooting for much of his own food.

Here more than once the Mistress and the Master had shared his sybaritic pseudo-simplicity. Here, now, they prepared to enjoy the first part of their visit as best they might, without their host.

There was an Adirondack chill and pungency to the balsam-tinged air when they awoke next morning. But the hoodoo of the preceding day had not yet spent itself.

First of all, as the Mistress and the Master repaired to the breakfast room, Gray Dawn came sidling shyly and self-consciously into the house from an early-morning ramble. A blind man would have known instantly just what horrible adventure the dog had met with. The Mistress gasped as he came unhappily toward her. The Jap rushed to throw wide such windows as were not already open.

In his casual strolling explorations Dawn had happened upon a black-and-white striped furry denizen of the wilds— an animal which seemed to have been afflicted with something akin to halitosis. Dawn had frisked over to investigate, with a jolly plan of chasing the kittenlike stranger up a tree. The result was known to everyone by the time his scared line of retreat brought him to within fifty yards of the house.

"Out!" yelled the Master, as the collie came ambling up to the Mistress and himself for sympathy. "Outside! STAY outside!"

Sadly the dog obeyed, withdrawing to the rocky patch of lawn which jutted out into the lake. The Master looked after him with a grunt of disgust.

"Dawn is the only creature I ever heard of," he said, gloomily, "that takes the pains to get up before sunrise to look for trouble. With his tendencies, he could find a day's supply of it if he didn't start his search till dusk. He——"

The grumbled plaint ended in a crash. The Master had put on a new pair of house shoes, for breakfast, to be changed later for his fishing boots. Now, as he turned back into the hallway after expelling the malodorous Gray Dawn, his sole slipped on the floor which the Jap had just oiled.

Down he went, with a jar that shook the building. As he

started to jump up, he changed his mind with much suddenness and sat down heavily. His left ankle had turned under
him as he fell, wrenching its every sinew and nerve, almost
to snapping. On this first morning of his fishing trip he had
sustained a decidedly bad and complicated sprain. It would
be days before he could hope to bear his weight on both
feet again.

"Dawn didn't succeed in cornering the trouble market,"
he observed, with what sorry philosophy he could muster,
as his wife and the Jap helped him into the nearest chair.
"There was a comfortable half portion of it left over for *me*.
I'll have to do my fishing on one leg, like a stork."

"You'll have to do your fishing on a couch, I'm afraid,
or in bed," said the Mistress sadly, as she examined the fast-
swelling ankle. "This ought to be treated at once by some
one with more skill than I have. Sato, is there a really good
doctor down in the village?"

"No doctor at all, down there, madam," answered the
Jap. "No doctor till Postville. Seven mile. Maybe six. If he
is home. Generally out."

"Go there as quickly as you can," decreed the Mistress,
"and bring him back with you. If he is out on his morning calls, try to find him."

"Why not save all that bother, by phoning him?" asked
the Master, grouchy with pain. "No use chasing all over
the state in a car for him when——"

"The telephone wires were blown down in that wind-
storm Sato told us about," the Mistress reminded him.
"They are broken in three places, he says, between here
and the village. Don't you remember? No, the only way

we can get the doctor is to send Sato after him. If he is out on his round of calls, Sato ought to find him without much trouble and get him back here before noon. I only hope he isn't on a fishing trip or away somewhere for the week-end."

Sato bustled off to the garage, giving a wide berth to Dawn, who moped malodorously on the lawn. The Mistress bent to renew the wet compresses on the discolored and puffed ankle. Presently she spoke again.

"When we were up here last September," she said, "Mr. Maclay told me about an old man—his name was Wyble, or else—yes, it *was* Wyble—an old man in that tiny mountain settlement we hiked to at the head of the lake—who set a broken arm for one of the maids when they couldn't get hold of a doctor. Mr. Maclay said the old fellow has a genius for surgery. He said a lot of the old-time mountaineers used to handle fractures and sprains as cleverly as any surgeon, but that Wyble is the last of them in this region who has the gift. Well, while Sato is looking for the doctor I'm going to paddle to the head of the lake and bring Wyble back here to look at your ankle. It can't do any harm."

Despite the Master's surly protests, she made him as comfortable as might be, and set forth on her quest of the mountaineer surgeon.

Maclay's cottage camp was built at the extreme point of a half mile of thin promontory which jutted far out into Rainbow Lake. The house itself stood at the apex of the promontory. For nearly two miles in front and for more than two miles in either direction the lake glistened in the September haze.

At the foot of the low promontory cliff, and almost directly under the cottage itself, stood the boathouse. Thither the Mistress hurried, stopping only to take the tagged boathouse keys from their nail. Down the steep little flight of rock-hewn steps she ran, Gray Dawn close behind her and seeking in mute appeal to win from her a word or a caress that should tell him he was in disgrace no longer.

The Mistress unlocked and opened the boathouse's iron-sheathed door. On the inclined plane in front of her were three fishing boats and a Lake George skiff and two canoes. A single braided steel rope ran through the prow rings of all of them. On each side of the boathouse the steel cable was welded into an iron stanchion. On one side there was a three-link break in it, with a stout padlock connecting the links. To get a boat out, it was necessary to unfasten the padlock and to draw the supple wire rope free from the prow rings.

The Mistress decided on the canoe nearest to the padlock. She was putting the second of the boathouse's two keys into this lock, when she became aware that the place was filled with a most ghastly aroma. Turning, she saw Dawn beside her, looking up into her face with an agony of mute appeal for pardon. No longer was there any mystery as to the source of the odor.

So concerned had the Mistress been with her husband's misfortune and with the need of getting to the lake-head settlement as quickly as possible, that she had not observed the unhappy dog. Now, seeing him, her brow contracted into a worried frown.

If she should forbid him to follow, he would obey her command. Dawn always obeyed. But in such case he would

trot to the Master for consolation. An excruciatingly painful sprained ankle was quite enough for her husband to
endure in her absence, without the added horror of such
scent as must fill the small house as soon as Gray Dawn
should enter. On the other hand, if she should take him
along in the canoe, she must have a two-mile close propin-
quity to him which would be even worse. Either prospect
was out of the question.

The Mistress snapped shut the padlock and left the boathouse, locking the door behind her and dropping the two
heavy keys into her sweater pocket. When she had visited
the mountain settlement with Maclay, they had gone on
foot, following a lakeside trail for two miles, and then
branching inland to the right, for another quarter mile to
the settlement.

The distance was shorter by land than by the widely
twisting lake route. By walking at her fastest gait the Mistress could hope to get to Wyble's shack as quickly over
the trail as in the canoe. The settlement was at some distance from the water; and in either event she would have
had some walking to do after getting to the head of the
lake. This latter distance was much shorter by way of the
trail.

Off she set at a swinging gait, Dawn bounding on ahead
of her. The collie's sense of disgrace was forgotten in the
prospect of this hike with the beloved Mistress, or else he
accepted the walk with her as a token of forgiveness. His
joyful return to good spirits kept him cantering far ahead
of her for the most part, during the bulk of the journey,
thus inflicting only a stray whiff or two of discomfort upon
her instead of the former unadulterated quantity.

As they hurried along, the Mistress resolved to send Dawn into the lake for a series of long swims later in the day, in the hope of making his presence more bearable. Even should the ice-chill waters of the spring-fed lake fail to wash him clean, they would lessen the nuisance. But all this must wait, of course, until the doctor or Wyble could reach the suffering Master.

Had she taken more notice of her dog she would have seen that Gray Dawn began to lose his exuberance and that he stopped several times to sniff the hazy air, as if he were seeking to tabulate some smell which was hard to recognize through the greater volume of his own unfortunate scent.

More and more uneasy he grew. Presently he ceased to gambol far ahead and came back to the Mistress, looking up at her in manifest worry, whimpering very softly. She signaled him to go on once more. For he was not a pleasant trail companion just now, when he pressed worriedly against her skirt as she walked. Meekly Dawn obeyed. But this time he did not bound forward as before. Instead, he slunk, tail between legs, head drooping, ill-hidden terror in every line and motion.

Again the Mistress was too intent in hurrying to her destination, to take heed of his behavior. There were other things she did not notice, skilled in wood lore as she was. The September sun stood high overhead. Yet it cast no rays. Ochre red it hung. It had not melted the mists. Indeed, the haze was growing thicker and thicker every instant, blotting out the vistas, making the mountain air strangely hard to breathe.

Back came Dawn again. He skulked at the Mistress's

heels, quivering as with a chill. There were foam flecks of fear on his mouth and on his pantingly lolling pink tongue. Once or twice he moaned. He seemed to be trying to keep as near to the Mistress as he could, to secure her human protection against a danger which stirred him to mortal terror.

And now, even to the Mistress's absorbed senses, came a reek which could be recognized above the baleful odor of the dog.

"There's a forest fire, somewhere," she told herself, hastening on.

Loving the woods as she did, this discovery ordinarily would have saddened her. To-day she thought only of reaching her goal. The lake was past. She was mounting the steep path leading to the settlement. Then the huddle of a dozen mean shacks was in sight.

At first glance the hamlet seemed deserted. But she saw a crippled child standing on a high rock just in front of her, peering to northward from under a curved hand. The Mistress called to him:

"Do you live here?"

The child started at the strange voice. He glanced around until he located her and the dog. Turning back to the more entertaining view from which she had distracted him, he made answer:

"Yes'm."

"Which house does Wyble live in?" asked the Mistress. "The old man who sets broken legs. Where does he live? Do you know him?"

"No'm," was the drawled reply, as the child continued

to gaze northward from under his shielding palm. "No'm.
I don't know him; not now. Nor yet he don't live nowheres.
He was my gran'dad. He went an' got hisself buried, back
last spring."

"He's dead?" exclaimed the Mistress, with a sinking of
the heart.

"Yes'm," said the child, adding in polite explanation:
"That's why he got hisself buried. He——say! It's gittin'
so's I c'n see it 'most all the time."

"What is?" queried the Mistress, wondering at his con-
centrated gaze to the north.

"The for'st fire, of course," he returned, as in amaze at
so silly a query. "Over yon. Ev'body has went to fight it.
They wouldn't leave me go along, 'cause I can't move fast
and they was afeared a back draft'd ketch me. They——"

The Mistress heard no more. She climbed to the child's
side and followed the direction of his stare: Above the tree
line hung a cotton-thick mass of smoke, shot here and there
by a lunging fist of flame. From afar came a continuous
muffled sound, like a mile-distant explosion of firecrackers.

"It's got around to where pop said it would!" the child
was orating. "Right back of that place where the land runs
way out into the pond for 'most a half of a mile. Pop said
if it was to git there, it'd clean that p'int right down to th'
ground, an' all Mr. Maclay's buildin's with it, pop said.
Gee! but I wish't I c'd see them buildings when they ketch
fire. They're due to in a few min'ts, now, from the way the
fire's been movin', jest the spell I been watchin' it. If you
stay here, you'll likely see it as good as me. I——"

But the Mistress had let herself down from the rock.

Dawn crawled forward to her on his stomach, his eyes bloodshot, his mouth slavering, his body one continuous shudder. He was moaning hoarsely, beside himself with terror.

The Mistress took no heed. She, too, was shivering. Her big eyes were dilated, her face was drawn and pallid. Her knowledge of the woods and her brief survey from the summit of the rock had told her the story, past all doubt.

Somewhere back in the drought-parched mountain a fool had dropped a cigarette butt or had knocked out a pipe or had neglected to kill his camp fire. Tinder-dry undergrowth and dead evergreens had lent eager fuel to the smolder. A forest fire had been born. A shift of wind had turned its murderous course straight toward Rainbow Lake.

Well did the Mistress recall the topography of that long tongue of narrow promontory on whose extreme edge stood the Maclay camp. Once let the fire gain a grip among its dead tamaracks and other tons of inflammables, and, with the wind behind it, the blaze must sweep every inch of the promontory. Not a stick would be spared.

In the inflammable cottage at the tip of that land-jut lay the Master; too crippled to walk a hundred feet, even with a cane. An athlete in the pink of condition could not have won his way through the fire to the mainland.

By the grace of Heaven, there was no need for that in the Master's case; she reflected gratefully. He could make shift somehow to hobble down to the boathouse; and in two minutes he could row out into the safety of the lake, too far from shore for any chance flying ember to reach him.

Then her wave of thankfulness ebbed with a suddenness that made her head swim. The boathouse door was locked. The boats themselves were locked to their metal rope. In her own pocket were the two big keys. With his helpless ankle the man could scarce hope to swim to safety.

The Mistress took a step forward. Her feet were weighted down, not by panic, but by a furry mass that had stretched across them as Dawn cowered there in crazy fright. She stopped, almost falling over the huge gray obstacle. She heard herself ask:

"Are there any boats at this end of the lake? Any boats that belong to you people?"

"Yes'm," was the annoyed answer, as the child dragged his attention unwillingly from the enthralling view of destruction. "One. Down yon. Below that big dead tree. Pop and them was a-goin' fishin' this mornin', till they heard tell about the fire. So the oars is in it, if you want to borrer it to git home in, wherever you come from."

The child was anxious to be rid of the bothersome questioner; at any price. She kept interfering pesteringly with his enjoyment of the fire.

He achieved his wish. Before he had finished giving his grudged information, the Mistress was running at top speed over the uneven ground toward the nearest shore of the lake. Dawn slunk quiveringly along beside her, tripping her in his eagerness to press as close to her as he could.

After an eternity of running and stumbling, she came upon a square-ended scow, half drawn up on the bank and with a pair of clumsy oars laid in the leaky bottom. With all her fragile strength the Mistress thrust the boat out into water. Then she paused and looked northward.

From here she could see the wall of fire had reached the landward neck of the promontory and was billowing outward toward the cottage-crowned point. Row as she might, she could not propel the slow and leaky old scow to the cottage before the fire should reach it. Then, out of despair, came her inspiration.

Picking up a sliver of wood, she cast it into the lake, bidding Dawn fetch it back. Ordinarily, the dog would not have waited for the invitation. Now he crept sluggishly out toward the stick, swam a wavering stroke or two, and came back to her without it. He had neither mind nor heart for such sport; when the smoke and the smell and the sound of the forest fire were striking blind dread to his very marrow.

As he came out of the water the Mistress was scribbling a word or two on an envelope back, with a stump of pencil from the little metal wrist bag she carried. This note she dropped into the wrist bag, and with it the two keys to the boathouse. She shut tight the bag and drew off her belt.

Deftly she tied the metal bag to the belt and the belt to Gray Dawn's collar as the dog crouched dripping in front of her.

"Dawnie," she told him, her sweet voice not quite level, "it all depends on *you* now. God never would have given you that steadfast look in the back of your eyes if you weren't to be relied on to the death, Dawn. And perhaps it *is* 'to the death,' dear old friend. But it's the only hope there is. Your coat is wet enough to keep from catching fire when you go through the thick of it. Master can't help seeing the bag on your neck as soon as he sees you. He'll understand and he'll open it. Then he and you can both get safely out on to the lake, Dawn. And—oh, it's the *only* chance! Do you suppose I'd risk your burning to death, if it wasn't?"

The voice no longer had the semblance of steadiness as she finished speaking. At the same time she finished binding the bag and the belt fast to the dog's collar.

The unfamiliar anguish in her tone made Dawn forget, momentarily, his own terror. He licked the busy little hands that wrought at his collar and he sought to wag his down-curved tail.

Then the Mistress was standing upright again, and her voice was as steady as a trumpet note as she pointed toward the far-off cottage and commanded:

"Master, Dawn! Find *Master!* Quick!"

He blinked at her, as though doubting that he had heard aright. Surely his gentle Mistress could never be sending him into that hell of flame and death! But the sweet voice cried out again, an agony of fierce appeal in it:

"Dawn! Find Master! *Master!*"

No, there was no mistake. She was calling on him to go to the Master. And she was doing it in a tone that never before had he heard. There could be no disobeying. From puppyhood, implicit obedience had been Dawn's life rule. She was sending him to a Horror from which his heart shrank in craven fear. But there was anguish in her dear voice that struck through him.

With a shuddering sigh the great dog lowered his head and set off at a hand gallop toward the point, traveling not by the trail, but in the straight and shortest line that dogs follow, by a mystic sixth sense, when they run to a goal.

"Faster!" called the Mistress after him. "QUICK!"

The words and the sob that followed them reached Dawn's ears as he loped on his mission. The lope merged into a tearing run.

For a half mile he sped on, over rock and windfall, up knoll and down gully, before he was lost to sight. Long before then the Mistress was rowing frantically toward the smoke-hidden cottage.

For a time the going was easy for the mighty collie. Then his eyes began to smart. The air was denser and increasingly hard to breathe. Unswervingly he thundered on, in no way slackening his express-train speed.

Well did Dawn know what he had to do. Well did he know what Inferno lay between him and his destination. The command had been given; with all the heart and soul and mind of the Mistress it had been impressed on him. He was to find the Master. Nothing else was to matter.

In less than another minute the smoke was stranglingly thick. The air was hot. The hideous sound of crackling wood was all around him. The roar of the tree-top flames smote into his brain.

In front of him danced a fence of fire. Swinging to the left, he sought to outflank it. He galloped around its fast-spreading fringe, and then into a momentary area of freer breathing.

But it was only a straggling skirmish line of the fire that he had outflanked. In a minute or so he was rushing toward a wall of conflagration three times as high and as fierce as the one he had skirted. This was the vanguard of the blaze —or of so much of it as had reached the landward end of the promontory.

Smoke-circled it belched and screeched and roared. Through the smoke on the hither side was a dim blur of hopping and scuttling human silhouettes—the fire fighters who had not been able to stop the course of the flame before it got to the promontory and who were making futile efforts to keep it from spreading to either side of its chosen path.

And now in front of Dawn the way no longer was clear. Between him and the fire wall was a furlong or more of ground over which the flames had passed. Charred and glowing, sputtering with tiny red spikes of fire—it could not be skirted nor flinched from.

Straight into it swept the galloping dog.

Well it was for Dawn that his coat was still wringing wet from his reluctant dip in the lake. Well it was for him, too, that he had the swiftness of a deer and the strength of a young bull.

But it was the flawless white heart of him—the stanch white heart of the Bruce-born thoroughbred—that carried him on; not his mere strength and speed. Onward he shot, over beds of sizzling weed coals, past hedges of flame points, amid a shower of golden sparks that stung and clung like so many super-hornets.

No longer could he see his way. The smoke was too thick for that. But his collie sense of direction kept him from swerving an inch to left or right. His flying feet spurned the red-hot coals. He hurdled a blazing windfall in his path, landing on its far side amid a geyser of fiery shreds and cinders.

He stumbled, was aware of the agony in his burnt feet

and hocks and of the strangling that gripped his sensitive throat; then he was up and on again like a silvern whirlwind.

Out through the murk toward him, all but colliding with the dog in a headlong plunge for safety, rushed a stag, antlers back, sides heaving. In another forty feet the collie's shoulder grazed the haunch of a lumbering black bear that blundered whimperingly past him in flight from the holocaust of flame.

For these fugitives there was a chance of safety—at all events the satisfaction of trying to escape. For the dog, there was no such sorry consolation. Voluntarily Dawn was diving, deep and deeper at every bound, into the hell that lay before him—he who could not endure to stay in the same room with a harmless hearth fire!

Then he was whizzing past two branch-waving men who blithered and bellowed aimlessly as he darted between them.

Next, instinctively holding his tortured breath, he was diving into the cyclone wall of flame that lay between him and the cottage. Instinctively, too, he shifted his course a little, to buck the line of fire at what seemed its shallowest and least terrifying point.

Into it he raced, a swirl of red-gold flame encompassing him; the incredible heat drying instantly his soaked coat, searing and scorching him well-nigh to the bone. Behind, ahead, above, underfoot, screamed and swirled that ocean of wind-whipped fire.

Moving wholly by instinct now, the dog tore on. Instinct kept his peerless strength in frantic play as his burnt and blistered body clove its crashing path through the wide wall of conflagration.

A blazing pine branch whizzed down from a dead tree, smiting him glancingly on the side and almost crushing him beneath its half ton of fiery weight.

He reeled drunkenly, caught his stride again, and lurched onward; a broken rib adding now to his mad torment.

By luck or else to lessen the intolerable burning, he was running with shut eyes. Sight would have been of no use to him in that world of fire and black smoke. Wholly by sense of direction he was galloping.

Then he was out of the furnace and on the far side. The smoke rolled ahead of him as blindingly as ever; and for a space the hornet sparks pursued him, falling on his scorched bare flesh. But the speed of the fire's advance was checked.

Here for a hundred yards was an outcrop of shale, with scarce so much as a blueberry bush or a patch of sweet fern straggling through its interstices. Here, too, ran windingly the car road to the cottage.

There was no fuel to feed the flame's onrush. The conflagration must needs content itself with hurling through the upper air great blazing masses of bark and twigs toward the shingle roofs of the cottage and the outbuildings. Already the nearest of these roofs—the garage's—was beginning to steam and to smoke.

In the garage tank was stored something like a hundred gallons of gasoline.

The Master, left alone, had tried to read and to forget the increasing throb of his hurt ankle. Then, bit by bit, he became aware of the strong reek of wood smoke. At last he hobbled to the door and looked out. To landward, the sky was hidden under a blanket of red-shot smoke. The wind was setting toward the point.

There was no time, even if he had not been lame, to cover the distance to the mainland before escape should be cut off. But there was time to make some kind of effort to save his host's home.

Having hobbled with the aid of a slender malacca cane to the pump house, the Master unrolled the long fire hose and started the pump to going. Thence, clumsily, he carried the hose nozzle outside, training it on the garage, to wet down the roof of this first building the flames must reach. In his haste he did not notice that the wind was beginning to shift away from the point.

Leaving the stream to play on the garage, he limped with greater difficulty to the edge of the low cliff, alongside the boathouse. Here, he remembered, flush with the brink, had stood in other years a shelter containing an emergency pump, for bringing lake water up to the bathrooms. If this pump were still in commission and if he could find another length of hose——

As he leaned across the edge of the little cliff to look, the fragile cane snapped beneath his weight. Over the verge he pitched, his head striking smartly against a knob of rock halfway down. Into the lake he splashed, senseless.

And over the edge of the ten-foot cliff, by the time the Master struck water, dived a hairless and hideous Thing, in pursuit of the man he had been told to "find."

Dawn had reached the garage just as the Master leaned over the ledge to look for the pump. Barely could the dog's bleared eyes make out the man's stooping form. But Dawn limped forward to greet him, at what speed he still could compass. Then he had seen the Master lose his balance and tumble forward. Instantly Dawn followed. There was no time even now, it seemed, to think of his own torture and sick fatigue.

The impetus of his leap carried Gray Dawn far under water. But instantly he was at the surface again, a yard or two away from the larger and moveless body that had just risen from its own plunge. With a rush, Dawn reached the supinely sprawling Master and caught him by the shoulder of his coat.

On every side from the point of the promontory the rocky bottom dropped off to a sheer descent of anywhere from ten to fifteen feet. In twelve feet of ice-chill water, the worn-out collie fought with all his fast-waning power to keep his master's head above the surface.

It was a hard task, for the man had not yet fully recovered consciousness from the rap on his skull. But Dawn put all of his own gay energy and devotion and unflinching will power into the tedious effort.

They had come to the surface close to the steep rocks, and some yards from the boathouse. Dawn towed the man toward the rocks, churning the water under his forepaws in the exhausting attempt. But here there was no foothold for either of them.

Water was trickling in through Dawn's open mouth and down his suffocating windpipe. He was strangling. Inch by inch, the Master's weight and the strain of keeping him afloat was pulling the dog's head under water.

Then, with a shake, the Master came to his senses. The

chilly immersion had done its work in startling his brain back into action. Dazedly he realized he was in the lake and that something was tugging with painful insistence at his shoulder. Roughly he shook off the incumbrance and looked about him, swimming feebly and trying to rid himself of the choking water that filled his mouth and throat.

Gray Dawn's work was done. The collie realized that, as he felt the Master shake him off. Often had they two swum together in the lake at home. He knew the man was no longer helpless. The thrust drove Dawn's head under water. It was a hard fight for him to bring it to the surface again.

He was one anguished mass of burns and scorches. The fire had done queer things to his lungs, too. He was half blinded. One of his ribs was stove on. He had swallowed much water through his windpipe. He was played out.

Now that there was time at last for him to afford the blissful luxury of quitting, he quit.

The Master, turning belatedly to learn what had hurt his shoulder by its vise grip, saw a huge scorched and pinkish object slowly sinking through the water. The head had submerged last of all, and the eyes were looking up at him through several inches of lake.

The eyes were the only recognizable part of the outlandish creature. But the eyes and their expression were enough to make the Master call upon what slight muscular force had come back to him, and to seize his drowning collie by the scruff of the hairless neck.

He yanked Dawn's head above the surface and held it there, himself struggling to keep afloat and to make his crippled leg tread water. He tried to tow the dog's inert weight toward the boathouse. But it was sorry progress and Dawn seemed unable or unwilling to help.

Twice the Master let go of the nape of the collie's neck. Both times the dog allowed himself to go under. Then, lifting him a third time, the Master called sharply:

"Dawn! Gray *Dawn!*"

The call pierced the mists which so mercifully had numbed the dog's tortured senses. Dawn made a weak effort to move.

It was then that the Mistress reached them in the scow.

To her husband's surprise, it was Gray Dawn she lifted first into the leaky boat, before helping the Master to climb overside. She was worn out by her frenziedly fast row in the unwieldy craft. But she was strong enough to lift to safety the loved dog that had been through hell at her command.

She knew the Master could hold out a minute longer, and she knew Dawn could not.

Outside, the late October blasts were howling. They racked the great oaks of Sunnybank. They buffeted the rambling gray stucco house that had withstood so many decades of their buffeting. They lashed the lake to white foam.

In The Place's pleasant living room, on the huge old brown couch in front of the twinkling log fire, sat the Mistress and the Master. The latter's left foot was shod in a loose slipper, though the ankle was almost well. In the Mistress's lap purred and blinked a green-eyed drift of gray fluff. Tippy loved to snuggle thus, on windy October evenings.

On the fur hearth rug, with the firelight flickering over him, sprawled Sunnybank Gray Dawn, his drowsy head pillowed on the Master's one boot.

It would have taken a second glance to recognize him as the magnificent silver-and-white collie of six weeks before. Still almost hairless and with his mighty body seared and mottled with scarce-healed burns, he was a travesty on his former beauty.

But the vets who had worked long and skillfully over him said that in another few months his coat would be as handsome and as shaggily luxuriant as before, and that, apart from his hairlessness, he was as well now as ever he had been. Even his deepset brown eyes were none the worse.

"It's queer how he has forgotten his dread of fire," commented the Master, stooping to caress the collie's scarred head with a new tenderness of touch. "He loves to lie here on the warm hearth, now. It is his favorite sleeping place. That's odd, isn't it? But then, everything about the grand old chap has always been odd."

"Everything about him has always been *glorious*," corrected the Mistress. "Every 'odd' thing he's ever done has somehow turned out beautifully. And it has been Gray Dawn himself that made it turn out so. He isn't like any other dog. He never was. He never will be. But that's the other dogs' loss, not his. As for his not being afraid of the fire any longer—well, if you had swum the Atlantic Ocean would you be afraid to step across a mud puddle?"

After-Word

IT HAS not been easy to write these Sunnybank Gray Dawn stories. Dawn's queer character and his tremendous personality have been as difficult to imprison in cold type as would be a thunderstorm or a toothache or a child's mischievous laugh.

But perhaps my clumsy attempt may not score a complete failure. For Dawn and I have lived together for eight years; and I have studied him with some thoroughness. Moreover, when these yarns appeared (in a more condensed form) in the *Ladies' Home Journal*, they met with unexpectedly cordial reception.

Here are two incidents that typify the two extremes of Dawn's erratic nature. Between the two boundaries is an infinite mixed area of white loyalty and bumptiousness; stanchness and puppylike flightiness; calm wisdom and tumultuously noisy idiocy: aggressive high spirits and the most painfully acute sensitiveness.

Dawn galloped merrily up to me, from behind, as I stood at the lake edge, and he flung his eighty-odd pounds of iron-

and-whalebone weight against my shoulders. (I was dressed for a wedding at which the Mistress and I were due in half an hour.) Even as I smote the deep water, head foremost, I wished with all my heart that I were carrying a gun or a bowie knife wherewith to slay the miserable gray clown.

Again, on a bitter night, I sat up with an ailing collie mother and her eight newborn pups. Gray Dawn followed me to the brood-nest shed. He stood outside it, on guard (stood, not lay or sat), for nine hours, waiting for me to come out. When I joined him there at sunrise his shaggy coat was thick with frost and he was stiff with cold and inaction. He had remained thus, on sentry duty, through the chill of the winter night, instead of seeking his warm kennel—just for the doubtful privilege of being near the human who was his god.

Gray Dawn is one of the most lovable collies of all the long Sunnybank line. He is not merely the professionally faithful dog of fiction, but rather—as the Mistress expresses it—an "own-your-own-soul dog."

Within a pitifully small handful of years, at very most, he will be gone. That is the way of dogs. All of them die too soon; though so many of us humans live too long. While still he is here, I want his stories to be read. Perhaps you may not like the stories. But I know you will like Dawn, himself. Everyone does.

ALBERT PAYSON TERHUNE

"Sunnybank"
Pompton Lakes
New Jersey